IN THE COUNTRY OF
THIEVES and GHOSTS

IN THE COUNTRY OF
THIEVES and GHOSTS

(The Diary of Troy Gaston)

SHAWN A. JENKINS

IN THE COUNTRY OF THIEVES AND GHOSTS
(The Diary of Troy Gaston)

iUniverse books may be ordered through booksellers or by contacting:

iUniverse
1663 Liberty Drive
Bloomington, IN 47403
www.iuniverse.com
1-800-Authors (1-800-288-4677)

ISBN: 978-1-4917-8003-9 (sc)
ISBN: 978-1-4917-8004-6 (e)

Print information available on the last page.

iUniverse rev. date: 11/16/2015

Be self-controlled and alert.
Your enemy the devil prowls around like a roaring lion
looking for someone to devour.
1st Peter 5:8

For his ninth birthday, Troy Gaston was given a diary. In his diary, Troy, in detail, would give accounts of his daily life and activities.

In the summer of 1982, at the age of 21, Troy joined a Christian retreat in Australia.

That same summer, while in Australia, both Troy and his diary went missing.

In 2011…only Troy Gaston's diary was found.

Something took place on Troy Gaston's journey, an incident that has baffled investigators for years. What Troy managed to document on the final pages of his diary can only be interpreted as sheer madness; interpretations of a sadistic…and possibly supernatural nature.

August ? 1982

I can't believe that I'm actually writing at all times like this. First off, I don't know what day it is, all I know is that the sun is up. I'm going to die; I know that much for a fact, so this will be my final entry. The last thing I want is to sound like a poet on his final leg. All I have to say before it all ends is that I wish to God I was dead now, so I wouldn't have to recall any of what I saw and went through. I really do wish I was dead right now. Please, God, please, just kill me.

CHAPTER 1

OKINAWA, JAPAN
JUNE 1982

"My God…please, have mercy." The short, pencil thin police lieutenant breathed behind his mustache as both he and his subordinates all gazed down the vast cliff that overlooked the ocean in utter amazement. "Who found this?"

Clearing his throat, one of the other officers replied, "A farmer that lives just down the way back there. His grandson told us that both he and his granddad were herding their sheep when they stumbled upon it, sir."

The lieutenant turned his head and began for his red and white cruiser that was parked just ten feet behind him. The crashing waves sounded angry that warm, cloudy morning, like they, too, were disgusted with the macabre scene.

The lieutenant wasn't as repulsed at the ghastly sight that lay below the cliff as he thought he would have been, but there was something about the sound of the waves that day that caused his stomach to churn, they only seemed to add a sense of anxiousness to an already startling situation.

"Sir," another officer said as he carefully approached his superior from behind. "Should we call the wagon now for—

"What time did the farmer report this?" The lieutenant hastily interrupted as he spun around.

Taken aback for a quick second, the officer answered, "Uh…I believe around six this morning. His grandson heard them sometime about three or so, but he never thought of calling the police in on it."

The lieutenant started for the edge of the cliff while taking a salty glance at the blowing trees all around him, as well as the old farmer and his herd of sheep that were all gathered behind a wooden fence a few yards back.

"How long is he going to be here?" The lieutenant grumbled.

"He wants to know how and why it happened, sir."

The lieutenant turned to the officer and grinned, "Oh really? Tell him to stand in line, Nagaowa."

"Sir, if I may be so bold, it is possible that they could have all just…been led to this."

"By who or what?" the lieutenant paused before reaching the edge of the mountain.

"Well, perhaps someone forced them, somehow."

"Like a pied-piper of sorts?"

"Possibly, yes."

The lieutenant stood solid against the strong wind that was determined to knock him backwards as he once again peered down at the violent beach below his feet.

"How many do you think are down there?"

"Officer Hiroki counts one hundred and seventy-eight, exactly."

The lieutenant turned to the officer in stunned shock before asking, "That many? Where could they have all come from, for God's sake?"

"Perhaps a shelter," the officer considered.

"It's impossible that a shelter could hold that many at once. Besides, there isn't a shelter within a hundred miles of this location."

"Lieutenant Shomata," another officer said, walking up beside the man, "this reminds me of a story I once heard when—

"I am in no mood to hear your stories, Miroku." Shomata rolled his eyes. "Your stories always begin and end with things that keep me awake at night."

"It's in the bible, sir."

"And he tells me, anyways." Shomata huffed.

"About the pigs that were—

"Enough, Miroku," Shomata obstinately ordered.

2

Lieutenant Shomata began a stroll across the edge of the cliff, seemingly unafraid of heights or the wind that at a moment's notice could possibly knock him off his lofty perch.

He was well aware of Officer Miroku's story, but that was the last place on earth he wanted to venture with the investigation.

His police division was a quiet one. The most recent disturbance that had occurred was over a landlord trying to extract money from one of his overdue tenants. What was laid out before him that morning was a sight that he never imagined he would envision. It wouldn't exactly turn his soul sideways, but it was jarring enough to cause his heart to skip a beat here and there.

Staring down the rugged cliff at the grisly crime scene gave him a sudden pause. There was something wrong with it all, the timing, the place, the mood. It all struck the man with such a forceful blow that his own two eyes were becoming foggy.

"This doesn't make any sense." Shomata droned on under his breath. "What a dreary day it is for such a thing. Why would this happen? What brought this on?"

"I'm sorry, sir? I didn't understand you." Officer Nagaowa said.

The lieutenant stopped pacing and responded, "Something…not someone, did this. That is the only explanation I have. Perhaps your story has some validity, Miroku, if you choose to believe such fables. But don't let it go to your head. C'mon, let's go down."

As the lieutenant and his two comrades began for the trail that led down the mountain, he couldn't help but to stare off at the old, grey bearded man and his little grandson who looked no more than ten years old at best.

The crusty looking elderly man appeared to be stuck in a hard gaze, seemingly unable to budge an inch from behind the crippled wooden fence that he and his grandson were standing.

Enthralled with the mysterious individual, the beleaguered Shomata suddenly paused and returned his own stiff glare at the man, studying him from head to toe.

Soon, out of nowhere, the old man began to speak what sounded like a foreign language. Shomata looked back at the two officers in a confused manner, as though he were listening to gibberish shoot from out of the man's mouth.

"My grandfather is from Korea, officers." The little boy said.

"What is he saying, now, son?" Shomata asked.

"He said that," 'they all jumped into the air and dropped. Like birds that were shot out of the sky. They just flew and fell.' The boy carefully explained before stopping to look up at his muttering grandfather and back again at the officers. "He said," 'God has forgotten about us. This is only the beginning.'

"Ask your grandfather if he saw or heard anyone out here last night." Shomata demanded.

The lieutenant watched and waited as the child looked up at his grandfather and interpreted his message in Korean.

"He said," 'No person was out here.'

"Okay," Shomata relented before carrying on towards the trail. "Thank your grandfather for all of his cooperation."

As he walked on, he could still hear the old man rambling on in his native Korean vernacular, the urgency in his weak voice sounded painstakingly disturbing.

"He said that," 'no person was out here!' The boy shouted.

Shomata once again stopped and looked back, trying to figure out whether or not there was a cryptic message in the old man's words.

Before resuming his walk, Shomata turned his head to the German shepherd that was perched behind the fence, just a few feet away from the boy and his grandfather. Judging by the serious, almost contemptible glaze in its eyes, it almost appeared as if the dusty coated animal wanted to say something. Its eyes just couldn't seem to tear themselves away from Shomata's.

Shomata rolled his eyes, not wanting to upset the animal and have it attack him and his partners. There was enough strange insanity that morning without having a mad dog on the loose.

Lieutenant Shomata and Officers Miroku and Nagaowa all began down the rough cliff that would eventually lead them to the one hundred and seventy-eight dead beagles that called the beach their final resting place.

CHAPTER 2

JULY 1982

"And don't you bring your white ass back here ever again!" The wild-haired black lady screamed before slamming her screen door right in Troy Gaston's face, leaving the stunned young man frozen stiff on the dilapidated porch, too overcome to even move.

Troy happened to glance over at the house next door to see three little black children all giggling at him as though the entire episode were the funniest thing they had ever seen.

With as much brave energy as he could assemble, Troy stepped down from off the porch and used a gallant walk to mask the pungent humiliation that was devastating him. Deep down, he knew that he would receive an attitude, but he never imagined that it would be as strong as it was just a moment earlier.

He waited as a brown Mazda rolled down the street before crossing over to a church and immediately stepping inside, slamming the door shut behind him as forcefully as he could. Troy then leaned up against the door and exhaled like he never had before in his life.

In his burning right ear Troy could hear footsteps rounding the corner near his vicinity. Instantly, he wiped the sweat from off his forehead before belting out an excruciating sigh and pulling himself from off the stone wall upon which he was perched.

With one hand, Troy brushed over his brown hair and watched as a burly, black man came walking into the front room with a determined purpose.

"Troy," the man, adorned in a black short sleeved shirt and minister's collar spoke amazed, what's the matter?"

5

Troy clinched his squishy body before saying, "Nothing…I just got back from across the street, that's all."

Troy tried his best to divert his eyes away from the man's, but it was virtually impossible, the gentleman was all too persistent.

"What happened?" The man questioned with a slight smirk attached to his face.

Hesitant to reply at first, Troy instead turned and started for the sanctuary that was just five steps ahead of him.

"Troy," the man continued, following in behind the young man. "Troy, what happened?"

Troy wouldn't stop walking, no matter how much the big man kept on calling out his name and urging him to hold up, there was no pause in his stride.

The second Troy saw the door that had the words *Pastors Study* printed on the front, he right away stormed in and dropped his tense body down into the first chair that he saw, directly in front of a desk.

Troy closed his eyes, he could hear the big man stumble in and sit down in his chair that sat behind the desk. The young man was in no state to explain his current, disheveled condition, but he was aware that a certain amount of clarification was going to be requested of him eventually. He just wanted to get it out of the way as soon as possible.

Troy opened his eyes, trying not to let the stinging tears flow. He saw the man seated behind his desk grinning at him as if his plight was mere, cute little amusement.

"So, what happened?" The man subtly sighed.

Troy lifted his heavy head and swallowed before saying, "I did exactly what you told me to do. I went all up and down the block, knocking on doors."

"Okay, and?" the man pressed on.

"And…when I got to Theola's house…she just started to cuss me out!"

The big man sat up in his chair and questioned, "What exactly took place?"

"Whaddya mean what took place?" Troy waved his arms in the air. "You know how she is! I asked if she was interested in coming to church, and she just went nuts! And you're just sitting there like it's all funny!"

The man got up out of his seat and sat down on his desk in front of Troy. Troy couldn't even look up at the man for fear that his tears would be seen.

The gentleman then handed Troy a tissue before saying, "Theola isn't exactly what one would call a rational person. She's been through a lot in her life."

Wiping his eyes, Troy asked, "And that gives her the right to yell at me?"

"Troy, you have to understand, these folks around here, they're not used to—

"Used to what, white people?"

The man paused before saying, "I was going to say that they're not used to people telling them what to do."

"All I did was give the invitation, it's not like I told her to come to church or else!"

"Troy, let me explain, not everyone you meet is going to be nice. I can't tell you how many people I approach on a daily basis and cuss me out simply because I'm a pastor. Theola is only one example. Read the book of Jeremiah, that brother went through hell trying to convince the Israelites to repent of their evil ways. Read of Paul's life, the man was beaten, ridiculed, tossed in jail and eventually beheaded trying to get the Christian church started. And you're upset because one person cussed you out? If only it were that simple, son. I haven't seen you this upset since we lost the interfaith basketball tournament three years ago."

Out of sheer frustration, Troy jumped up from out of his chair and stared out the window. Every word the pastor was saying to him was going in one ear and out the other. All he could see in his aching head was his girlfriend and her smiling face. For a very brief second, her image brought him a much needed relief.

"I dunno, maybe I'm not ready for all this yet." Troy murmured as he turned back around.

The pastor stood up from off his desk and approached Troy saying, "I really do wish you would take time to listen to God."

Troy rolled his eyes and said, "I do listen to him, but I feel like sometimes he's not listening to me."

The pastor laughed before asking, "What, are you expecting God to just talk to you face to face? Troy, sometimes God speaks to us through our obedience to him. Psalms 31:24 says 'Be strong and take heart, all you who hope in the Lord.'

Troy turned his head, once again trying not to let the pastor see his tears of embarrassment. He honestly couldn't feel the compassion come from the man, it all felt more like he was putting on a show.

"Let me ask. Has Jill discussed her little…trip with you lately?" The pastor winced.

Troy turned his head somewhat; another subject that he didn't want to discuss had suddenly reared its ugly, malformed head.

"Uh…not lately," Troy meekly replied. "I guess you could say that I've been avoiding her."

"Avoiding her?" The pastor snickered. "How can you avoid your own girlfriend?"

Troy tossed up his hands and said, "I guess I don't have the guts to tell her the truth."

"The time is almost here, man."

"I know, and she's been pressing me more and more. I even have Chris running interference for me whenever she comes by the house. Do you know how it makes me feel to have my own little brother lie for me?"

"Well, just make sure she doesn't push you into something that you're not comfortable with. What may be good for her may not give you same the remedy."

Out of all the words that the pastor had uttered to him over the course of the past few minutes, it was the subject of Jill that seemed to captivate his off- kilter attention the most. He heard the man loud and clear, without any pause.

"Look, um…I need to go get Chris." Troy huffed.

"I understand," the pastor said. "Can I count on you tomorrow for alter service?"

Troy just nodded yes before quietly stepping out of the study and outside to his brown and maroon 1979 Chevrolet Caprice Classic and hopping in. The entire car felt like a hot, soupy mess, thanks to the heat of the day. But that was all easily shoved aside.

Troy sat and sulked before reaching into the glove compartment and pulling out his *Journey* tape and pushing it into the deck. Then, beyond the clutter, he whipped out a little black book, along with his blue ballpoint pen and began to feverishly write.

July 10th, 1982

I'm both pissed and confused. I just got through doing what Pastor Reynolds told me to do and I get cussed out for it by this black lady. She's crazy anyways, but I didn't deserve that. I don't understand these people. Why are they so belligerent? And all Reynolds could do was just sit there and smile like it was all a damn joke. The guy actually laughed. And then to top it off, he asks if I will be in tomorrow to serve.

I have to be out of my mind. I could be at UCLA right now, playing ball with Mike and Kevin. But no, I'm stuck here in Bixby, Ohio, going door to door begging drug dealers and welfare moms to come to church. I feel like a complete moron.

I know I keep harping on California, but I can't help it. I'm beginning to believe that all of this isn't even worth it anymore. If God does talk to people, I wish he would talk a little louder, or else just leave me the hell alone.

At that, Troy placed his diary down into the passenger seat before glancing at the picture of his girlfriend that was taped to the sun visor. With his index finger he rubbed across the Polaroid while reminiscing on the time they both met. As in times past, just the simple remembrance of the event was a sobering occasion for him, like a moment of clarity in an otherwise bleak state of dismay. It kept him stable, despite certain circumstances.

Wiping the drenching sweat away from his brow, Troy turned on his car before taking a hard, scornful stare over at Theola's house from the rearview mirror.

With as much enthusiasm as he could gather, the young man ripped out of his parking space and away from the church as fast and angrily as he could.

CHAPTER 3

BOSTON, MASSACHUSETTS

His hair was snow white as it stood straight up on his wrinkled head. His pencil sharp nose was just as studious as the eyes he used to see the piece of paper that was sitting in front of him. He was a white man of his mid to late sixties.

The old one was seated on a massive stage, surrounded by countless, unmanned musical instruments. The bright light that shined down upon him didn't provide him with the adequate illumination he required, for there was a dimming in his eyes, so much so that just seeing a simple page in front of him was becoming more difficult with the passing minutes.

To his right on the floor was seated a cup of steaming tea. With a shaky hand, the man reached down and picked up the cup before sipping on the rim and momentarily shutting his eyes as to say the drink were a reliever from his current dilemma.

Once the man was done sipping, he gently placed the cup back down onto the floor and studied the blank sheet of paper that sat before him on his conductor's panel. His white t-shirt that was always too tight for his body itched unbearably, but it was an agony that could be ignored for the time being.

With an exhaustive sigh, the old man squeezed his foggy eyes, and with a ball point pen in his left hand, he began to scribble away. At first, the words that he wrote were chicken scratch. He didn't even notice that he was writing so appallingly until he reached the very bottom of the page.

Once he realized his misfortune, the man ripped up the piece of paper and tossed it to the floor before taking another sheet, squeezing his eyes and exhaling as hard as he could.

My dearest Captain. Yes, I still call you my Captain after so many years. I am afraid it is such a habit that the likes of myself cannot be rid of.

It has been for so long that we have heard from one another. So long that even your face has become foreign to me. Either age or the wanton desire to forget that has taken your blessed image away. Nonetheless, I am always at ease whenever just a faint remembrance occurs.

My life away from my mates has been one of trials and triumphs. I am here in America, of all places on God's earth. The talent that my departed mother handed me as a child has developed into a sort of crusade if you will. I am a wealthy man. Not so much wealthy by worldly standards, but by a standard of peace. Just as you yourself once mentioned, our lives are not measured by coins, but by amity. Yes, you have lost your mind, and so have I, my friend.

However, with all of that being mentioned, I sit here an old, suffering man. My time here in this earthly realm is drawing nigh. You must understand, Captain, I choose to forget the past because of all of its misgivings and judgments. Of all of its coarse rigidness. We were men of bitter wickedness, I am afraid. Men, who much like our adversaries, were out of place in a world that already saw us as not much more than war machines at best.

I am a frightened old man. At first, my dreams were that of notes, delightful, inspirational melodies that seemed to bring so much elation to so many souls. Now, now I am besieged by another dream. A dream that is dark, darker than any other nighttime terror I have experienced.

They are chasing me, Captain. Chasing me down like the fox in the forest. They both are as striking as hell's embers. They have found me, Captain. After so many years, they have sought me. And now I fear even more, they are coming for you.

I realize that your belief in a higher power has kept you at bay. The once violent urges you once possessed have all but been eradicated, but they are aware of our existence. It is not our blood they require, but rather our very souls to carry with them back to perdition.

I have slept not for three nights straight. I cannot eat, I cannot concentrate. My very occupation, my passion, is all but spent. My life, my existence is a dread. The last hope I cling to is you, Captain. You must escape, for they are as relentless in the netherworlds as they once were in this.

I have come to the conclusion that my only relief is to deny myself the only thing that has brought me so much ecstasy.

They seek me now as I write this to you. Be ever so mindful, my friend, and if prayer be your shield, then use such a device. Always bear in mind, they are vicious, cruel and wicked, even more so than we once were. But I need not remind you of that.

Sincerely yours,

First Mate, Mr. Leor Hastings.

"Good afternoon, Leor!" A young, Asian woman said out loud as both she and a little girl of equal identity stepped onto the stage.

Leor ever so hastily wrapped up his letter and stuffed it into an already stamped envelope. He then felt the hard bulge in his right pocket before raising his head and smiling.

Squinting his eyes sharply, Leor by then could only make out one tall blur and one smaller blur beside that one.

Trying to search for any benevolent word to blurt out at that instant, Leor said in a polished Australian inflection, "I see you brought tiny company this day, Leah."

"Yes, she's so excited about tonight. Since Tanya has been here in the states she's never seen

Like a loving grandfather, Leor held out his arms and waited as the little girl came to him. "And can you remember what section your mother plays in, my dear?" He kindly asked.

Tanya stood and contemplated for a moment before saying, "Uh…the bassoon section, sir."

Laughing out loud, Leor happily remarked, "Very good, darling, very good! Your mother is quite the reflection of beauty when it comes to her craft. Perhaps one day you, too, will be as such."

"She's already practicing five hours a day. Her father won't have it any other way."

Leor sat and smiled at the distortion in front of him. With every passing minute, the brightness in the room grew vaguer.

Taking his envelope and placing it in Tanya's small hand, Leor said, "Do you know of the mailbox outside, around the corner right next to the traffic light, my child?"

"Um…yes."

"Good." Leor grinned. "I need for you to take this and place it inside for me."

Leor sat and watched as the blur skipped away from him, with his letter in hand. It was the very fact that there was speed in her stride that caused his heart to melt all the more.

"She is such a delight, that child." Leor softly stated.

Stepping forward, Leah said, "Yes, she's already at the top of her class in algebra, and she's only in the sixth grade."

"How wonderful," Leor remarked as he attempted to reach down and pick up his warm tea cup, only to have it drop out of his hand.

"Oh my," Leah fretfully shouted as she came running to Leor's aid.

"Do not make a fuss over me, my friend. Remember, I am only an old man who writes music."

"You are a remarkable man who writes music." Leah said as she picked up the cup. "We only arrived early so I could take in a little practice. I still believe I'm a little flat on the E harmony section."

Leor's ears could pick up every word that she was saying, but even the velvet virtue in her voice seemed out of sync to him. It was as if he couldn't even recognize her any longer.

"I hear that the Prime Minister from France is to be here this evening, Leor. Is that true?"

Leor sat and helplessly watched as the lights in the room, as well as the various instruments that surrounded him, gradually began to vanish right before his eyes. All the old man could do was sit perfectly still and wait until blackness took over his once vibrant eyesight.

"Did you hear me, Leor?" Leah spoke louder.

All that was left for Leor was a shimmering effect, like sunlight trying to glisten through a tiny sliver.

Leah cautiously approached Leor while holding out her hand and saying, "Leor…can you hear me?"

But before the woman could even place one finger on his body, both Leor and the chair that he was sitting in slid across the floor about four feet away from Leah.

The young woman jumped back at that moment. Leor sat absolutely still in his chair while an idyllic smile lay across his face.

"Stay back, my dear." Leor calmly ordered. "I love you, Leah. I always have."

Leah said nothing; she stood absolutely motionless in the middle of the floor while watching her conductor pull out a 38.revolver from his right pocket and point the thing directly at his temple.

Holding out her frightened hands, Leah screamed as loud as she could, "God, no!"

With his smile still in place, Leor pulled the trigger before falling out of his chair and landing on the floor in a heap. The blood from his wounded head quickly oozed all over the stage floor while his body shook and quivered from convulsions.

Leah stood for a few moments out of complete shock before eventually turning and racing away towards the back of the stage.

Leor's body lay on the floor for a few more minutes before the same invisible force that moved it seconds earlier snatched it right off the stage floor and into the bottom section of the podium.

Chapter 4

Like a wild, unchained stallion, Troy charged past just about every other player on the basketball court just to dunk the ball through the hoop as hard as he could. Most of the other players stood in awe at the way the man played so recklessly. Charges of foul should have been called out moments earlier, but instead they were held in out of fear that an argument might ensue with the furious demon that dwelt among them.

From left to right Troy bounced the ball, giving an evil eye to each opponent while daring them to steal the ball from him; most just stared at him as though he were just being cool and arrogant, while others were seemingly becoming more irritated by the minute.

"Get the fuck outta the way!" Troy hollered while barging past one black man on his way to the hoop for a graceful layup.

"Damn, Troy," the frustrated black man roared while picking himself up from off the gymnasium floor.

Troy looked back at the angry man that was approaching him as fast as he could with fire in his eyes. Troy dropped the ball to the floor and braced himself.

"What the fuck was that, man?"

Troy just shook his head while carelessly smiling, "Look, I guess I didn't see you, and—

"You didn't see me? Shit, I'm six-foot four! How can you not see me?"

Troy turned his head and began to walk away, but not before the man snatched him by the arm and yelled, "What the hell is wrong with you?"

The gym in which they were playing wasn't exactly filled to capacity, in all, it was Troy and his group on one end of the court while clear down on the other end was a cluster of young boys playing their own pickup game. Seated on the bleachers were perhaps five or six others just waiting their turn to play. But the moment they saw the brewing skirmish erupt between Troy and the other player, that was when all eyes were focused upon them and only them.

Troy looked down at the man's forceful hand that still had a powerful grip on his sweaty arm. He did see him clearly before charging past him, but that day he was completely oblivious to anyone's feelings, he had his own to sift through. Inside, Troy wanted to lash out, but not that badly.

"I'm sorry, man," Troy muttered in a skittish sort of tone.

The man stared at Troy with a disgusted glare before eventually relinquishing his hold and storming away. The other players followed in suit, like they, too, were sickened by Troy's behavior. After so many seconds Troy looked up to see only himself on his end of the court. Trying to play off the disruption, he nonchalantly bounced the ball and sank a few three pointers before a young white boy came racing down the court towards him.

"Hey, man," Troy said before taking the ball and tucking it underneath his sweaty armpit.

The boy used sign language to ask, "Were you and Calvin gonna fight?"

Troy only smirked before answering, "No, we just had a little disagreement, that's all; nothing to worry about."

"James thinks that you could probably beat him up." The boy signed with a smile gracing his face.

Troy only giggled and said, "I wouldn't count on it, Chris."

Troy tossed the ball to Chris, and just like that they began to shoot hoops. Feeling a little less aggravated, Troy dropped his ultra-machismo as he played basketball with his little brother before losing his attention at the sight of a young white woman that had all of the sudden sat herself down on the bleachers.

Chris looked at his brother in a curious manner before signing, "What's the matter?"

The second Troy saw Chris' fingers move he quickly snapped back to reality and pointed to the young lady. Chris looked back before turning to his brother and blushing.

"What are you smiling at, squirt?" Troy grinned before handing the ball to Chris and making his way over to woman.

The girl stood up and attempted to hug Troy, only to have him pull away. "I'm a sweaty mess, babe."

"I don't care; I haven't seen you all day." She smiled before wrapping her thin arms around Troy's neck.

Troy returned the sentimental gesture by sliding his arms around her waist and squeezing; the second he let go he immediately noticed a blushing appearance form on her freckled face, right away he knew just what was coming.

With sheepish eyes, the young woman looked up at Troy and meekly said, "Pastor Reynolds told me what happened."

Troy cut his eyes away and twisted his lips before asking, "What, is it worldwide news now? Why doesn't he go ahead and tell Sam Donaldson, too?"

"Don't be mad at him, Troy."

"Jill, the guy laughed at me!" He griped.

"You know how Pastor Reynolds is, he's a lighthearted guy."

Troy rolled his eyes and exhaled, "Jill, all morning long I went up and down that block, knocking on doors and asking people to come to church. Some were cool, some just simply said no, but—"

"But when one person was mean to you, you just up and quit?"

Troy stared pensively at Jill before saying in a contemptuous tone, "I didn't see you out there today."

"I had to babysit my brothers, you knew that."

"Yeah," Troy frowned, sounding as though he could have cared less about her excuse.

"Troy, don't act like that."

"Act like what, Jill, like I'm sick and tired of being everyone's punching bag?"

Troy watched as Jill turned her head like she was ashamed to look at him any longer. Troy himself blushed before taking Jill by the hand and walking her towards the gymnasium's door.

"I'm glad you didn't see me act like an ass in front of everyone."

Jill looked up at Troy and asked, "What do you mean?"

"I guess I was a little too ferocious for the guys earlier; they'll probably never want to play with me again."

Jill giggled, "You sound like a little boy."

"I behaved like a little boy."

As they were strolling along, Chris all of the sudden jumped in front of Troy and Jill and began signing excitedly as though his very life depended on it.

"We'll go as soon as I get a shower in." Troy said before opening the door and letting Jill exit the building before him.

"What did he say?"

"He and Billy want to go the arcade." Troy replied before taking off his tank top to reveal a white t-shirt that had Bela Lugosi as Dracula printed on the front.

"I can't understand why you insist on wearing two shirts while playing basketball."

"I burn more calories that way." Troy smiled as he took Jill by the hand and began to walk around the track.

As they wandered along, Troy couldn't help but to lock his eyes on a group of young ladies dressed in hip high shorts, standing directly in the middle of the field talking and laughing. Most of them carried on amongst themselves while two or three gawked back at Troy.

Without saying a word, Jill redirected Troy's waning attention back to their conversation by using her hand to turn his head around.

Troy blushed and said, "Oh…I guess I got a little distracted."

"That seems to happen to you a lot." Jill cracked a demure smile."

For what seemed like minutes, there settled among them both a deep quiet that began to get underneath Troy's skin like the humid sun that was bearing down upon him. He wanted Jill to say something first, he honestly had nothing else to utter.

"I guess you haven't thought on what we've been talking about for the past three months, have you?"

Troy continued walking while holding his breath in the hopes that he could conjure something rational to say at that moment. He had wished that she would have at least given up hope on the aforementioned subject as time went by, but as it appeared, luck wouldn't have it any other way.

"Troy turned to Jill and said, "Jill…it's just that—

"It's just what, Troy?" Jill hastily jumped in.

Troy once more held his breath for as long as he possibly could, hoping that the seconds that were passing by would help him think up something that wouldn't upset Jill.

"Jill, Australia is a far cry away from Ohio. I mean, can't you find any missionary groups in Canada or somewhere else close?"

Jill sulked as her feet began to drag across the steaming hot pavement. Troy stared down at the ground with a miserable doom gaze; as usual, what he was thinking came straight out of his mouth.

Troy wrapped his sweaty arm around her shoulder; much to his chagrin, it was time to suck up once more.

"It's not that I don't wanna go, it's just that you've backed me into one helluva corner, Jill."

"How so, Troy," Jill raised her voice. "What else are you doing here? I thought you wanted to go."

"I do, but I just don't wanna be pushed into it. Jill, you're asking me to travel to another continent, for God's sake."

"Oh, I see, so you say yes when you think you're gonna get sex, but it's a question mark on anything else? Is that why you've been avoiding me these past few days like the plague?"

Troy blushed at that instant, not quite knowing how else to react. He had consoling words to say, but pulling them out of his dry mouth was another hard-fought mission.

"I do everything I can for you, Troy." Jill urged. "I went to see that Rocky Three with you, and believe me, I wouldn't exactly call that intellectual entertainment."

"Jill," Troy chocked, "that was a movie! We're talking Australia here!"

Jill stopped walking so she could place her right hand on Troy's chest. "I realize that going to a whole new place for two months is jarring, but it's for a really good cause. It's what God wants us to do, to help those in need."

Troy enveloped his arms around Jill's waist and pulled her close. The strong scent of her strawberry perfume caused him to momentarily close his eyes and inhale. It was such a comfortable fragrance that he didn't want to let her go.

With his lips to her left ear, Troy whispered, "I am with you, always, wherever in the world we may end up, as long as we're together."

Jill didn't say anything, she didn't even look up at Troy, all she did was wrap her arms around his neck and squeeze as tight as she could before giving him a peck of a kiss on the lips.

"I gotta go to the store and pick up some beef and onions for my mom." Jill said as she released herself from Troy. "The woman will go into cardiac arrest if she can't make beef stew tonight for dinner. I love you, Troy."

"I love, sweetheart." Troy said as he watched Jill walk back to her car and pull away.

There he stood in the middle of the track while a million and one thoughts raced through his head like a school of spawning fish. In all truth, Troy could hardly recall what had just taken place just a few moments earlier, all he could seem to recollect was something about a movie and beef stew.

After nearly a whole three minutes of standing in the sun, Troy carried his stiff body to his car and got in. From the glove compartment, he whipped out his diary and pen.

July 10th, 1982

She came at me again today with it, right on schedule, no less. She is determined to wear me down. I feel like a man waiting to be executed. I don't know if I'm coming or going anymore. I hate feeling like this, like I have no say in the matter, but I love Jill so much, even if she keeps holding out on me, (which I will admit is really beginning to piss me the fuck off).

I know that I've been stalling for as long as I can, and yet, I can't seem to get over the fact that I'm not doing anything here either. Just work and church, oh, and getting cussed out by crazy black ladies with curlers in their hair. Yeah, boy, it's been one hell of a day.

CHAPTER 5

"What the hell are you doing, kid?" A large construction worker hollered at Troy from behind.

Side stepping the angry individual, Troy knelt down and started to scoop up each and every cinder block that he had carelessly dropped back into the wheelbarrow before resuming his long trot down a dirt burdened path.

Sensing his co-worker's rage, Troy did his best to maintain both his balance and sense of sanity without allowing another mishap to take place before day's end. He could feel every set of aggravated and worried eyes bear down upon him as he tarried on. He was already on work probation from his superior, the last thing he needed was to be terminated, and that excruciating thought alone only gave him the extra boost of strength he needed to at least make it for the remaining two hours that he had left in his shift.

Without taking a momentary breath, Troy immediately began to unload one cinder block after another onto a concrete slab before laying down globs of wet cement where the bricks were eventually going to be placed.

The boiling summer sun soaked right through his yellow hard hat, causing sweat to stream down his face like a dripping faucet. Brick after brick was hastily positioned onto the slab while wet cement funneled onto the ground. When Troy looked down beneath him, a cinder block fell right on his left foot, followed by another and three more after that, which in turn caused his wheelbarrow to tip over and knock the bucket of cement to the ground as well.

Rather than get down and clean up his unruly mess, Troy instead looked up to a partially constructed building to his direct right to see a tall white man staring poisonous arrows directly back down at him, as though he were telepathically cursing at Troy.

Troy took off his hard hat and wiped his drenched forehead before turning and walking away from the site and back to his car that was parked in the makeshift lot.

He slammed his helmet onto the hood and dropped his head. He was waiting for it, like a coming storm that meteorologists had been relentlessly predicting for days.

The longer he waited the more the sweat seemed to flow until it started to sting his eyes. He couldn't find it in his self to turn around; there was too much burning shame behind him.

"You wanna tell me just what the hell all that was back there?" A deep, irate voice griped from behind.

Without exhaling, Troy spun around to face the tall man. "Dad, it was a just a simple accident.

"Simple accident," the man asked. "Dammit, you almost dropped those fucking bricks on someone's head! What the hell is the matter with you, anyways? You've been walking around here for the past few days like you have your own head up your ass!"

Troy swallowed, trying to bide himself time so that his father would at least try and calm down before the next wave of attacks began.

"You know damn good and well that this project has to be completed by September, and here you are, fucking up! Either get it together or else I'll find another man to take your place!" The loud man ranted before turning and marching back to the construction site.

Much like his shadow that stood tall and firm against the sun, Troy remained silent as he looked on at his enraged father. He was all too familiar with the script; it was something he had memorized all his life. He didn't have the nerve to tell his dad just what was on his mind; he didn't even have the guts to stand up to his own girlfriend, for that matter.

Troy gathered the remains of his melted pride before snatching his hard hat from off the roof of his car and carrying on back to the site.

* * *

Both Troy and his father pulled into the driveway at the same time. There was something inside the young man that wanted to ditch his dad on the drive home and simply take off for the next state; he didn't quite know just what had stopped him from doing so; perhaps not wanting just yet to leave it all behind him so soon.

Troy had hoped for at least a little time to himself before confronting his father, but that was completely out of the question, the man was hot on his heels on the way inside the house.

The second Troy flung open the backdoor he saw Chris and another boy both seated at the kitchen table, trading basketball cards back and forth.

Without saying so much as a hello, Troy stormed into the living room and waited. He was thirsty and hungry all at once, and yet, eating or drinking was the last thing that he wanted to do at that instant.

"Go home, Jason!" Troy's father roared from the kitchen before slamming the door shut behind him.

Troy could hear his dad's bellowing voice all the way in the living room. The young man couldn't even let his own lunchbox slip out of his tight right hand; he held it with such an aggressive force.

Troy watched as his father sprinted into the living room before he asked, "Okay, just what the hell is up your ass?"

Troy held his breath before replying, "Dad, I just have some things on my mind."

Troy's father put his hands on his hips and asked, "Things, huh? What kind of things? Jill? Your buddies on 10th Avenue? Spit it out!"

Troy turned before dropping his lunchbox to the floor. It was on the tip of his parched tongue, all he had to do was pull the sentence out and hope that his feet wouldn't be too wobbly to cut and run.

With a skittish stutter, Troy said, "Jill…there's this thing in Australia, and Jill wants me to go."

"Jill," Troy's dad replied as he rolled his eyes and exhaled. "You gotta be kidding me. What thing is this?"

"It's a missionary retreat."

Troy's father scrunched up his face before asking, "Missionary retreat? What the hell? What is it, some hippie commune down there? Did Pastor Reynolds put you two up to this?"

"No, dad, he has nothing to do with it."

"So let me get this straight, you wanna leave a perfectly good job down at the site just so you can go with your girlfriend to some country to become a missionary?"

"I'm not gonna be a missionary, dad. It's just helping people down there and—

"You got people here that need help!" The man barked. "When the hell are you kids gonna grow up? I don't understand you, Troy. One day you wanna be a basketball player. What do you do? You turn down a scholarship to a good school and stay here to serve at some church. Now you want to go to butt-fuck Australia to help people? For the love of God," the man raved before turning around and leaning his body up against the wall.

For the first time in his life, Troy saw his father defeated; the man that had dropped his shoulders to the floor was completely alien to him.

"I don't get you, son." The man quietly uttered, sounding exhausted. "When your brother was little, he wanted to be an astronaut. Last year he wanted to be a firefighter. Just last week he wanted to be a professional wrestler after seeing some guy jump off the ring and land on another guy's face. But your brother is only twelve. You're twenty-one, and now you're playing the 'I have to find myself' role. I can't believe this is happening."

"Dad, it's only for a couple of months." Troy contended. "It's not like I'll be gone forever."

Troy's father sighed. "You must really love Jill to want to go to another continent with her."

Troy's lips never parted, he looked past his dad and into the kitchen to see Chris standing in the middle of the floor with a deadpan look on his face.

Troy's father then pulled his body off the wall and began to advance towards him. "You don't even know a damn thing about that country. It's not exactly Canada."

"Dad, it's something I have to do."

"Really?" the man sneered. "Give me a break, kid, you're a man, and no man runs off to another country with a woman without knowing that he'll get something from that woman in return.

"It has nothing to do with that!" Troy defensively struck back.

Troy's dad smirked ghoulishly at his son before snickering, "Missionary retreat? What are you guys gonna do down there, sing hymns at kangaroos?"

Troy rolled his eyes at his father's callousness; in a way it was like listening to himself whenever he and Jill would speak on the subject, and that stung him to the very core.

"You know, it's funny, when you first started this whole church thing, I thought to myself, 'okay, he dropped college, maybe this will put him back on the right track again.' "But, Australia," the man questioned with a painful angst cursing his face. "I feel like I'm gonna have this same conversation with you when you turn thirty-one. Jill is a nice girl, and I'm sure she means well, but this is something that stupid liberals do whenever they can't hack it in the real world."

Troy really had no other alternative but to stand and listen to every word that came from out of his father's mouth. The man was saying all the things that Troy himself had been thinking for months.

"This whole thing just didn't pop out of nowhere. When are you supposed to leave?"

"On the thirty-first," Troy sheepishly answered.

"I see," Troy's dad lifted his head, as to say that he wasn't surprised. "When did Jill first approach you about this little expedition?"

Troy held off a reply at first, trying in earnest to conjure a lie, or at least something that sounded reasonable enough to keep from appearing like a total idiot in front of the man that already saw his own son as grade A goofball.

"Back in April," the young man carefully muttered.

Troy's dad only stood in place and stared on as though he were gazing at a complete fool. Troy had seen the same look in times past, and that was the problem.

Shaking his head from side to side, Troy's father sternly said, "I love you, son. I love you. But…sometimes I wonder just what the hell is on your mind. You're twenty-one, and all you do is spend your days clowning around at work, chasing after your girlfriend and writing in that damn diary. What guy keeps a diary, anyways?"

Troy couldn't even lift his head, listening to his dad was like hearing a recording that would never stop repeating itself.

The two grown men paced the floor like a couple of boys that were ashamed of some mischievous act that had just taken place. The bitter silence between them both lasted for at least a minute before Mr. Gaston stopped walking, turned to face Troy, and said with his teeth gritted, "I love you, Troy, I truly do. But sometimes you make me so damn mad!"

Troy looked up to see his father walk out of the warm living room and into the kitchen, right past Chris who had been standing in the same position ever since the argument first started. The man never once bothered to look back at the Troy who himself was wearing a quizzical glaze upon his face, like he was completely lost within the world in which he dwelt.

Troy turned and began for his bedroom. He could hear his father's car start up and rip out of the driveway like he was racing in Daytona.

CHAPTER 6

"President Reagan, and U.S. Secretary of State, Alexander Haig both met yesterday to discuss the continuing conflict in Lebanon. President Reagan discussed whether or not U.S. intervention would be necessary in the conflict that began last month. The President stressed a quote, unquote, short war, pleading with Israel to wrap up the occupation in Southern Lebanon as quickly as possible. Meanwhile, around the nation, it is hot, hot, hot. Temperatures reached triple digits in Austin, Texas yesterday, topping out at one hundred and five. While here in Bixby, it looks like another steamy, humid day with our high reaching ninety-five. Now, we take you to the obscure town of Alexandria, Minnesota where a truly bizarre and frankly unsettling occurrence took place just last evening. We take you now to our ABC affiliate in Alexandria, KSAX and Mitch Foley who is live on the scene. Mitch, can you elaborate on just what folks there are dealing with?

"Thank you, Roy. I'm here in front of First Light Episcopal Church where an absolutely jarring event has unfortunately taken place. As you can see behind me here, the church itself seems to be…bleeding. According to Sheriff Paul Walton, the exterior of the building seems to be secreting a blood-like substance. Now, if you think that isn't bizarre enough, take a look at the ground in front of the church. Four horses were found lying dead this morning right at the front door. Sheriff, can you shed some light on this situation, please?"

"Well, it appears that sometime early this morning, a little after midnight, this substance began dripping off the church."

"Okay, just to confirm, is this or is this not real blood?"

"We have forensic scientists who are informing that yes, this is real blood. Blood from who or what, however, is still the mystery."

"*What about the horses, Sheriff?*"

"*The horses are still a mystery as well. No ranches in or around the area have reported any of their steeds missing. But from what we are being told, the horses all seemed to have suffered from what appears to be massive brain hemorrhaging.*"

"*Sheriff, could we be looking at vandals or perhaps a cult of sorts?*"

"*Right now it's hard to say. We're still trying to figure out just how the church is managing to secrete this blood.*"

"*Thank you, Sheriff. Well, as you can see, this unbelievable occurrence has attracted a lot of onlookers who most are in total shock. Who's to say? We'll keep you apprised of any leads, should they arise. For KSAX, I'm Mitch Foley. Back to you, Roy.*"

CHAPTER 7

"To my man, Troy, the only white guy in the world that can slam dunk a basketball, and he's not from Jupiter!" A young black man with a Jeri curl said out loud.

All at once, Troy and his two black friends, along with a young white woman, all gulped down their individual cans of *Pabst* as hard as they could.

Grandmaster Flash and the *Furious Five's*, *The Message*, blared on the loud speaker that was tucked behind a bush outside the garage where everyone was gathered.

Troy bobbed his head up and down to the music while sipping on his beer and laughing and carrying on with his two friends who were both seated on opposite ends of him.

For Troy, reveling amongst his longtime buddies was one of the few sparks of satisfaction that he had left in his life. The time that was high school flew by like a breeze, and immediately after graduation came work down at his father's construction company. The young man was determined above and against all odds to enjoy at least one final glimpse of merry before leaving to fulfill a destiny that he didn't even really want anything to do with.

Laughing, Troy blurted out, "So after that, she brings up the fact that she went to see Rocky Three with me, like it was the most grueling thing in the world to do."

"Wait a minute, she compares seeing Rocky to going all the way to Australia?" One of his friends asked while puffing on his cigarette. "I know Jill is one cold blooded chick, but this trip had better be worth your time, man."

"It's like she wants me to go with her so bad or else she'll hang herself. After a while, I felt guilty about stalling and eventually just broke down."

"Man, you still haven't got in between those legs, either." The other fellow snickered. "I would have told her to give me some and then I'll go with you."

Shaking his head, Troy said, "Jill is too much of a Christian to do it before she gets married."

"And she's too fine to be holding all that pussy all to herself, too!" Troy's friend laughed out loud.

Troy joined in before lighting a cigarette and asking, "Do you guys remember what Mike did before he left for California?"

"Yep, that nigga fucked just about every girl from the senior class, even the ugly ones. He lied and said that he was dying from cancer."

"Man, he was crazy." Troy shook his head in a fond sort of way.

"Man, Troy, just think of all the things you're gonna be missing when you're gone. Rax, basketball, TV. I wonder if they have any fine ass women down there."

"I dunno," Troy sulked, "but I do know that me getting my Delorean is becoming more and more of a fantasy."

Troy's Jeri curled comrade sat up in his lawn chair and leaned forward to Troy whispering in his ear, "If you need a little work when you come back, come on by and see us, man."

Troy was well aware of just what kind of work he was referring to; it was the same work that he had been struggling to avoid for years while trying to maintain his longtime friendship with his shady friends.

"Either that or you can go to New York and become a Guardian Angel. Wearing your little red beret and chasing bad guys down the street." One of the friends giggled, sounding as though he were nearly drunk.

Troy chuckled alongside him before settling back down and saying, "I dunno, I love Jill and all, but…I just wish she would consider my feelings, too."

"It's sad that the woman you love treats you like that." The young white lady purred from behind Troy.

With the music blasting in the background, the garage area suddenly grew eerily silent at that second, as though something drastic had just been uttered. Both of Troy's friends nervously glanced at Troy, and Troy back at them. It didn't help the young man that it was in the mid-eighties that late evening, which in turn only made him sweat even more abundantly.

"Have another beer, my man." Jeri curl said with a crafty grin while handing a cold can to Troy.

"Yep, it won't be the same without you, Troy. Everyone is leaving, Mike, Kevin, now you. But you never know, maybe you'll find what you've been looking for." One of the buddies pondered with his hand on Troy's shoulder.

Troy lowered his head to the ground beneath him and tried to reconsider the single most momentous decision of his young life. Life and death.

*　*　*

After hours of loud, thumping music, the tunes had been leveled to that of distant hums in the background. With both of his friends passed out in their individual lawn chairs, Troy shot one three-pointer after another through the hoop that was lanced upon the front of the garage.

Seventeen consecutive shots and not one missed. Each time all that could be heard was the blissful swishing sound of the ball as it sank through the net. With each shot, Troy would reflect on his relationship with Jill, while keeping in mind the first time they met way back when. Troy had come to the startling revelation that that one day could have possibly been the only thing that had kept him with the woman for so long, and would eventually take him far away from home for two months.

"You were always really good at that." The young white woman said as she all of the sudden appeared from behind a bush with a beer bottle swinging back and forth between her fingers.

She was a thin girl with auburn hair that was tied up in a ponytail. Throughout all the years that they had been familiar with each other, Troy realized that she had never once changed; she was a "pass around" amongst his friends. But in the times that they had encountered each other, Troy couldn't seem to find it within himself to see her like that.

"If you ask me, you should have gone out to California. With shots like that you'd be near the NBA by now." Tucking the ball underneath his arm, Troy blushed and muttered, "I guess, but anything can still happen."

Sashaying herself closer to him, the girl said, "I guess that doesn't matter all too much to Jill, though."

"She means well," Troy replied, bouncing the ball, "she's just really passionate about God."

The young woman giggled, "God? Does she think she can find God all the way down in Australia?"

Troy shot a surprised eye at the woman before turning and sinking his eighteenth three-pointer straight through the net. He honestly didn't know just how to react to her snide comment that sliced right into his skin like sharp ice.

"If it were my man, I would have let him go so he could fulfill his dreams. I bet your father sure didn't like knowing that his son was running off to Australia."

With a bashful smile, Troy replied, "It's not like I'll never return. I've still got a lot of life ahead of me. I can always go and play in Europe."

The woman sat her beer bottle on the ground before stepping up to Troy. Feeling an overwhelming sense of entrapment, Troy took a slight step back before looking down at the young lady and taking a whiff of her perfume.

He could feel his manhood begin to stiffen in his pants the longer he stood next to her. Troy knew full well what she was doing, but he never expected the event to be so blatant and up front.

No words were uttered between them, only the music in the background that was softly playing *Planet Rock* made the only noise as they both swirled about one another like two inseparable magnets.

For an inexplicable reason that he couldn't explain to himself, Troy couldn't take his eyes off the girl. Her brown eyes seemed to carry a spell-like power that compelled him to no end.

Just like that, the young lady took the basketball from out of Troy's hand before placing it on the pavement and leading him into the house.

Troy held on for dear life while being led inside. His hands became sweaty all of the sudden as they passed through the kitchen and into the living room where *The Tonight Show* was playing its opening sequence on the television.

Troy couldn't tear his eyes away from her; as far as his mangled brain was concerned, he might as well have been on the moon because he was completely oblivious to his very surroundings.

Straight ahead, past the TV was a dark hallway; to Troy, it resembled something from out of a scary movie. He was familiar with the entire layout of the house from front to back, and yet, on that evening, the home that he was so accustomed to had become a house of horrors.

He could feel the young lady tug at his hand, trying to pull him along like a stubborn mule. Troy watched as she looked back at him with the most confounded glaze on her face.

"What's the matter?" She grinned. "Are you afraid of me after all these years?"

Troy cracked an uneasy smirk before shuffling his feet and following her down the blackened hallway that led straight to a closed door.

The very second she opened the door, a dim light seared Troy's vision enough to where he had to squint. In his head, Jill's name kept on repeating over and over again like a skipping record. The young man was far from stupid, he was well aware why he kept on hearing her name, it was almost like something or someone were telling him to stop what he was doing and run away.

Troy's heart dropped the moment the woman closed the door behind her. It was at that instant that the name Jill had ceased racing through his head.

He was numb.

CHAPTER 8

Survivor's, "Eye of the Tiger", played on the stereo that sat near the swimming pool. Jill's three little brothers took turns jumping into the water while her father stood over the grill poking and prodding at the steaks that were simmering over the open flame.

Troy, with a can of *Coke* in hand, sat on one of the lawn chairs while watching both Jill and her mother come out of the house dressed in matching blue one pieces.

"You sure you won't change your mind about taking a dip, Troy?" Jill's mother waved.

Smiling back at the woman, Troy replied, "No thanks, I remember what happened the last time I got in that pool!" "We promise we won't try to dunk your head in again, Troy!" One of the little brothers splashed about in the water.

Troy only twisted his lips before gulping down the last ounces of his soda. Out of everyone that inhabited the pool, Troy kept his eyes locked on Jill. It was only a few hours removed from his time with Amber. His stomach wanted to come out through his mouth. Just looking at the woman seemed to give him a headache. The sun that was already blazing hot and steady in the sky only beat down upon his brow all the harder.

Troy wanted to turn his head away, but he couldn't, he was stuck in his current position, watching the Carter's frolic about in the cool water. If the man wanted to move it would have been the single most gut wrenching experience he had ever faced in his life. He just couldn't take his eyes off of her.

"Hey, Troy," Jill's father waved for him to come over.

With every muscle in his neck, Troy turned his head and used his reserve energy to propel his steaming body up from off the chair he was stuck to.

Smiling from ear to ear, Troy met the man by the grill he was attending to. Looking back and forth, from the pool to the steaks, Mr. Carter griped, "If I hear that accursed song one more time I'm going to upchuck all over our lunch here."

Troy only giggled and said, "It's a popular song, how can you not like it?"

Stroking his beard, the man responded, "I liked it the first three times, after that, the radio station plays it almost every half hour."

Troy took another long gander at Jill in the pool. Much like seconds earlier, his eyes would not relent in their staring duty; it was almost as if her very image had cast a spell upon him.

He wanted Amber out of his head forever, but Troy was wise enough to realize that deleting her face out of his memory banks would be virtually impossible, for at least a long time to come, or as long as he and Jill would be together.

"Come with me, Troy." Mr. Carter commanded before placing his tongs down beside the grill and walking towards the garage.

Troy followed in behind the man until they met inside the cool shade of the garage. Parked inside was a vehicle that was covered in a long, white sheet. Mr. Carter opened a small refrigerator beside a door and took out a sweaty can of *Tab* before cracking open the lid and sipping away.

"The song got on your nerves that much, huh?" Troy cracked.

Subtly laughing, Mr. Carter said, "That and the heat. You and Jill are going to have a helluva time down under. If you think this is hot, just wait."

"Yeah, tell me about it." Troy's eyes rolled.

Mr. Carter strolled about the covered vehicle for a few seconds before removing the sheet to reveal an all-white, 1960 Chevrolet Corvette. Troy stood back in awe at the sheer elegance of the car, from its chrome grill, all the way to the shiny rims.

"No way," he gasped, "you finally finished it?"

With a haughty appearance on his face, Mr. Carter answered, "Yep, last week to be exact. I had to order the headlights from a dealer all the way in Italy."

Troy placed his empty soda can down on the garage floor before taking a grand tour of the stately car. It looked brand spanking new, and with it being a convertible, Troy wanted nothing more than to hop right in and take off.

"I gotta make sure to keep it away from the boys or else they'd be in here all the time messing around with it." Mr. Carter grumbled.

"I hear you." Troy replied while still ogling over the automobile.

Placing his hands on the hood of the car, Mr. Carter stood and looked hard at Troy. "So, how are things down at the construction site?"

"So, so I guess." Troy sighed. It's still just a job to me."

"Just a job," Mr. Carter frowned. "Do you know when I was your age I would have killed to be a part of Bixby's newest building foundation? That place is gonna bring in some pretty heavy wheelers and dealers to this city. You should be on your hands and knees thanking your father for such an opportunity, son."

Troy soaked it all in. His father saw it one way, while Mr. Carter saw it another, but to Troy, it was yet another pair of cement shoes that kept him stuck in place.

"Troy, I want you to be honest with me."

Troy held his breath, he didn't know exactly what was going to come out of the man's mouth at that juncture, and it terrified him all the more that he happened to pause before saying what he had to say.

"What all do you know about this Hudson fellow?"

Troy had to stop and think for a second or two before saying, "Oh, that guy. Well, besides what Jill told me so far, not much." Mr. Carter turned around and rooted about in a small box behind him before handing Troy a pamphlet. Troy took the piece of paper and studied the invitation that Jill had presented him with months earlier.

"I'm curious, if this Pastor Hudson is as famous and experienced as Jill makes him out to be, how come no one but her knows the man?"

Troy placed the pamphlet down onto the hood of the car before saying, "I don't know, sir. All she's been telling me for the past few months is how great the guy is."

Mr. Carter pulled himself away from his car and stuffed his hands into the pockets of his hip high shorts before wandering around the garage. "It's funny, Jill came to me and Mrs. Carter with the news that she was going to Australia to see this man. I've never seen such stars in my little girl's eyes before. I've never seen her so mesmerized, Troy."

Troy stood and listened attentively at the man carry on about the same woman he, too, adored. Over the course of the past few months Jill had seemingly become a brand new person, and it wasn't up until departure time that everyone began asking why.

"I'll admit, I'm not the Christian that my wife and daughter are, but that doesn't mean I don't believe in God all the same." Mr. Carter explained as he approached Troy face to face. "Troy, you're the only man Jill has ever loved. You're a good man, you come from good stock, and I know I can trust you to keep her safe."

Troy stood and stared pensively into the man's grey eyes. He couldn't move at that point. It was agonizing just listening to such resolute words exit his mouth.

Clearing the dryness from his throat, Troy stated in an amused tone, "I'll never let her out of my sight, sir."

Mr. Carter's face never budged from its serious demeanor, which in turn gave Troy the impression that the man was not only dead serious, but that perhaps he knew something that even Jill didn't.

"I know you won't, son." He gravely murmured.

"Howard, the steaks look like they're done!" Mrs. Carter shouted.

"Just turn them over, they got about five more minutes, honey!" Mr. Carter announced. "Well, we'd better get back to the party. Oh, and try not to mention the car to the boys, will you?"

"You got it." Troy grinned.

Before both men could meet up with the rest of the group, Jill, with a towel wrapped around her soaking body, ran up beside Troy and asked, "Dad, were you showing Troy you're car again?"

"Keep it down; I don't want the boys to find out." Mr. Carter whispered before going over and attending to the food on the grill.

Troy could smell the chlorine emanate off of Jill's body. The softness of her wet hands felt soothing on the scorching day in which all had succumbed to.

"So, I know you and daddy weren't in there all this time talking about his car." Jill said in Troy's ear. "What else was going on?"

Troy just looked down at the young lady for a few seconds. "We were just talking about Australia, that's all."

"Oh really," Jill squared her eyes. "What about Australia?"

"Oh, just the sights and sounds down there."

Jill kept her suspicious eyes glaring hard at Troy before she asked, "What did your father say about the whole thing?"

"Let's just say that he's less than thrilled."

Jill and Troy stopped walking. Jill then stood face to face with Troy, and with a worried look on her face she said, "Troy, if you going to Australia is putting a rift between you and your father then you don't have to come with me."

Troy actually contemplated for what seemed like an eternity before he took Jill by the hands. "Look, you know my dad, if I'm not sweating like a farm animal down at that site, then he's not happy. We'll be okay, I promise."

"Are you sure this is what you want?"

"Are you sure this is what you want?" Troy asked back.

Jill never parted her lips, she just shook her head yes and squeezed Troy's hand. Troy then lightly kissed her on the lips before resuming their trek back to the patio deck.

All Troy could now ponder was his life, and the rest of it.

CHAPTER 9

"Australia has only six states, and we'll be stopping first in Darwin, which is located in Northern Territory." Troy carefully explained to Chris as they both sat on the couch in the living room examining a thick and heavy encyclopedia. "Then we'll be going to Western Australia in Perth."

Chris turned the pages of the book and eyed the various pictures of Australian landmarks, people and animals.

"A Tasmanian Devil, "Chris eagerly signed.

"Yeah," Troy grinned, "they look like mutant rats."

With a smile, Chris motioned, "I hope they're not like the cartoon character."

"If they are then I'm staying home."

Troy and Chris continued to ogle over the strange creatures that inhabited the far off land. They marveled at the size of a kangaroos claws, as well at how tiny their offspring appeared right out of the womb. When they came across a page that contained information and photos pertaining to Aborigine people, right away Troy sat back in subtle awe.

"Those are strange looking black people." Chris signed.

"Yeah, they must be of a whole different tribe of blacks. I sure hope their nicer than the ones here in America." Troy grimaced.

"Look at how hot it gets down there, one hundred and ten degrees in the outback. Are you gonna be there?"

"I sure hope to God not, I can't stand the heat here in Ohio, let alone in some desert."

Chris pulled himself away from the book just so he could reach over to the coffee table beside him and gather a collection of papers.

"Me and Jason got to draw these really neat pictures of these naked women that we saw on TV." The boy excitedly signed.

Troy scanned over each and every well drawn depiction of the two female characters while a devious smile developed across his face. "I thought HBO didn't show dirty movies until after midnight."

"We saw it on this laserdisc thing."

Troy sniggered before saying, "You better hide these before dad gets home, or else he'll have another stroke."

Suddenly, and without warning, Chris shoved aside the drawings and sulked in his seat. Troy looked over at his brooding brother with a worried face.

"What's the matter, man?"

It took a few seconds before Chris could sign. "Why didn't you tell me that you were leaving for Australia sooner?"

Troy sat for a moment and sighed, trying to figure out a way he could explain himself to the one person in the world that he didn't want to disappoint.

"Chris, when Jill came to me about going down there, I really didn't know what to think, or even how to explain it to everyone."

"I feel like you wanna leave us."

Troy wrapped his arm around Chris' shoulder. "That's not it, I just feel like this is something I have to do. Jill is real passionate about it, and…some am I. Besides, it'll only be for two months, I'll be back by October."

"Does she mean that much to you?"

Troy paused before replying, "Yes, she does. But so do you. You're the only reason I would think about coming back. There's nothing else left for me in this town. Dad was right; I have to think my life over."

"Maybe you can still go to UCLA." Chris beamed.

Troy only rubbed the top of the boy's head before closing the encyclopedia and exhaling, "We'll see, champ. In the meantime, I wanna see if I can—

But before Troy could even finish, his misty attention was taken over by the extra-long sheet of manila paper that was seated on the other side of Chris' lap.

Troy reached over, picked it up and studied the crude colored drawing with a steady eye. At first glance, the various, multicolored images were difficult for him to clearly make out. He had to squint real hard just to see the two odd shapes that seemed to stand out the most.

"What is this, Chris?" Troy frowned strangely.

Without looking at Troy, Chris signed, "Do you think dad will calm down once you leave?"

Troy stared down at Chris for a few seconds, he was somewhat startled that he had ignored his question altogether. Troy once more gawked at the bizarre drawing.

The more he looked the more he could begin to make out the two forms that appeared to be roughly drawn human beings.

"Chris," Troy urgently pressed on, "what is this? What is that," he pointed. "Is that blood all over these two? Are these men or boys?"

"Hey, Troy, watch Jerry Lawler slap Andy Kaufman, it's gonna be real funny." Chris eagerly signed at the television while still ignoring his brother.

Troy pointed his head to the TV to watch the burly professional wrestler pop the skinny comedian right across the face live on the David Letterman show before the channel suddenly flipped to the movie Nosferatu without the use of the remote control.

Frustrated and a bit scared, Troy grabbed Chris by the shoulders and spun him around. He then gazed forever into the boy's eyes and watched as he coughed and gagged right there in his arms.

Troy released Chris before frantically screaming, "Chris, what's the matter?"

But Chris continued to cough until spurts of blood shot out of his mouth and onto the floor. Troy leapt up from off the couch like it was on fire. He stood back and watched in amazement at his little brother, too stunned to make a single move.

After nearly two whole minutes of convulsing, Chris calmed down and caught his breath. Troy knelt down in front of the child and took a hold of his face. "Chris, are you okay?" He stammered, holding on to his cheeks as tight as he could.

Chris stared into his brother's eyes and smiled before turning from side to side and saying, "Look... your... favorite... movie... is... on."

As though struck by lightning, Troy stood up and looked down on Chris in absolute astonishment. For the first time in his life his brother was actually speaking. It was those six words alone that caused Troy's heart to flip over repeatedly.

With tears streaming down his face, Troy sat down on the couch and yelled, "Chris…it happened, you can talk! I can't believe this shit! If dad and Carla could see this, now," Troy wept on, seemingly too enthralled to be still. "Say something else…anything!"

Chris looked directly at Troy for a few moments before saying in a deep, scratchy and unfamiliar tone, **"You will be all alone."**

It was right then that Troy's eyes amazingly opened to find himself lying in his bed. Soaking from head to toe in a pool of sweat, the young man sat up and gazed all around his blackened bedroom. He could feel his heart beat out of his chest like it was ready to explode.

Troy wiped the sweat from off his bare chest before reaching over to the nightstand to grab his diary. But the very moment he picked up the book, he paused and suddenly realized that perhaps he wasn't all too ready to document such a staggering dream as the one he had just escaped.

He slid the book back onto the nightstand and got up. Before he could take two steps, he nearly tripped over his bible that was strangely lying on the carpet in front of him. Troy crouched down and picked up the book, mesmerized at how it managed to find its way onto the floor.

Too drowsy to contemplate the mystery, Troy placed the bible onto the nightstand before taking a quick glance at his large Nosferatu poster that was nailed to the wall and carrying on out of his room and into the hallway in only his blue swim trunks.

From the hallway he could hear faint sounds of a man yelling the name God over and over again. The television was still one, trying its best to grab the attention of Troy's father who was snoring away in the recliner.

Like a ghost, Troy crept quietly into the living room to see Pastor Oral Roberts carrying on in front of a massive crowd of people about the book of Romans. Right before cutting off the television, Troy found it within himself to pause and listen for a few seconds.

He never bothered to give the man any attention in times before, but as Troy stood over the TV, he waited endlessly for Mr. Roberts to say something, anything, one sentence or word that would possibly give him the indication that his trip to Australia wasn't exactly the wisest course of action to undertake. He wanted any excuse he could find, any subliminal message that would possibly slip out of nowhere just to stay behind and continue to lay down bricks in the overbearing summer sun.

When countless minutes passed and the pastor's sermon was complete, Troy, feeling as hopelessly disheveled as he could, cut off the television before moving on to Chris' room.

The door just happened to be cracked open, so Troy didn't have to worry all too much about waking the boy. He peeked in to find Chris fast asleep with a comic book lying idly on his chest, about to fall to the floor.

There were portions of Troy's dream that he wanted more than anything to be all too true, but the fantasy of Chris speaking was something none of the Gaston's enjoyed talking about; in their minds it was all but a *Disney* dream down the drain. For the time being, Troy was satisfied with the sight that he was privy to seeing that early morning.

Trying to hold on to what little sleep he still had stored in his foggy eyes, Troy went back to his room. Before he could even shut the door behind him, his long feet once again managed to stumble upon an object on the floor. Troy wanted to shout an obscenity in the air, but instead he held his fuming tongue and reached down to pick up none other than his bible.

Troy gawked oddly around his room, waiting breathlessly for something or someone to suddenly appear out of nowhere, anything that would give him a clue as to just how the same book that he hadn't cracked open in months ended up on the floor, not once, but twice in the same night.

Troy was never one to entertain asinine ramblings; it just wasn't in him to give much attention to things he couldn't explain. It was late beyond late, and his mind was still cluttered with travel, females and the little brother that he would be leaving behind.

Troy sat his bible down onto the dresser before climbing back into the bed and closing his eyes.

However, no more did ten seconds pass by before he opened his eyes once again, to stare at his bible.

Chapter 10

July 31ᵗʰ, 1982

I know it's been a while since I last wrote, but sitting here on this long plane ride, I just have to let loose. Here I am at zero hour, still trying to sort through my emotions. For starters, Christopher. The look on his face as I left the house will stay with me forever, even when I do come back home. I feel like I let him down. Like I tore out his guts and just stomped on them, all for a woman. If I could honestly turn back time then I would have told Jill the truth when she first brought up this trip.

Then there's dad. Ever since our spat weeks back, he and I did a good job of keeping a safe distance from one another. Usually when we get into it, I hear about it for days after, but the man didn't say hardly two words to me for days. He didn't even say goodbye when I got into the cab for the airport. All he said was good luck. I honestly don't know what to expect when I come home.

Then of course there's the matter of the going away party that I've chosen to shove aside. Amber has always been a nice girl, but I can't help but to think that our one hour together that night will come back to haunt me sooner than later.

I wish Jill and I could find a common ground. I wish she would see things from my perspective rather than her so called godly slant. I love her to death, but flying across an ocean just to join some, as my father would put it, "hippie commune", doesn't exactly fit into my life plan. There has to be a compromise. But of course, I'm saying all of this as I'm cruising over an ocean, as far away from Ohio as humanly possible, which in itself is one hell of a wonder. Canada was nice back in '77, but I wouldn't quite call the place an exotic land.

I guess all I can hope for in this journey is that Jill finds what she's looking for so she and I can go back home and settle down. That's all that will be on my mind for the entire duration; a life free of worldwide expeditions, and a woman that will be content with the life that she has at home. Or am I asking for too much?

Troy closed his diary and slid it into his pants pocket before reaching under his seat and pulling out his Walkman. He glanced over at Jill who was sleeping away on her pillow that looked more uncomfortable than soft and restful.

There laid upon her face a peaceful manifestation, like she was aware even her slumber that everything was going to turn out for the better.

Besides the minor details that she let him in on, Troy had no idea what to expect at the retreat. All the studying he did on the continent didn't seem to grant him the much needed assurance he had been in search of, rather, it may have only been a deterrent.

He couldn't help but to take his hand and softly rake it across her face in an endearing fashion. He was happy just to see her happy. For the past few months he had seen her so wound up with furious anticipation that at times he wanted to ship her first class airmail himself. The last thing he ever wanted was for her to be disappointed, he was determined on that fact.

Trying not to wake Jill, Troy slipped on his headphones and pushed the play button to hear *"Flock of Seagulls'", I Ran*, before turning his head to the black sky outside the window and the full moon that shined gracefully down upon the sprawling, infinite water.

* * *

From the airport, and a serious, almost nauseating case of jetlag, both Troy and Jill hopped into a cab that shuttled them from one end of the city of Darwin to the other before arriving at a small bus depot that was bound for Western Australia.

The very second they were informed that the bus trip would take one day and twenty hours, Troy's entire body sank into itself. He was still a bowl of jelly from the plane ride.

As they traveled along the vast, dusty highway, both trekkers couldn't help but to marvel at all the open mountain scenery, as well as the rugged bush that was home to innumerable creatures, most of which Troy had already studied at the library.

Kangaroos vigorously hopped from one end of the road to the other as though they alone owned it. And of course, the ever so tenacious Tasmanian Devils that raced like hell on wheels across the sandy plan.

For Troy, experiencing the brand new world upon which he was immersed didn't seem as jarring as he first envisioned. In all his twenty-one years he could say that he had been somewhere else besides Canada. It would be a badge of honor to take back home with him.

"Perth Port," the strange sounding bus driver loudly announced to the passengers aboard.

Troy and Jill gathered their luggage and followed in behind the other travelers off the bus. The second Troy's long legs hit the dirt, he dropped his bag and stretched for all he was worth.

"Why in the world did a day's long ride feel more like a month?" Troy yawned before looking back at the ragged bus that was roaring away down the road.

Jill smiled and said, "Because, silly, it was a day's long ride."

Clothed in a pair of hip-high blue shorts and a tank top that read UCLA Bruins, Troy watched as Jill strolled about near a mound of dirt. Even though it would be the very first time she had set foot on the continent of Australia, she appeared as if she had returned home. There wasn't a single sign of regret or fear emanating from her, just total satisfaction and relief.

"Isn't this place amazing, Troy?" Jill asked as she came walking up beside him.

Troy's lazy eyes meandered around at the humid and hazy landscape where all he could see in front of him was boundless desert land, and behind, nothing but choppy sea water. It was well over a hundred degrees that morning, and Troy could already see his skin turn apple red right where he stood.

"Yeah," he sarcastically chuckled, "it's a blast."

Sounding as though she were overjoyed, Jill said, "I mean, just look around you. Did you ever think you would end up here, of all places?"

Troy didn't bother to reply to her elated question. Instead, he stared around at the countless characters that were milling about the seaside port.

Aborigine salespeople were pawning off their wares while children raced through the harbor at breakneck speeds. Troy could see and smell the food that was being sold at a nearby counter, but from where he was standing it all looked too unfamiliar to his eyes, he was still longing for American cuisine.

"I don't think I've seen you this happy ever since that prince was born last month in London." Troy mentioned, wrapping his long arms around Jill's waist.

"How can you not be happy?" She smiled wide. "This is the experience of a lifetime. And to think, were going to be doing the Lord's work down here."

Once more, Troy retreated into himself, like hearing the Lord's name had somehow unsettled his aching body even more.

"Do you need someone to carry your bags for you, sir?" A little Aborigine boy adorned in a ragtag t-shirt and shorts asked as he tugged at Troy's shorts.

Troy looked down to see the boy as well as another boy beside that one both waiting for a response. It took a few moments before Troy could actually gather what the child was saying in his broken English.

"Uh, actually, we already here, we're gonna go catch a boat in a second." He carefully grinned.

The boy looked around a little bit before saying in a glum tone, "Okay…catch me if you can!"

At that, the boy reached into Troy's pocket and snatched out a collection of slim papers before tearing away with his partner in crime behind him.

"You gotta be kidding me!" Troy hollered as he attempted to break off after the robbers.

"I'm afraid you're not gonna be able to catch those little buggers!" A short, pudgy white man who was wrapping fishing net said as he stepped down from off his small boat and onto the pier. "Those little scamps are as fast as the devil himself."

"But they got my travelers checks!" Troy griped.

"That's the number one thing everyone seems to overlook once they step off that bus, never leave your money in your pocket." The man grinned. "G'day, the name's Finch."

Troy stood and helplessly watched as the two boys vanished into a crowd of other Aborigines before turning around to see Finch button up his blue t-shirt in front of Jill who seemed more than happy to shake the generous man's hand.

"Are there any cops around here?" Troy breathlessly asked.

Finch blushed before saying, "'Fraid not, mate. There's not a bloomin' constable for at least an hour of here."

"Well, where's a phone? At least I can—"

"Troy, I think what Mr. Finch is trying to say is, there's no way you're gonna get your money back, darling." Jill patiently stepped in.

"But that was a whole month's pay, Jill!"

"Troy, where we're going we won't need money, anyways."

"I take it you two are headed past the Coral Coast?" Finch asked.

"Yes, there's a community there we're supposed to arrive at." Jill replied.

"Ahh, the Sinai Village," Finch smiled somewhat. "I know exactly where that is. I can get you both there at no charge, being that I witnessed the whole crime with my own two eyes and all."

Troy sighed as hard as he could before turning around and looking at Jill who appeared giddier than ever before. All that was separating her and her so called destiny was half a sea.

Gathering what was left of his crushed humility while trying to conceal his burning rage, Troy snatched up both his and Jill's bags before climbing aboard Finch's boat.

"Where are my manners?" Jill caught herself. "My name is Jill Carter, and this is my boyfriend, Troy Gaston."

"G'day to you both," Finch happily responded, helping Troy settle the bags into a compartment within the deck of the boat.

The instant both Troy and Jill situated themselves on the boat Troy right away ducked his head to the floor and brooded over being taken so easily.

Jill placed a compassionate hand upon Troy's sweaty palms and whispered, "If you need any money then I've got us both, honey."

Pulling his heavy head up, Troy glanced over at Jill and sat while she kissed him on the cheek. The kiss wasn't going to quell his temper, but at least he could take solace in the fact that the boat ride was free of charge.

Turning over the boat's loud engine, Finch looked back and asked, "Have either of you ever been on a boat before?"

"I have, but I was nine years old then." Jill answered.

"Well, the one thing you both need to always remember is to stay seated at all times. These are dangerous waters for a number of reasons.

"How so," Jill asked, still rubbing Troy's hand.

"Well, for one, there are a lot of sharp rocks, and the current can get downright bitchy, if you catch my drift. And two…the sharks," he groaned before pulling out into the open water.

Just then, Troy awoke from his angered stupor and worriedly questioned, "I'm sorry, did you say sharks?"

"I sure did, mate. All kinds of beasties out here in the Coast," Finch said.

Troy looked overboard to see the foamy water pass by before sitting back down and clasping his shaky hands. Just the very aroma of the salty water caused the young man's stomach to bubble.

"Have either of you ever been to Australia before?"

"This is our first trip." Jill responded.

"Well, let me be the first to say, welcome!"

Troy happened to glance back at the pier that was becoming more distant with every passing minute. Before him laid a infinite body of water that contained the aforementioned beasties. He had totally skipped that part of the trip back at the library.

"Uh, just what kind of sharks are we talking about?" Troy questioned in a mild stutter.

"Mostly whale sharks and carcharodon carcharias," Finch gladly replied while steering.

"You mean…great whites?" Jill's eyes opened.

"The one and only, girlie," Finch declared.

Troy once more dared to look overboard. With a pair of quivering eyes he spotted two, large tail fins protruding from out of the water and sailing past the slow moving boat at great speeds.

"Do you two know a lot about sharks?"

"Only what we've seen in the moves." Jill replied, sounding a bit tense.

"Ahh, your Hollywood." Finch snickered. "Well, when it comes to sharks, there is only one thing that is predictable, and that is their unpredictably. About thirty percent of what you see in the movies is fact, the other is make-believe. There are only two rock solid truths that pertain to all the devils; they have an incredible sense of both hearing and smell. They can smell drops of blood from up to a mile away, as well as any irritants."

"What kind of irritants?" Troy spoke up.

"Mostly urine, "Finch looked back. "You wouldn't believe how many tourists come down here just to surf and end up pissing in the water! For sharks, all that does is call them to dinner. It's like one of us humans smelling sulfur. Yep, the Coast is definitely one of a kind." Finch proclaimed.

"You sound like you're proud of that." Jill noticed.

Finch laughed before saying, "There's really not much else here to be proud of, love. Did I mention also that they can grow up to at least thirty feet?" Troy couldn't rip his eyes off of the scaling water and the two massive shark fins that just wouldn't leave the vicinity of the boat.

For Troy, the village that awaited him on the other side of the Coast would be kissed with a zealous passion the very second they docked.

CHAPTER 11

It took nearly an hour and a half for Finch's boat to reach Sinai Village. No one on planet earth was more elated than Troy, however. With the energy of an Olympic athlete the young man grabbed both he and Jill's luggage before sprinting off the boat and onto precious dry land.

"You might wanna be a bit more careful there, boy-o!" Finch called out. "Last time I checked they were still trying to cover up all the sink holes in the ground!"

Troy stopped on a dime and looked back asking, "You mean… quicksand?"

"You betcha," Finch replied.

Troy carefully studied the ground beneath his Nike's and murmured to himself, "I'm on Death Island."

Finch then came running up beside Troy pointing, "That there trail will lead you to where you both need to be. If you see nothing but bush then you've gone too far."

"Too far," Jill questioned with a worried frown.

"Beyond the village is nothing but miles and miles of desert. Stick to the village and only the village." Finch kindly warned as he began back for his boat.

"Wait a minute," Troy frantically yelled, "where will you be if we wanna get back to the mainland?"

"They have flares here, boy-o! I'm never too far away! G'day!"

Troy held his breath for what seemed like minutes before looking over to see Jill picking up her bag and politely saying, "Well, let's get to walking."

He stood and watched as his girlfriend trekked her way down the dusty trail before he gazed back at Finch who by then was already halfway out of the dock.

Plastered all over his sunburnt face was a dreadful look of despair. Never before in his life had he felt such a sense of utter and complete trepidation. Oceans, seas, continents and islands all stood between both him and Bixby, Ohio.

Troy snatched up his bag from off the ground and ran after Jill who was nearly a hundred yards ahead of him.

"Did you hear that?" He huffed. "They don't have phones here, Jill, only flares."

"Oh, Troy," Jill sighed, "I'm sure if something happens then they will be more than prepared to handle it."

"Are you kidding?" Troy urged on. "This is like something from out of the late movie show. Two young adults walking down a dark path towards God knows what."

Without looking in his direction, Jill happily replied, "You're right, only God knows what is beyond this trail."

Troy stopped walking to watch Jill carry on down the road as though she were being dragged. For as long as he could recall he had never seen her so determined, so hell-bent on doing what she felt was the right thing to do.

It should have inspired him, he thought to himself, but all her vigorous walking seemed to invoke instead was aspirations of basketball. He, too, was determined at one time.

Troy resumed his march behind the love of his life, leaving more space between him and home.

*   *   *

From behind a cluster of thorn bushes Troy could hear the boisterous sounds of people laughing and carrying on as if a party were afoot. Thankfully the walk down the trail was only ten minutes, but to Troy's rubbery legs that had to endure a long plane ride, as well as a day long bus trip, ten minutes of walking felt more like ten hours.

The second they cleared the trail, a huge painted sign immediately stared both Troy and Jill in the face. **To all brothers and sisters in Christ Jesus, we welcome you to Sinai Village Baptist Church,**

and our 1ˢᵗ annual Sinai Revival Retreat. Our study will begin in 1ˢᵗ Samuel 2: 12.

No sooner had Jill finished reading the sign, she immediately bolted away from Troy and into the mess of humanity that was all gathered in front of the somewhat sizeable church.

Troy closed his eyes before reading the sign again and venturing into the madness. Men and women of all races and nationalities conversed and swarmed about the grounds, laughing and hugging as though they had known each other for years. In Troy's eyes there had to be at least well over two hundred people gathered. Not once in all the times that Jill had mentioned the retreat did she bother to bring up the overwhelming crowd. He never imagined that it would turn out to be the big, worldwide event as it appeared.

As Troy began to mingle about, he found himself being bumped into and smiled at by numerous people who carelessly wished him peace and God's love. He saw African's talking with Russians, Asians giving testimonies to Hindus. Old men and women sitting down in chairs praying with one another. There were Aborigine village children racing back and forth in reckless abandon like the yard were a playground all their own.

After so much socializing, Troy began to lose his breath, and it didn't help that he had lost track of Jill altogether as well. He had to sit down; he had to break free of not only the crowd but also the overbearing heat that was causing his clothes to stick to his body.

All of the sudden, all Troy could think of was his father. There were a lot of things that had come out of his father's mouth over the years that in Troy's ears was all blustering criticism, but on that day, in that village, the man's voice never sounded more rational.

"Where the hell is a bathroom at around here?" Troy muttered to himself before leaning up against a eucalyptus tree out of exhaustion.

"I've been asking myself that same question ever since I first arrived here." A mild voice said from the other side of the tree.

Troy dropped the bags that were in his hands and spun around to see a bearded white man dressed in a N.Y. Mets ball cap and a sleeveless shirt and shorts. Just hearing another person speak perfect, clear English was enough to make Troy want to jump for joy.

"With a relieved grin, Troy asked, "You're an American?"

"You better believe it. The name is David Sollenberg." The young man smiled, extending his right hand while extinguishing his cigarette on the grass.

Troy shook his hand and grimaced for a few second before asking, "Wait a minute, Sollenberg? Uh…aren't you in the wrong camp?"

David put his index finger to his lips as to tell Troy to be quiet before saying, "You and I know that, but to these poor saps, I'm David Jones. To them, I'm just another, quote, unquote, hapless Christian on the road to redemption."

Troy stood back, outwardly perplexed by who was standing in front of him, he could sense that David had an angle; Troy was just waiting for the man to let it out.

"Are you here with anyone particular?"

"Yeah," Troy timidly glanced to the side, "my girlfriend."

David grinned and asked, "Oh yeah? By the sound of it, I take it she coerced you to come here?"

"Yeah, you can say that."

"Wait a minute, you came all the way down under just for your girlfriend?" David shined his teeth at Troy.

Slightly embarrassed, Troy hurriedly replied, "Yeah, that's me alright."

"The things we do for love. I kinda figured you weren't here for the brainwashing treatment these others showed up for. Where are you from, anyways?"

"Bixby, Ohio," Troy exhaled, sounding a bit vexed with all the questions.

"Never heard of it," David squeezed his eyes.

"It's a small town about two hours northwest of Columbus."

"Oh, home of the Buckeyes." David shook his head, seemingly amused.

"What about you, where are you from?"

"I was born and raised in Queens, but I work at the New York Times. My editor brought this little shindig to my attention a couple of months back, I couldn't pass it over. This is just too rich, people from all over the world converging to this one place in the ass crack of Australia just for a revival. C'mon, there's gotta be something else to it all."

Troy neared closer to David and whispered, "You don't think that this is one of those cults, do you?"

"That's what I'm here to find out, buddy. If so, then you can call me Mr. Pulitzer." David smugly stated.

Troy turned his head for a moment or two at the large mass of people before looking back at David. "Jill can sometimes be a little… headstrong, but she's no bird brain. I believe that she came here for a spiritual awakening. I just wish we could have talked about it more in depth."

"That son of a bitch Reagan has everyone believing in Santa Claus, the Easter Bunny and Leprechauns. The guy can't even pull his own head out of his ass long enough to do something about Lebanon." David obstinately griped. "Look, I'm not saying that your girlfriend is out of her mind, but you have to admit that this just doesn't happen every day. This all could have taken place in any other city in the world, but no, it's all the way out in the middle of the bush, for God's sake."

"Who's in charge here, anyways?" Troy asked with a hint of worry in his tone.

"A guy by the name of Tobias, but I haven't even seen him yet. I've been here now for over four hours and all I've seen so far are people hugging and kissing each other. I feel like I'm trapped in a Coke commercial. In about an hour or so we'll be singing Kum bah yah to each other and praying for rain."

Troy retreated once more into his mind, trying his hardest to give Jill the benefit of the doubt. What he told David was the truth, Jill was no bird brain, but whenever she put her mind to something, there was no turning back. He wanted ever so badly to discover just what kind of awe-inspiring hold Sinai had on its followers, all the while, making sure not to forget his way back to the pier.

"Troy…Troy," David yelled.

Troy suddenly awoke from his stupor to see David standing next to an old Aborigine woman.

"She says you can find the dunny behind the church."

Troy stood and scrunched up his face before saying, "The what?"

David stepped beside Troy and whispered into his ear, "I believe it's an outhouse. Didn't you say you had to use the bathroom?"

Troy shook his head yes before scooping up his bags and racing around to the back of the church where two slender sheds were located.

It was completely quiet back there, so quiet that even the raucous clamor from the front was hardly audible. It was the first piece of calm the man was able to receive since arriving in Australia.

Troy sat his bags down on the grass before opening the door that had a male stick figure painted on the front and unzipping his shorts.

Like a rushing geyser Troy let it all flow into the stinking hole in the ground. For just mere seconds all the man desired was to be alone, and if he could stay inside the outhouse any longer than that then he would be blessed.

Just as soon as he zipped up his shorts, a deep scratching racket disrupted his peace. Troy spun around to face the door. It sounded like someone or something was clawing at the wood, wanting ever so much to get in.

"Uh…I'm almost done in here!" Troy stammered.

But the longer he hesitated to the open the door, the more incessant the clawing grew until it sounded like it was circling the shelter.

Troy realized that he was in unfamiliar territory; he had hoped that it was another human being on the other end, idiots came in all races, he pondered to himself.

Wanting to escape the outhouse as quickly as possible, Troy whipped out a switchblade from his back pocket before carefully grabbing hold of the door's knob and slowly pushing it open while pointing the blade straight ahead.

The very second he stepped out Troy felt a furry creature land on his back. The man fell to the ground screaming for dear life before turning over and finding a koala bear licking his sweaty hair.

He then looked up to see two little Aborigine boys standing to the side laughing like jackals. Troy concealed his switchblade before getting up from off the grass. He watched as the startled animal ran to the boys.

Trying to regain his self-esteem after hollering holy Hell, Troy patted down his hair and stared closely at the giggling boys to notice that they were twins. He watched closely as they both petted the koala and used sign language to converse back and forth. Troy looked on at the amused children and gave a sort of smile at them, believing that they had no idea that he himself knew sign language.

With a smirk, Troy both signed and said out loud, "Yeah, I know, us white men are pretty dumb."

Both boys stared back at Troy in stunned amazement. The laughing that they were reveling in just seconds earlier had all but dissipated.

Without another word, Troy picked up his bags and grudgingly carried on back around to the front of the church to see Jill standing next to and talking with an Asian and Mexican woman.

"Troy, I was looking all over for you." Jill excitedly smiled. "This is Guadalupe and Soon-Ba."

But rather than greet the women, Troy rolled his frustrated eyes and dropped himself underneath a tree far from the church.

Jill sat down next to him before rubbing his sweaty back and asking, "What's the matter?"

Troy looked over at the young lady like he was two seconds away from wrapping his hands around her neck and squeezing as tight as he could.

"'What's the matter', she asks." Troy gritted his teeth. "Let's see, first, I get robbed by some kids, and then I have to walk with my luggage down some dark trail. Then on top of all that, I get mugged by a koala bear, of all things. But other than that, I'm good."

"You got attacked by a koala?" Jill froze up.

"Yeah," Troy's eyes grew. "Do you know how sharp their claws are? And then these two kids laugh at me. Boy, Jill, this is real fun." Troy sarcastically sulked.

"You don't have to say it like that, Troy."

At that point, Troy couldn't even look Jill in the eye; her passiveness was like a burning knife slowly grinding into his neck.

With her warm hand on his, Jill said, "I see you made a new friend."

"That guy," he grunted. "I wouldn't say he and I are bosom buddies, I hardly even know him."

"Well, you have plenty of time to—"

Before Jill could wrap up her response, beyond the multitude of people suddenly stood a tall, slender white man who appeared as though he were in his mid to late sixties. The second he clapped his hands the gathering of humanity saw fit to quiet their clamor and direct their attention to the front of the church where the man was standing.

"G'day to you all, and welcome home!" The man gently greeted in a polished Australian tenor. "My name is Tobias Hudson. I am both blessed and honored that you are all here! Today begins a miraculous journey that none of you will ever soon forget! A journey that I pray will draw you to a closer relationship with the Holy Spirit!"

Leaning up against the strong tree and listening to another person speak of the Holy Spirit wasn't exactly what Troy had in mind when it came to uprooting himself from Ohio. But there was Jill, seated next to him with a blissful smile gracing her lovely face. She stared at Hudson with the kind of admiration and anticipation that would have a person believe that she was listening to an impactful world leader who was delivering a speech that would become immortalized throughout the annals of history.

Troy couldn't take his eyes off of her. She was an incredible sight to behold. He felt as though she had forgotten that he was seated next to her altogether. The passion in her brown eyes, the quivering of her soft hands upon his, it was almost frightening to a certain degree.

"If there is one thing that I desire from each and every one of you is that you leave from here at the end of September with a better, more in depth closeness with Christ, and with one another! Think of this not as a retreat or a vacation, but as an odyssey into eternal peace with God! Now, I realize that there are some here that may not believe! Some that feel as though this is some sort of cult! Do not believe me or take my word for it! Believe in the Son of Man! Believe in the life giving water that only Christ Almighty can provide!"

Troy saw fit to look around for David who was standing underneath a nearby tree smoking his cares away and waiting for Hudson to say the wrong thing.

"Disregard the world and all its snares and allow the Spirit to take over every aspect of your life!"

Troy sat and listened as Hudson continued on and on about the love of God and redemption in Christ Jesus. The man even detoured into the book of 1st Samuel for good measure. By the time his speech was over, Troy's legs had fallen asleep. He looked at his watch and noticed that the man had spoken for almost an entire hour, in the oppressive sun no less.

"Wow, wasn't that great?" Jill shined.

"Oh yeah, I can't wait for the next speech." Troy cracked a cynical smile while getting to his feet.

The masses began to disperse, which in turn gave Troy the much unneeded notion that he was going to lose track of Jill all over again.

As he started to pick up the bags, Troy felt the familiar sharpness of claws raking across his back once more. He turned around and saw the twins, Pastor Hudson, a large Aborigine man, and a short woman of equal origin all standing there with curious glares painted on their faces.

"So, I see Ju Ju likes you." Hudson smiled at Troy.

Caught completely off guard and trying to pull the squirrely animal off of him, Troy stuttered, "Uh…yeah, I guess she does."

"Joshua, get Ju Ju." The light skinned woman ordered one of the boys in a broken-type of English.

Joshua did as he was told and immediately retrieved Ju Ju.

"The boys tell us that you understand sign language." Hudson said.

"Yes, I learned it back home."

The woman then began to whisper something in the large man's ear which in turn caused him to smile at Troy.

"My name is Ardan, and this is my wife, Josephine. These are our boys, Joshua and Jacob."

Troy shook everyone's hand, including Pastor Hudson's, before reaching down to pick up the heavy luggage.

"My wife and I were thinking, perhaps since you know how to sign, you would like to stay with us in our house while you visit here?"

"Yes, your skills could be incorporated in our services to those who are in need of them." Hudson chimed in.

Troy glanced over at Jill and back again at the pastor before hesitantly saying, "Well, I don't—

"That would be wonderful!" Jill jumped in.

"Good," Ardan beamed. "Our home is just a few yards behind the church. Allow me to take your bags for you."

Troy watched as Ardan, his family and Pastor Hudson all carried on around to the back of the church.

"Great," Troy pouted, "I get to live with Heckle and Jeckle, and their pet."

"Stop that," Jill chuckled before taking Troy by the hand. She then stared deep into his eyes. Troy was expecting a long, drawn out kiss for all the abuse he had suffered so far. "I just wanted to thank you for coming with me, Troy."

It was at that moment that Troy saw such tenderness in Jill's eyes, the same soft kindness that caused him to fall in love with her in the first place. He was hungry, thirsty, sleepy and aggravated all at once, and yet, it was Jill's eyes that caused all of his festering emotions to take a backseat and relax for the time being.

"C'mon, Jill," one of her newfound friends called out.

"I have to go and get my room! I'll see you later!" Jill excitedly shouted as she ran off in behind her female cohorts.

It wasn't exactly the Hallmark moment he longed for, but Jill was his, and that was all that mattered in the here and now.

CHAPTER 12

August 1, 1982

Where the hell do I begin? Let's see. We get here to this tiny island, meet a whole bunch of people, sit out in the hot sun, and, oh yeah, I also get attacked by a koala, not once, but twice. So far, it's shaping up to be a great summer down under.

This Aborigine family is letting me stay at their place while we're here. They seem nice. The husband, Ardan, reminds me of a dark skinned James Earl Jones. It's just him, his wife and their two mute, laughing boys, plus their killer koala.

The guy that runs the place is called Pastor Tobias Hudson. It's kind of hard to make him out just yet; with all these people it's going to take some time to get to know him on a one on one basis. I think it's funny though, there's this guy from The New York Times here, he's writing a hit piece, trying to see whether or not this place and everyone in it is on the up and up. If dad were here he'd call David a stupid, liberal bastard. But I digress.

Then there's Jill. I've never seen her so happy before. It's a kind of happiness that not even I could have given her. I don't how to feel about that. It's like I'm having a Grinch moment. All the money I've spent on her all these years and in the end I find out that none of it ever mattered. It's not the material things, but the spiritual. What a moron I am.

Anyways, all I can do is just hope that our time here will fly by at warp speed. They've got both me and Jill separated; they don't allow males and females to share beds; it's a Christian camp, so I guess it makes sense.

Another thing that is brand new to me is all the foreigners here. Wait a minute, I just had an incredible thought, I'm a foreigner, too. I feel like I'm at the United Nations. I don't think one nationality has been overlooked here. I just hope that Jill will keep me from making a complete American jackass of myself. She's real good at doing that.

Troy slid his diary into his suitcase and listened as numerous, light sounding feet came in from the kitchen and into the small living room alongside him.

Both Jacob and Joshua came in with towels and washrags in their hands, as well as a bed sheet and a pillow.

"Thanks, guys," Troy smiled before getting up from off the couch and layering it with the sheet.

"I do hope that this couch will be comfortable enough for you." Josephine said as she entered the living room with a small basket.

Troy peeked into the basket and eyed the contents. Inside was a bundle of small, red items that to him resembled raspberries. With a courteous smile, Troy looked up at Josephine and asked, "Uh, what is it?"

"There are tart tomatoes." She smiled back, with the basket still pointed at Troy's face.

Troy didn't mind the tomatoes, but tart tomatoes were something completely new to him. Trying not to appear rude, he picked one out of the basket and popped it into his mouth. Before even swallowing the sweet tasting treat, Troy knew that he had stumbled upon a new passion.

Right away, he grabbed a handful of the tiny tomatoes and began to happily pluck one after another into his already full mouth like he was eating popcorn.

"He likes them," Jacob excitedly signed to his mother.

"Yeah, they're actually really good." Troy continued to gulp.

"Do they have tomatoes in your country?" Joshua signed.

"We sure do, but they're a lot bigger than these." Troy replied before sitting down on the couch.

Josephine sat down next to Troy and asked, "Where did you learn how to sign?"

Seeming a bit apprehensive at first to reply, Troy swallowed a couple more tomatoes before saying, "I have a little brother; he was born mute, too. I figured if he can learn, so can I."

"Both of the boys were born not being able to speak or hear, but when they turned five that is when their hearing came to them. We pray to the good Lord that he will send them speech as well, one day."

"How old are they?"

"They are ten."

The boys signed back and forth to each other while giggling.

"You both know better than to be laughing around others, it is rude."

Blushing, both boys turned to Troy and signed, "Is that white woman you were with your wife?"

Troy's face turned its own shade of red at that instant. He looked over at Josephine before glancing at the boys and grinning, "Uh, she's just my girlfriend. But I hope to make her my wife one day."

"Now, boys, you do not ask people questions like that." Josephine lightheartedly scolded the two.

"It's okay, my brother is the same way, sometimes."

"I see you are getting situated, my friend." Ardan said as he strolled into the living room with a pleasant smile upon his chubby face.

Immediately, Troy sat up and said, "Yes, sir, everyone is taking real good care of me."

"Very good, "Ardan replied. "Service will begin in a half hour. I will walk with Troy over to the church, we will meet you there." He then said to Josephine.

As both men exited through the front door, Troy couldn't help but to feel as if he were being set up in a way. He couldn't explain it to himself, it was such a nagging feeling that nearly made him want to race back inside and eat tart tomatoes for the rest of the evening.

"I pray you are having a good time here." Ardan said, patting Troy on the back.

"Uh, yeah, so far," Troy coughed. "I just wish I knew what was going to take place here."

"Christ will take place, my friend. That is why you came, isn't it?"

Troy kept his mouth shut on his response, choosing instead to grip his lips as tight as he could while nodding.

The unrelenting heat began to die as the large sun started to fade away behind a cluster of clouds. It wasn't going to get cool overnight, but at least with the sun asleep for a few hours it would feel somewhat tolerable for a good night's rest.

"So, what is it you do here?" Troy asked.

"I am Pastor Hudson's deacon. He and I have been side by side for years now. I've known him ever since I was a child. He is the one that helped us build both the church and our community. He is a very good and godly man."

"What was it like before Hudson arrived?"

"Very bad," Ardan sighed heavily." A lot of sexual abuse went on here. A lot of us were fighting one another. My three brothers were all killed by guerillas. It was like our village was cursed. When the pastor came, he prayed, and then others followed. Soon, everything just started to come together. That is when I became a believer in Christ."

Standing just a few feet away from the church's backdoor, Troy could already hear the uproar of humanity inside.

"Just how many people do you think showed up for this gathering?"

Unlocking the door, Ardan responded, "Including yourself, two hundred and seventy-four people. And that is added to the two hundred and twelve that already reside here in the village."

Troy found himself momentarily immobilized. The sheer number of people all gathered inside one building never once seemed to weigh down upon him as it did right then.

The second Ardan opened the backdoor he proceeded to lead Troy down a dark corridor that eventually twisted around a corner and straight into the mammoth sanctuary. It was a lot bigger inside than out, Troy noticed. There were pews layered all over the place, from the balcony, all the way down directly in front of the pastor's pulpit.

Beside the pulpit stood a tall, golden crucifix and a glass stand that stored a large, black bible inside that was lit up by a collage of rainbow colors.

Troy stood back and viewed the organized chaos that was Sunday evening church service. He tried in earnest to find Jill amongst the assembly, but spotting one person out of countless others was a task for one of greater ability. No matter how hard he bobbed his head up and down, Jill could not be seen.

"Hey, buddy," David suddenly appeared beside Troy. "How do you like your accommodations?"

Troy modestly grinned, "It's not so bad. Have you ever heard of tart tomatoes?"

David turned up his face and answered, "I'm afraid not. Is it some Aborigine dish?"

"From the way they taste, it's more like sour grapes, but they're damn good." Troy said as he, with David beside him, began to mix and mingle amongst the crowd.

"Have you found out anything else about Hudson?" Troy asked David.

"Not yet," David answered with his hand concealing his moving lips. "The people I'm staying with tell me he's on the level. I'm bunking with this Japanese fellow who swears that Hudson is Jesus in the flesh. You already know what my tribe thinks of that."

"Ardan said that including the visitors and members, there are exactly four hundred and eighty-six people here."

"I'm not surprised." David rolled his eyes. "Four hundred and eighty-six people all drinking the proverbial punch. Can you say Jim Jones?"

Troy stood and watched as David swam into the crowd before eventually vanishing out of sight. He then resumed his search for Jill while bumping into various people and shaking hands along the way.

As outlandishly overpowering as the whole experience appeared, Troy found it sort of enlightening in a way to meet so many people of different races and backgrounds.

Everyone seemed so glad to make each other's acquaintances. But in the back of his mind Troy realized that once the dust had settled, the very moment when weeks felt more like months and months like years in such close quarters, the amiable, warm environment would soon melt into a fusion of ill-tempers and short fuses. People who became fast friends on the first day would eventually end up forgetting one another the second a hairbrush went missing or because they were standing too close to one another during church service.

He definitely didn't want to mirror David's pessimistic attitude, but in his twenty-one years, the man had experienced it first hand, and in more times than few, the end result usually went south.

"Troy," Josephine enthusiastically ran up beside him, "there are some here that are hearing impaired. Can you sign for them, please?"

Right then, Troy's entire warm body began to shiver in his own clothes. "Uh, I dunno," he shrugged. "I guess I could."

"Praise God," Josephine glowed before taking Troy by the hand and leading him up the altar. "Now, all you have to do is sign everything that the pastor says."

With a parched mouth and jittery eyes, Troy asked, "Up here, in front of everyone?"

"Yes, so everyone can see you."

There were no words, or thoughts, for that matter, that could possibly explain just how Troy felt at that stomach churching moment in the evening.

With more and more people filtering into the already crowded church his feeling of total and complete anxiety caused his head to swim. The more his fidgety eyes gawked around at all the individuals, that was all the more solid his body became, like a piece of iron that wouldn't bend.

Up above on the top floor, Troy spotted Jill seated amongst more of her friends, waving and cheesing a wide smile as though she were cheering him on.

Without moving his stiff head, Troy noticed Pastor Hudson stepping up to the pulpit; just like that, the crowd started to calm until the entire church grew to a startling silence that even caused Troy to look around in startled awe.

"Let us open our hearts and allow the Lord to come into his house of worship!" Pastor Hudson, with his arms spread eagle, said out loud.

Troy stood and waited for Hudson to continue, but when there came over the church an inflated pause, he found it in himself to turn his head and see the pastor staring back at him with a blank expression on his face, like he were waiting for Troy to do something important.

All of the sudden, Troy managed to snap back to his senses. Without delay, he tried to remember Hudson's words from just a few seconds earlier before using his clammy hands to sign.

With his eyes still shifting from one end of the church to the other, Troy happened to catch both Jacob and Joshua giggling in their pews next to their mother who was trying to settle them down.

Once Troy was able to slip into a sort of rhythm, he carried on with his reluctant signing duties. He didn't have the nerve to look up at the balcony at Jill.

His eyes couldn't take themselves away from the dim front entrance where he saw two dark figures lurking about.

Too consumed with the persons at the doorway, Troy found it difficult to maintain his concentration on Hudson's sermon on the book of 1st Samuel. The young man was entirely too transfixed with the entrance and the two mysterious bodies that he couldn't seem to make out beyond the dimness.

CHAPTER 13

With a letter in one hand and his eyeglasses in the other, Pastor Hudson ventured down past the wooded path and to the pier in the middle of the still night. The crashing waves belted the edge of the deck upon which Hudson was perched.

The man had a serious look on his face as he peered out into the black never-ending sea. His tears were robust and unrelenting. The cool, night breeze wanted so badly to rip the letter in his right hand away, but Hudson held on as tight as he could all the same.

With a heavy head he looked up at the starry sky and gazed on and on until the half-moon came into sight. He couldn't stop the tears from falling down from his eyes; it was as though everything around him was crashing and left for dead.

With a trembling mouth, Hudson stuttered to the sky, "Is this a fate complete, my Lord? Is this to be my final accomplishment? I have sinned in my life, but I have made atonements, and I have served you. I have—

But before Hudson could go any further, he was stopped by a voice that he and he only could hear. It startled him so that even the trembling in his jaw seemed to pause.

"Yes, my Lord, but why now does this ungodliness come about? Why now, at all times, does it choose to resurface?"

Once again, the voice caused Hudson to stand back in awe and listen in reverence at its wise council.

"But, my Lord, are they prepared?" Hudson pointed behind him. "Are they willing?"

Hudson kept his face to the sky as his entire body began to shudder right there on the pier where he stood.

"There is another?" He froze. "Who such a person, Lord?"

Hudson listened carefully before spinning around and asking, "I question not my master's wisdom, but…how is that possible? The person you speak of is so…young. Younger than I was when you took me aside."

At that second, listening closely to the voice, a whimsical grin came across his face. It was so charming that he could hardly believe that he was smiling at all. It actually granted him the measure of peace he had been wanting ever since reading the letter that was mailed to him.

"I see, my Lord." Hudson quietly spoke. "Tell me what to say, and I shall obey."

Pastor Hudson stood a bit longer on the edge of the deck before allowing the rigid sea breeze to snatch the letter from out of his hand and carry it out into the abyss.

CHAPTER 14

August 10th, 1982

Well, here it is. It's been okay here so far. Nothing extravagant, but okay. I remember the Jim Jones thing, but as of yet, I don't see any of that here. David is looking for something, anything that will prove that this whole experience is some cult, but all he can seem to do instead is bitch and moan about the heat and not having TV to watch.

The days here are filled with cluster prayer groups, most of which last until the evening around bonfires. I must have heard at least over a hundred testimonies from various people. I've heard all kinds of stories from members, accounts of how terrible their lives were before coming to Christ. People from third world countries who are not allowed to praise God. Some have been sexually abused and even worse, and yet, it's God that they hold on to, no matter what.

I myself haven't had any mind-blowing, life altering experiences yet, I've been far too busy signing for the deaf. And if I'm not doing that then I'm helping the other men build an adjoining chapel next to the church. If it's not that, then I'm running back and forth from the house, making food deliveries or handing out mail and the such. I feel like a fucking courier. Like I'm the only person around here with two working legs.

I've managed to put up a makeshift basketball hoop behind Ardan's house. It's really nothing more than a small wooden crate lanced onto a tall branch. Josh and Jacob seem to love it. They know of the game, but they've never played it before. Imagine that, a lanky white guy teaching two black kids how to play basketball.

It amazes me at how full of life the boys are. It's like they have no worries or problems in the world, despite their disability. I see the same from Chris, all he ever wanted was to be like the other kids, not wanting people to treat him differently because he couldn't speak. These two guys are like cartoon characters, and I like them both, and they seem to like me, too. All they do is laugh and play, like kids are supposed to do.

Jill seems to remain in good spirits. I never realized just how much this whole thing means to her. In all the years I've known Jill, I feel like at times I don't know her. Or could it be that I just never really cared to become familiar with that aspect of her life? I'll be the first to admit that I'm a horndog when it comes to women, but it actually kind of makes me feel like shit knowing that I never really had any interest in her pursuits. I only wish I had realized it sooner.

But I honestly have to confess that these past few days I've grown closer to her. Sure, it's hot as hell here, and doing all the odd jobs is worrisome, but when I'm around Jill, it's hard to explain. I'm actually falling in love with her all over again. Not that that's a bad thing, I just never imagined that it would happen down here in the land that time forgot. The way she and I look at each other sometimes makes me feel something I've never felt before. Uh oh, cliché-hole.

Sure, I would give her the world, but now, she deserves the universe.

*   *   *

Minute by minute the evening breeze grew more intense, but not strong enough to have everyone running for shelter. For most of the guests from warmer climates the wind was a welcomed visitor from the sweltering heat that they were living amongst for the time being.

Troy, clothed in a black Count Orlock t-shirt and a pair of shorts, took a bucket full of cold water and poured it all over his head in the hopes that it would cool him down. Totally ignoring the fact that he was wet from head to toe, he carried himself out of the half constructed chapel and into the courtyard where various people were walking and conversing with one another.

Finding himself just aimlessly blundering, as he ended up doing almost every evening at Sinai, Troy happened to stumble upon a darkened patch of land located just a few yards past the church. From a close distance in the dark, he could see Pastor Hudson, along with several others, surrounded by thin poles of fire that were wavering to and fro in the breeze, just praying on their knees in the grass.

Ironically, standing at the foot of the patch was David, who had his hands lodged in his pants pocket, just watching the pastor.

Curious by the entire scene, Troy stepped up behind David and whispered, "What's going on?"

Without turning, David whispered back, "The villagers that live here tell me that he does this every night for at least two hours, sometimes more, just praying amongst the fire."

Troy fixated all of his attention on Hudson who appeared oblivious to the fact that there were two people standing watching him with intrusive eyes.

"I guess I never really noticed that much." Troy said. "Usually around this time I'm trying to catch up to Jill."

"Yeah, I can't imagine how a human being can stay in the same position for so long. The guy has to be a machine. Hell, he preaches for over an hour every night. It's like he enjoys hearing himself talk."

Troy giggled from his stomach before watching the pastor and his prayer partners all get up from off the grass and greet one another before starting back his way.

"Perfect timing," David cooed, sounding like he was preparing for battle.

"Good evening, brothers." Pastor Hudson kindly greeted both Troy and David as he and his comrades passed by.

"Yeah, it is a good evening, isn't it?" David turned around.

Hudson, as well as his three prayer partners, all stopped before spinning around. Hudson shot a suspicious but gentle eye at David as if he was well aware of what was coming his way.

"I enjoyed your sermon last night on 1st Samuel, just as I did the night before, and the night before that." David said.

"I'm glad, Brother David."

"Yeah, we have a priest back in New York who can preach for hours. Tell me, do you always preach so long?"

"The word of God can never go on too long, my friend."

"I guess, but I was just curious, how were you able to convince everyone to come here all at once? I mean, let's face it, this isn't exactly Fantasy Island."

Smiling from ear to ear as though he were amused, Hudson replied, "Brother David, the people that are here have chosen to come to share their Christ experiences with one another. No one was forced. Following God is a choice, not a command."

"Perhaps, but how can anyone be sure what your true motives are for this little gathering? C'mon, Hudson, spill it, who are all these people…really? Are they props for a photo op or what?"

Troy caught himself feeling a bit embarrassed as the pastor, as well as the other three all glanced at him before turning back to David. He wanted to say something to David, something that would hopefully cause him to pull back his attack on Hudson. But before he could even make a move, the pastor, in his usual manner, stepped up to David, face to face, placed his hand on the man's shoulder and smiled at him with such a compassionate warmness that it almost appeared as if Hudson were going to hug him.

"Tell me something, brother," Hudson said, "do you believe in evil?"

David glanced back at Troy before turning around and answering, "Great, now were getting into a good vs. evil argument."

Holding on to his smile, Hudson said, "It's a simple yes or no question, David."

Pausing for what seemed like an eternity, David simply stated, "I believe that there are some dirt bags out there in the world. Manson, Berkowitz, the Republican Party."

"Do you believe me to be evil?"

David stood and stared hard at Hudson like he was studying an ancient piece of art before saying, "What I believe is inconsequential."

"What you believe is of great importance, brother. Your beliefs are what keep you going in this world. In my life I have experienced great, unimaginable evil, and wonderful goodness. But none of that can compare to the grace of God, the one who saved me from myself."

"You make it sound as if you were this horrible monster at one time."

Pastor Hudson took a moment to stand and look at David with a good-natured smirk before saying, "You are loved, Brother David. More than you will ever know. I pray you find what it is you are searching for. Let not your heart be dismayed."

And at that, Pastor Hudson, along with his prayer partners, all went on their way, leaving both Troy and David speechless in the middle of the grass.

Troy could sense that David was confounded by the confrontation that he had expected to go his way ever since first hearing about both Hudson and his Sinai Village. The man's hands were still stuck inside his pockets while his tongue fumbled and flickered about in his own mouth like it were trying to find something to say.

"You see that?" David conceitedly grinned at Troy. "That's exactly how all these religious types sleaze out of these conversations, by using God as their shield."

Troy only gave a slight smile as if to say he was tickled at David's stubbornness before uttering, "I don't know, the guy is cryptic, but I don't believe that he's evil for one moment."

"Yeah…we still have plenty of time before this whole event is over. I've got to get him alone, though."

"What for," Troy questioned.

"Usually, whenever a person has others gathered around, getting the truth out is as hard as fishing for guppies. We got two months, buddy, we'll meet up again. Speaking of cryptic, you never did tell me why you love vampires so much." David pointed to Troy's shirt.

Troy looked up and said, "Oh, well, I guess when I was little I had a lot of…issues, with a certain someone who will remain anonymous. Anyways, I figure vampire movies were my only escape."

"Whatever helps, I guess." David sighed before pointing to one of the shacks and saying, "That Hawaiian chick stays here."

Troy looked forward while trying not to be knocked down by the sturdy wind that was gaining momentum with the passing of time.

"I can't remember her name." Troy mused to himself.

"It starts with a K. She's gorgeous, but she's also clinically insane."

"How so," Troy questioned.

"Did you hear that story she told the other day in church? The one about her how her uncle molested her when she was six? Christ, I thought she would never shut up crying."

Troy only shook his head as to say David was a completely ludicrous individual. The man's callous nature was beginning to wear thin on Troy, but there was still something about him that seemed so original and familiar. Besides himself and Jill and David, there were only six other American visitors, and they were all females.

"I could sure use a Tab right about now." David sighed before attempting to light a cigarette.

"My dad says that Tab is a soda only for the feminine breed, if you catch my drift."

Before David could retaliate, Jill and two of her roommates came walking out of their shack with laughs and giggles like school girls after class. Right then, Troy's entire body lit up with exuberant excitement at just seeing Jill enjoying herself to no end.

"Hi, baby," Jill glowed as she kissed Troy lightly on the lips.

"Uh, oh," David chimed in, "someone call Ali Mcgraw and tell her that she's being upstaged."

Both Troy and Jill gazed over at David with exasperated looks on their faces for the sarcastic man who could never be pleased no matter what.

"What," David shrugged as though he were completely lost on everything.

"Do you always have something silly to say?" Jill asked before taking Troy by the hand and beginning to walk around the courtyard.

Running up beside them both, David said, "No, but it sure helps when you're as far away from civilization as we are. What, didn't Jesus ever laugh?"

Troy once more looked over at David, but instead of handing him a tired glare, his face became more disgruntled, as to say he was fed up with the crass remarks, especially around Jill.

Snorting, Troy explained, "I think what David is trying to say is that sometimes we all need to just let loose."

"I know what he meant, Troy." Jill murmured, sounding like she was ashamed to speak out loud.

Troy could hear the disappointment in her tone; it nearly tore him in half. He wanted to hand David a few more poisonous daggers to the eye, but two streaks of bright lighting from the west caught his attention instead.

"I feel like a fucking beatnik among all these people." David griped.

Jill all of the sudden stopped walking alongside Troy and faced David, adamantly asking, "Just what people are you referring to?"

But before David could throw out some sort of quick-witted response, hard and heavy rain came pouring down, so hard in fact that it was blinding.

Everyone broke for the nearest shelter. The various lanterns that lit up the village at night were knocked out by the ensuing wind that was blowing more ferocious than before, leaving the courtyard completely black.

"Maybe we should go inside the church!" Troy shouted at Jill.

Without pause, Troy, Jill and David all began for the church, as did the other members and visitors of the village, but before any of them could even reach the church's front yard, the wind that was unruly only moments earlier had grown to the intensity of near hurricane force.

Most people were being knocked and pushed into one another, while others fell to the ground in a heap, totally discombobulated with the situation at hand.

Two men were able to reach the church's door, but they both found that the doors wouldn't open or even budge, for that matter. A vast majority of the attendance began to race for their own shacks, which were starting to lose their integrity in all the bluster; they had nowhere else to go.

"Where is the pastor?" One of the visitors screamed out.

Ardan came out in front of everyone and began yelling to each and every person to remain calm, but no matter how hard he tried to convince the masses that everything was going to be alright, that was all more frightened everyone seemed to become.

Troy held on to Jill's hand as tight as he could, fearing that if had let go she would have blown away into oblivion. He watched as Ardan, with his two boys by his side, raced down the trail that led to the pier.

Shuddering in Troy's arms, Jill screamed out, "Where are they going?"

"I dunno," Troy yelled back, trying his best to keep a secure grip on Jill's wet body.

Eventually, others began to follow in behind Ardan, much to both the shock and dismay of Troy. He knew that if the rest of the group was headed off, there went Jill right behind them.

"They must be crazy," David hollered, "the fucking pier is down that way! Those waves must be way past high tide! And you know what that means!"

Troy shielded his eyes from both the wind and striking rain before watching Jill rip away from him and race down the trail where the others were headed.

"Jill, come back here!" Troy bawled at the top of his lungs before taking off behind her.

The lighting provided the much needed brightness he required for going down the trial at night. Like a soldier ducking and dodging bullets in war, Troy skipped from side to side, trying to elude falling branches that were flying all about in front of his face.

The second he cleared the trail he saw all the visitors and villagers gathered together by the pier. Each one of them had their frayed attention seemingly focused upon an object in front of them. Rather than give any thought to what they were looking at, Troy tried to spot Jill though all the rain, but no matter how hard his eyes tried to see or how intensely the lighting flashed, Jill was nowhere to be found, just scores of people all huddled together watching something ahead of them.

"Do you see her?" David screamed as he ran up beside Troy.

Troy didn't have the wherewithal to reply to David's question, or even pay much consideration to the bolt of lightning that had struck just seven feet away to his left. If it wasn't Jill, it wasn't worth his time.

"Jill...Jill, can you hear me!" He hollered with all his might.

As Troy began to move about the ground, he caught sight of two persons standing side by side near the base of the pier. Unlike the rest of the community that were holding themselves and shielding their faces from the rain, the two bodies stood as still and calm as though the vicious storm were nothing more than a sweet lullaby.

As Troy started to advance towards the pier, out of the corner of his left eye he saw Pastor Hudson standing at the foot of the beach getting drenched and nearly drowned by the colossal waves while singing.

With only his hands waving in the air as if he were an orchestral conductor, Hudson persisted in his chorus, apparently no more fazed by the storm than the two onlookers that were still standing hand in hand next to the pier.

The second he realized that the crowd was focused on Hudson and not the two individuals, Troy turned around to David and yelled, "Do you see those two guys standing over there?"

David squeezed his eyes before saying, "Yeah, who are they?"

"I think I saw them at church the other night! They must be—

But before Troy could even finish, the blazing lighting in the sky shined long enough for him to catch a glimpse of Jill who was standing directly at the foot of the beach, watching Hudson carry on.

"I see her," Troy gleefully cried out.

"Can you believe this guy?" David shook his head. "In the middle of all this, he's singing! I told you he was crackpot!"

Without giving David another thought, Troy made a break directly for Jill while trying not to lose his balance against the wind. When he reached her, he could hear her and most of the others sing the same song the pastor was singing; it was a familiar tune, one that was sung at his church back home on various Sundays.

Troy stood in awe and listened as Jill sang, *Lift high the cross*, alongside her fellow Christians. The wind and rain was overpowering, and the lighting was bright enough to blind a person had they looked into it directly, but none of that seemed to weigh heavy upon Hudson or the others.

Troy couldn't tell if Jill was even aware that he was standing right beside her, all that seemed to matter to her was her song and the man that was leading it.

Troy gawked around at the others for what seemed like endless minutes before the wind gradually began to die down to a firm breeze. The blistering lighting that ripped across the sky became nothing more than mere flashes, as though someone were clicking a flashlight off and on. The only element that remained prevalent was the rain that continued to pour down in saturating chorus.

The waves behind Hudson progressively simmered down to that of a playful splash on the heels. The storm was slowly passing, but that didn't stop the crowd from singing to their hearts content.

Trying to catch his breath, Troy glanced over at Jill who was soaking from head to toe. In any other situation, seeing the young lady dripping wet would make Troy as jumpy as a dog in heat, but he was too engrossed with her entranced state of melody that never once skipped a single note. It was nearly haunting on every level as far as he was concerned.

Distant rumbles of thunder rolled across the sky and eventually out of earshot as Troy looked over to the pier's base to see the two calm persons turn and casually walk away into the darkness behind them.

On one hand, Troy wanted to know just who in the world they were, on the other hand, Jill was by his side, safe and sound, there was nothing else.

CHAPTER 15

August 12th

It's been two days since the storm, and surprisingly things are coming back together quicker than I expected. At first I envisioned people wailing and crying their eyes out over all the damage. I foresaw devastation from start to finish, but instead of all of that, these people are actually praising God and rebuilding whatever damage had taken place. According to Ardan, these crazy storms are rare, perhaps two times a year rare, but when they do occur, the villagers know exactly how to batten down the hatches and hold on for dear life.

But besides the storm that nearly took my Fruit of the Loom's out to sea, the other strange occurrence that threw me for a loop was Pastor Hudson. After he stopped singing, the guy just simply walked back to the church and went to sleep. The man calmed down a storm, and he just goes to sleep like nothing ever happened. What the hell? I understand faith, but this joker takes it to a whole new level.

I still can't believe Jill, however. After the storm had died down and everyone began back for the shacks, I expected to have to stay up all night with her, calming her down and telling her that everything would be okay, but instead, she smiled and hugged me on the neck till I could hardly breathe. I honestly don't know what kind of effect this place is having on her, but whatever it is it has her breathing in a brand new life. Mind you, diary, this is the same girl that stayed up for three nights straight after going with me to see An American Werewolf in London last year. But when she stands right smack dab in the middle of a violent lightning storm, she fucking smiles. Don't ask me, I'm still having a hard time believing that I'm in another continent.

There's some rebuilding to do, but that's to be expected. The chapel that me and some of the other guys were building is a wreck, so I can't say that I'm going to be looking forward to picking up the pieces there, but at least every life is accounted for.

"Okay, are you two finally through using the bathroom?" Troy asked before placing his diary down on the ground and picking up the red ball that was lying next to him.

He watched as both Joshua and Jacob raced out of the outhouse and into the yard like they were ready to tackle Troy to the dirt.

Bouncing the ball, Troy said, "Okay, so far its twenty-two to your sixteen."

"But you're taller than we are." Jacob protested with his hands while carrying a playful smile upon his face.

"What's that got to do with anything?"

"You can dunk and we can't." Joshua's whined.

"Did I mention that I can shoot, too?" Troy laughed before turning around and landing a three-pointer straight through the crate.

"That's not fair," Joshua exclaimed before running towards Troy and trying to snatch the ball away from his hand.

With the ball held high over his head, Troy taunted, "C'mon, you guys said you could beat me, so let's see it."

The brothers jumped up and down, struggling to reach the ball that seemed like miles up in the air from where they were standing.

"Boys, come in, it's time for bible study!" Josephine called out from within the house.

"Ok, fellas, that's all for today." Troy said as he tossed the ball to the boys. "Tomorrow I'll teach you how to shoot three-pointers."

"What do you write in your diary, Troy?" Jacob questioned, looking down at the book.

Troy simply shrugged, "Just stuff about how my day went. I just got through writing about the storm from the other night."

"Do you have storms like that in Ohio?" Jacob asked.

"We have storms, but not as ugly as the one here. Have you guys ever heard of a tornado?"

The boys looked strangely at each other before shaking their heads no.

"Well, a tornado is a—

"Motherfucker," Troy overheard David squeal from the nearby half-constructed chapel where he was working.

Sensing the need to remove the boys from the vicinity, Troy said, "Um, okay, guys, why don't you two get inside and I'll tell you more about tornadoes later on. They're really cool."

The boys sighed before unenthusiastically going inside the house. Troy realized just how much they enjoyed playing basketball, and even though he never told them, he enjoyed teaching it to them all the same.

As soon as the backdoor closed shut, Troy reached down to pick up his diary before making his way over to the dilapidated chapel to find David and six other men banging hammers and picking up debris from off the ground. Ever since the storm, David had become more agitated with his surroundings, it was like he was beginning to crack under the pressure. Even though Troy anticipated that he would be the first to break down.

Ever so carefully, Troy stepped into the structure that had no roof to speak of. From left to right, men of varying races all worked diligently, while David, in a corner, cursed and fought with himself.

Picking up a hammer from off the floor, Troy glanced over at David's heavily bearded face before taking a nail and starting to drive it into a piece of wood.

"Glad you could take time out to help today." David remarked with a sense of scorn in his tone.

Troy chuckled nervously before saying, "I was here early this morning, David, but you were still asleep."

David said nothing for a few moments; it looked as if he were trying to find something sarcastic to reply with.

"I'm surprised this fucking place has electricity." David groaned.

Troy looked around at the other men who were glancing back at David with worried glares on their faces.

"Hey, uh, maybe you should keep the cursing down to a minimum." Troy whispered. "Remember where you are."

At that moment, while pounding a nail into the wood, David smashed his thumb with the hammer. He cursed yet another stream of obscenities into the air before turning to Troy and saying out loud, "You want me to keep my voice down? While you were out shooting hoops with Pixie and Dixie, I was in here smashing my fucking thumb with this fucking hammer all morning long, just like I've been doing ever since I first got to this Godforsaken hole of village!"

Troy stood back and watched as a brand new appearance took shape all over David's already angered face. Behind the beard sat a look of both absolute contempt and lethargy. Troy could definitely tell that David was at his wits end, but there was something else hiding behind the hair.

Ever since David first arrived at the village, he was a ball of arrogant, yet quirky pessimism. But there in the half-finished chapel, David Sollenberg had become something out of the ordinary. In his red eyes laid a disdain that Troy could not recall seeing from another human being. It was sinister enough to make him step back and grip his hammer all the more tighter.

With his hands waving in the air, David ranted, "I mean, look at this, were in here fixing up some chapel for someone else! Is this the big experience that's brought everyone down here? We almost get killed in storm! Hell, we couldn't even get into the damn church because the doors were locked!"

"You heard Ardan, he said that when it rains the doors become stiff." Troy urged.

"Ardan," David rolled his eyes. "That guy is probably off somewhere eating Twinkies right now, for all we know! And speaking of Ardan, how is it you get to stay in a nice house while the rest of us get cooped up in shacks like were prisoners of war? I feel like I'm in Auschwitz waiting to be gassed!"

All Troy could do was just stand still and listen. He had to catch his breath momentarily after losing it. David was saying all the things that he himself had been feeling ever since first arriving.

"David, c'mon," Troy insisted, "the kids out there can hear you."

"Fuck those little niggers!"

Just then, a deafening pause covered the makeshift sanctuary, it was such an ominous silence that even the birds that were chirping saw fit to shut up.

Suddenly, one of the workers, a short Hindu man, boldly approached David as though he were going to either do or say something in retaliation.

David just stood back and callously snickered, "Great, now I got Gandhi coming at me, with a hammer no less!"

Like a temperamental child, David threw his hammer to the ground before storming out of the structure. Everyone man inside, including Troy, all stood in place without one word being said amongst them.

Still kind of stunned, ever so gradually, Troy placed his hammer down onto a tool table before slipping out of the chapel and back into Ardan and Josephine's backyard where he saw fit to kneel and tie his tennis shoes. Troy needed time to collect himself, to gather the thoughts in his head and erase them all. Yes, he had felt every emotion that David was experiencing up until his racist remark was dropped. That was very last place he wanted his feelings to wander.

Just as he finished tying his shoes, Ju Ju crept her way out the backdoor and crawled on all fours to Troy. Troy picked her up and asked, "What are you doing here?"

Troy cuddled and played with the animal before beginning back for the house.

"Hey," Jill shouted, stepping up behind Troy.

Troy turned around and said, "Hey."

Jill then wrapped her arms around Troy's neck before grinning, "It looks like you two are finally getting along."

"Oh yeah," he shrugged with a dryness in his speech, "I hadn't noticed."

Jill stopped for a second to stare up at Troy. With a concerned expression, she asked, "What's the matter now?"

Troy sighed, "Its David."

Jill rolled her eyes, "What did he say now? Is he telling you how crazy I am for bringing you here?"

"No, it's something else. He went berserk just a while ago about having to stay in the shacks, and how the church doors wouldn't open the other night during the storm. But after all that, he said the…N word."

Jill's eyes widened at that instant in a state of shock before she asked, "Are you serious?"

"Yes, I thought Jantu was going to rip his head off with his hammer."

"What is wrong with him?"

"I think it's all just getting to him. Maybe he just needs to go home."

With Ju Ju snugly wrapped around his neck, Troy took Jill by the hand and started to nonchalantly stroll out of the yard and onto the main pathway where children were ripping and running about, as well as various adults milling around the twenty-five shacks that lined the trail.

"I think he just needs to be to himself for a while." Jill suggested.

"I don't know, the look in his eyes made me…made me second guess him. I just hope he doesn't go nuts and go on a rampage."

Nearly a whole minute passed by without a word being spoken between the two. Then, after so much quiet, Jill breathed, "Do you think I'm nuts for coming here?"

Troy chuckled before replying, "No, I don't think that, although the other night had me a little worried."

"You mean the storm?"

"Not so much the storm, but you and the way you behaved. I mean, you just took off after Hudson and started singing. Jill, you have to admit, that's a little startling."

"I know, but the truth is, I wasn't even afraid. All I saw was the pastor, and nothing else."

Troy listened carefully as Jill articulated all that she felt that evening. It derided him to know that everyone but him was not overwhelmed by the wild storm.

"I know you don't like talking about it, but, some of the others would really like for you to come and join in on the bonfires. I mean, all you do is hang out with David."

"And don't forget, I also help build the chapel and run errands for everyone." Troy obstinately added.

"Okay, you do all that, too, but it would be nice for you to just come and sit with some of the other groups as well, Troy."

Troy sucked in his gut and exhaled, "Okay, perhaps I'll join you tonight at your meeting. It'll do me good to stay away from David for a while."

"Good," Jill smiled from ear to ear. "You won't believe who I got a letter from today."

"Who," Troy asked, feeding Ju Ju a shred of eucalyptus.

"Pastor Roberts."

Troy handed Jill a coy smirk before asking, "Is he still laughing at me?"

"No," Jill shook her head. "He said that everything there is fine. And you won't believe it, but Theola came to church, too."

A bit touched in his stomach, Troy looked up and asked, "Really?"

"That's right. Pastor Roberts said that she actually asked about you." Jill proudly smiled. "Do you see what happens when you keep trying and trusting in the Lord?"

As furious as he was at the woman after all that time, Troy couldn't help but to feel a sense of assuredness at the unexpected news.

"Do you miss home," he asked.

Jill looked over at Troy and laughed, "Yes. I miss *Burger King*, *Dallas* and *One Day at a time*. But I miss my parents and brothers the most."

"I miss my brother, too. Sometimes I feel like I let him down by coming here."

"You shouldn't feel that way, honey. I'm sure he understands."

"Yeah, but I can't help but feel like he needs me right now, more than ever."

"He's always going to need you, Troy, you're his big brother."

Feeling heavy as a ton of bricks, Troy hung his head low and watched as the dusty ground moved alongside him.

"You know, I have to admit, I'm still kind of surprised that you came all the way down here with me."

Troy looked up and responded, "Really?"

"Yeah, I mean, I realize that I was asking you to make a huge life change, but I never imagined that you would do this."

Troy pulled Jill underneath the cool of a nearby tree before placing Ju Ju down on the ground. He then took her by the hand and said, "I know it seems that I've been real selfish ever since coming here. But I…I just want you to know that I'm glad you're having a great time."

"Troy, it's not about me having a great time, it's about gaining a closer relationship with God. I realize that a person doesn't have to come all the way to Australia to have that happen, but I know in my heart of hearts that Christ called me here. All the others feel the same way. And besides, I understand why you haven't exactly been enjoying every moment here. After all, you've been robbed, coerced into signing at church service, and you were almost swept away in a storm."

"Did I mention, too, that Ju Ju stole my socks the other night?" He grinned.

Jill laughed and said, "No, you didn't mention that, silly."

"I dunno," Troy exhaled, "I like to think that this place is doing something to me."

"You really haven't sat down and told me just how you really feel."

At that moment, Troy stood and stared pensively into Jill's brown eyes, struggling as though he were trying to pull some important, life-altering message from out of his head.

"I uh…I just want you to know that these past few days with you have really made me think about a lot of things."

Troy stood with wobbly legs as Jill gripped his sweaty hands in her own wet palms. The look on her sun-tanned face was that of anticipation, like she was waiting for him to reveal something miraculous to her.

Troy's mouth at that instant grew dry and scratchy as the rough ground that he treaded upon on a daily basis. For years he had never had a closer relationship with anyone. Jill was always the one that he had shared a kindred spirit with, but just then, he felt such a claustrophobic anxiety that even his tongue seemed to want to stick to the roof of his mouth.

Out of nowhere, Troy opened his mouth and said the first thing that came to mind. "Do you remember back in the tenth grade when you, me, Mike, Victor and Amber all skipped sixth period and ran off to Dairy Queen?"

Appearing slightly dumbfounded, Jill cracked a timid smile and replied, "Uh, yeah. I definitely remember what Amber did with both Mike and Victor after school that day, too. You would think she would have been ashamed of—"

Without even thinking, Troy cut in and stuttered, "Will you marry—

Before he could even finish stumbling over his words, Troy's wavering attention was snatched away from Jill and to the numerous people that were running like marathon competitors down the trail that led to the pier.

"What's happening?" Jill frowned strangely.

"I don't know." Troy said before picking up Ju Ju from off the ground and staring oddly at the runners.

Although it seemed like the entire village gathering, only perhaps a handful was taking off at an unstoppable pace.

When Troy noticed that David was among the sprinters he stepped forward and yelled, "Dave, what in the world is going on?"

But David didn't answer; he kept on racing as though he heard nothing at all, much like all the others that were seemingly oblivious to their friends who, too, were calling out their names.

Without even glancing at one another, both Troy and Jill curiously followed in behind the odd ones, as did the rest of the village, down the path that led to the pier.

Once they made it to the edge of the trail Troy and Jill found the runners all perched around the dock, staring endlessly at the raging waters that was recklessly splashing onto their bodies.

Without looking at him, Jill stammered, "What are they doing, Troy?"

Trying to find something to say, Troy muttered, "I dunno. There must be something in the water that—

At that second, every word that Troy was going to utter next had been forcefully snatched right out of his mouth. The man handed Ju Ju to Jill before running towards the entranced crowd like a man on fire.

"Where are you going?" Jill screamed.

"It's high tide!" Troy frantically hollered before resuming his stride to the pier.

The closer he neared the pier the more he could see the blank faces of those who were just standing idly by the water, watching the massive waves crash by.

Just before Troy could reach David, one by one, all the runners began a quiet and solemn march directly into the violent water.

"David, don't!" Troy strongly screamed.

"Troy, don't follow them!" Pastor Hudson called out from behind.

"But there going into the water!"

Hudson stopped right before Troy and stood and watched as the hapless zombies all drifted deeper into the water.

That was all Troy could stand. Immediately, he, along with a gathering of other men, chased after the mindless drifters, hoping that he could at least grab David, if no one else.

But just as soon as Troy reached the edge, he stopped to see one floating body suddenly be snatched right underwater. One body was followed by another and three more after that. Troy froze up, too afraid to even budge at that point.

He helplessly looked on as David's body bobbed up and down in the water like a buoy before a row of sharp teeth exploded out of the water and grabbed a hold of the man, whipping him from side to side like a flimsy doll.

The water turned a deep red as countless bodies were torn and shred in half before being taken under by the great whites that inhabited the mighty sea. Oddly enough, not one scream came from the ill-fated victims, instead, all the yelling and hollering that was taking place emanated from the women and children that were gathered on land.

Troy viewed a graphic scene play out before him as torn human bodies floated about on the water and legions of seagulls all descended upon their feast for the day.

Troy's head managed to turn around to see Jill crying and shouting her eyes out in the arms of one of her girlfriends. He then looked to see upon Pastor Hudson's face a stoic manifestation, like he were taking the entire event in without allowing it to show on the outside.

Troy looked back at the water where he could see fins swarming about in the waves; some sharks, as massive as they were, leaped in and out of the water as if they were trout in a stream, seemingly delighted for the free meal.

CHAPTER 16

August 18th, 1982

It's been six days now since the 86. That's what I call the massacre, because that's how many people were eaten by sharks that day. To say that I have nightmares about it all is an understatement. I can still see those teeth tearing those people apart. Those wide open mouths swallowing everyone like we humans devour popcorn or something of that nature.

I can't help but to think of poor David and the way he looked that day standing at the pier. I can't even remember the belligerent way he acted before being killed, all I can see is him running to his death. I can't say that he and I were friends, but we were cool. He could get under a person's skin in the worst way with his smart ass remarks, always sniggering whenever Pastor Hudson would begin to preach or whenever someone would become filled with the Holy Ghost. But all around, he wasn't that bad of a guy. All in all, I'll never forget the empty look on his face that day, along with the others. It almost looked like they were trapped in a doom gaze or something.

Body parts are still washing ashore, and of course Brother Troy, along with most of the other men, is called upon to help scoop up the remains. I'm having a hard time trying to figure out what's worse, watching the actual feeding frenzy or having to haul dead carcasses off the beach and into their own makeshift graves for a burial ceremony.

And the fucking smell. Granddad Gaston would always talk about being in battle back on Omaha Beach and smelling the bodies of dead men all around him. At first, I thought it was all the ramblings of a man that had been shot in the head, but now, I have more respect for the old man than ever before.

Pastor Hudson is a peculiar one, and that's putting it mildly. On the night of the killings, the man delivers an almost two hour sermon on the book of 1ˢᵗ Samuel, of course. He also talked about how demonic forces will mock the Holy Spirit by doing certain things in three's. Don't ask me what the hell he means. As calm and reserved as he appears, I think deep down the man is beginning to lose it. He mentioned that a hungry evil has descended upon the village, and that we all should remain prayerful and fast. He would mention a fast just as soon as I get my appetite back.

As for Jill, the only thing I can say for her is that she's not the same girl she was before the deaths. Even though she's trying her best to regain her bearings, it's all taking a toll on her. She missed prayer meetings for two nights in a row and she's hardly eating. Jill is already thin; if she misses anymore meals she'll be worse than Twiggy.

Even Josh and Jacob are having a hard time dealing with everything. For the past few nights they've been waking up having nightmares about these two guys chasing them down in the bush, and having something horrible happen to Ju Ju.

I'm working up the nerve to suggest to Jill that she and I should leave and go home. I'm not only creeped out by the killings, but also by the way it seemed to happen. They just jumped into the damn water. We all yelled and screamed for them not to, but they did it anyways. Shit like that doesn't just occur out of the fucking blue. Something drove them to do what they did. A person just doesn't run to the edge of a pier, at high tide when the sharks are closer to shore, no less, just to jump in and be eaten. And to think that a "Doubting Thomas" like David would do such a thing is all the more unbelievable. Once again, I do remember the Jim Jones thing, but this just nixes that whole sick nightmare down the toilet.

Also, ever since that day, there's been an eerie, almost inescapable feeling swirling around here. That wonderful, life-altering, Holy Ghost sensation that was present when we all first arrived is all but gone. And just like I had expected, tempers are beginning to burst. One Cambodian guy got pissed at this Eskimo woman for sharing his bible in service the other night. Ardan had to actually hold the Cambodian fellow back from tearing the poor lady apart.

It's not that I wanted people to be at each other's throats, and I wish to God that I would have been wrong, but I have a feeling that things are going to get a whole lot worse before they get better. I only hope that Jill and I can get out of here before it's too late.

* * *

Troy pushed an old Aborigine woman along in her wheelchair out of the small, shack-like infirmary and down the trail that led to the church. Much like on any given evening, he found himself lost amongst the crowd of able-bodied individuals who as well were pushing the twenty-two invalids along. But on that warm dusk, Troy wasn't watching where he was pushing the woman he was charged with attending; instead he was in search of Jill.

When it came to pointing out one single person in the church melee, it was a mission that not even a skilled Marine could undertake successfully; it was like everyone wanted to grab their own specific seat before someone else planted their selves there first.

On that particular evening, however, bodies were slow walking down the trail. Crowds filtered into the church like they were shoving off to listen to their own eulogies. Their strides were sluggish and melancholy, almost like they didn't want to be there any longer. Even the anxious chatter that everyone brought with them every other evening was all but clamped.

Troy anxiously bobbed his head up and down before finally spotting Jill entering the church all by herself. Her usual pack of friends that she would be seen fraternizing with were nowhere to be found.

Troy turned to one of the other wheelchair attendees and asked, "Gabriel, can you take Usa into the church for me, please?"

The young, white man complied and took hold of the woman's chair. Troy then began to barge his way through the shiftless humanity on his way inside the church. Right before Jill could take her seat Troy grabbed her arm and pulled her to the side.

He peered strangely into her blank eyes as though he were searching for something inside to take hold of.

"Jill, I've been wanting to talk to you about something." He seriously said.

Jill's flushed faced looked as if it were about to melt all over the floor. She opened her mouth and dragged, "What's the matter, Troy?"

Trying to conceal his words from the rest of the congregation, Troy neared close to Jill's ear and said. "I think we should go home."

Jill immediately snatched herself away from Troy before a disgusted frown formed across her face. It was like his words were blasphemous to her ears.

"Leave," she questioned with wide eyes. "Troy, I need this place."

"Have you forgotten what just happened?"

Jill grew sullen at that second, trying not to look Troy in the eye. "No, Troy, I haven't forgotten." She rolled her eyes.

"Jill, I'm sure you can find what you're looking for back in Ohio." He persisted.

"I don't wanna hear this now." Jill replied, wiping her misty eyes dry. "I have to go, I'm ushering this evening."

Troy stood and watched as Jill left his side and skated her way down to the front of the church. At that point, his church duties were all but a side matter; the "eighty-six" incident was traumatic, and it wouldn't leave his mind anytime soon, but to see Jill so downtrodden and depressed made him sick to his stomach.

Troy shoved his way past a barrage of people all trying to find their seats in the pews before he made his way to the alter to prepare himself for service.

Just as soon as he climbed the three steps that led up to the alter, Troy saw Pastor Hudson thumbing through his bible. The stern looking man stared broodingly at his trusty book behind his pencil thin reading glasses while the rest of his body stood as firm and still as though he were beginning to turn to stone.

Troy couldn't help but to keep his eyes fixated on the uncharacteristic man. They didn't exactly have the closest relationship, even when he would visit Ardan and Josephine on a nightly basis, Hudson would only say hello and goodbye to Troy. But it wasn't the fact that their so called affiliation was kept to a mile wide distance that upset the young man, Pastor Hudson was entirely too well kept and composed. Troy didn't expect the man to bawl and cry like a child at the drop of a hat, but there was no emotion whatsoever from him. He was stalwart like a battle hardened soldier, unshakable and nearly invincible. And as hard as Troy stared at him, Hudson just wouldn't pull his face away from his bible.

"Let us all settle down and begin our service, please!" Hudson announced with his eyes still nailed to the book in front of him.

Gradually, the entire congregation began to calm until it became incredibly quiet inside the church.

Troy gazed down at both Jacob and Joshua who were seated in between their parents in the front row. Their usual giddy behavior was absent that evening, it was instead replaced with bored glances that would have suggested that they would have rather been anywhere else but at church.

"Let us open our bibles to the book of 1st Samuel, chapter two, verse twelve." Hudson said.

Troy rolled his eyes before a faint chorus of moans echoed from the balcony. Within the back came a feeble sob; it was such a quiet weep that the pastor ignored it altogether.

Hudson preached as usual on the book of 1st Samuel as diligently as he could. As Troy signed away, he could see the various eyes in front of him drifting away from the pulpit. Some people were conversing between one another while others chose to stare at the windows. Troy actually had to wonder if anyone was even paying attention at that point. Even Jill, who was standing next to the pulpit, seemed weary and introverted, like she were losing the will to care anymore.

Nearly thirty whole minutes dragged on, and Pastor Hudson obstinately continued with his nightly rant of 1st Samuel. By then, the congregation, even the ones in wheelchairs and the hearing impaired, seemed more inconvenienced by the entire experience. Time just seemed to grind along endlessly that evening.

Like an attentive interpreter, Trot listened to every word that the man was preaching, but his eyes couldn't help but to wander about the church, much like they did every other night. From the balcony he could see two people with their arms dangling lazily over the railing. Down to the bottom, just seven rows back, one young woman was snoring away while the man seated next to her saw fit to steal a peek down her blouse.

Troy's blundering eyes then caught sight of Joshua and Jacob who by then had all but managed themselves to fall asleep. Usually, Josephine would slap them both awake whenever they chose to drift off, but that evening, she sat still and nonchalant, seemingly indifferent to her boys' lackadaisical behavior.

Just as soon as Troy was about to cut his attention away from the children, he all of the sudden caught a glimpse of the two of them awakening simultaneously and turning to the stain glassed window to their left which bared the image of Saint Peter.

They sat and stared strongly at the window for what seemed like an eternity before Joshua, without any warning whatsoever, just got up from out of his pew and knelt down to the floor. Jacob soon after followed in suit. Everyone that could see looked down at the two boys in a subtle bewilderment. Pastor Hudson, however, continued on with his ever important sermon as though nothing at all were happening before his very eyes.

Meanwhile, Troy, who was trying to keep up with the words that Hudson was saying, happened to gawk down at the boys in an odd manner. He watched as Josephine got up and tried to sit them both back into their seats, but no matter how hard she struggled, the woman just wasn't able to hoist their inflexible bodies from off the floor.

Then, from out of nowhere, Jacob began to cough, and cough violently. Joshua, too, coughed, but his retching fit seemed more tempered than his brother's.

The boys coughed and gagged out spurts of both phlegm and blood before dropping completely to the floor. Ardan got up and ran over to attend to them while Josephine, in earnest, rolled the children over onto their backs.

Pastor Hudson halted his sermon at that instant before stepping down from the pulpit to investigate the situation closer. Clear in the back of the church a refrain of female sobs cracked into the air. Troy, too, stepped down from the altar to see if he was needed.

After nearly five whole minutes of coughing, a sound began to gurgle from Jacob's mouth. The sound of what appeared to be a word, of all things dripped from the child's lips. Josephine nearly fell over onto her backside at what her ears were hearing at that second.

Joshua as well started to babble something before hacking out another glob of blood onto the messy floor beneath him.

Troy stood back while his brain began to entertain all sorts of wild and ridiculous ramblings. His mind was trying to recall something miraculous but fictitious at the same time. For the strangest reason, he couldn't register the images all at once inside his head.

On his knees before his mother and father, Jacob looked up, and in a slow, garbled tone, asked, "What…happened?"

The entire congregation, which was already on their feet, all gasped in unison at what was taking place.

"Mama…I'm…in…church." Joshua's rough sounding voice mumbled.

"Thank you, God!" Josephine wailed aloud as she pulled both of her sons to her bosom and hugged the life out of them.

Just then, like an explosion, the whole assembly blasted out into yells and sobs of joy and wonder at the miraculous sight that they were privy to experience.

Everyone that was seated up in the balcony flew down the stairs, some were so excited that they managed to climb over the railing and jump down to the bottom floor like uncoordinated acrobats.

Troy stood in place and watched as everyone gathered around the two boys and their weeping parents that were thanking the Lord for the unbelievable phenomenon.

With Jacob in his strong arms, Ardan turned to Pastor Hudson and cried, "God has done this! God has blessed us once again! Praise be to the Most High God!"

Pastor Hudson took off his glasses and yelled out to the overjoyed congregation, "Please, we must all pray for God's discernment upon this matter! We must ask the Lord if this is his will or not!"

But no matter how loud Hudson spoke, his words were all the more drowned out by the boisterous noises of his elated congregation that couldn't stop praising God and crying.

Jill, as well, was in tears as she and some of her friends all knelt down next to the boys and their parents and prayed their hearts out.

Troy stared at Joshua and Jacob in utter perplexity. He watched as their confused faces returned to the far window that they were staring at just moments earlier. Troy, too, turned to the window, but saw absolutely nothing but Peter.

He honestly couldn't explain it all to himself. There was something nagging at him, like a thousand mosquitos biting him all at once. There wasn't a soul on earth that could have budged him out of place as his mouth hung wide open.

Even though his body was immobile, his eyes were still functional. Troy happened to glance over at Pastor Hudson who also seemed to be nailed in place. The man stood outside the animated crowd, appearing as though he were too afraid to join in the commotion.

Troy could no longer see the boys; they were enveloped inside the massive huddle of humanity. At that point, Troy's brain had completely shut down for the evening. It had taken in far too much at one time.

CHAPTER 17

August 19ᵗʰ, 1982

Now I remember. It was that damn dream I had last month. I never told anyone about that dream, not even you, diary. It was Chris that was talking. I'm still kind of lost by it all. I don't know whether to be happy for the boys or pissed off at God. Sure, he gave Josh and Jacob their voices, but Chris is still without his. It pisses me off more that it was all a dream that night, too.

There are a lot of things that are making me mad right now. This steaming hot village, Jill's stubborn ways, and that damn Pastor Hudson. All the guy does is troll around with his holier than thou attitude, like he is God's gift to the fucking world.

I remember what Pastor Reynolds talked about once back home, he said that God puts us through all kinds of tests in our life. I can't help but to wonder if all of this is just a test, or just one big, dumb joke that is amusing God. Either way, I can't get Chris and that dream out of my head. I don't believe this is actually happening.

*   *   *

Troy, along with most of the other visitors and villages, stood at the foot of the infirmary and watched as Finch closely examined Jacob and Joshua.

With a small flashlight, Finch peered into their mouths and down their throats. He then meticulously turned their heads from side to side, trying intensely to find something that could possibly explain the unexplainable. The man even studied their boney chests, just for good measure.

When he was through with his probe, Finch sighed, stood to his feet and said to Pastor Hudson who was standing beside him, "Well, I can't explain any of it, mate. I've never seen anything like it before."

"But we were told that they would never be able to talk." Josephine rattled on from behind the boys.

Finch apprehensively glanced over at Hudson who was wearing a disturbed glare on his fatigued face. The portly Finch then said in an exhausted tone, "I'm sure you were told a lot of things, girlie, but the fact remains, this shouldn't be happening."

"This is truly a day the Lord has made, Pastor!" Ardan loudly rejoiced. "The Lord God has blessed us! His faithfulness endures forever!"

Troy watched as a subdued grin crossed Hudson's face just then. It was so forced that he thought the pastor would crack into pieces just trying to smile at his longtime friend.

"Yes, Ardan," Hudson patted the man on the shoulder, "his faithfulness does endure forever." Hudson then turned to Finch and asked, "Uh, Mr. Finch, can I have a word with you, please?"

Troy stepped aside as both Finch and the pastor made their way out of the infirmary. The moment he spotted Jill within the crowd outside, he immediately shoved his way past the scores of onlookers just to reach her.

"We need to talk." Troy seriously stated as he took Jill by the arm and practically dragged her over to a nearby tree.

"What's the matter?"

Out of amazement, Troy jumped back and asked, "What's the matter? Jill...do you see that in there?"

"Yes, I see it, Troy, it's amazing!" She marveled.

"No, it's not, it's weird."

Jill exhaled and said, "Troy, you have to believe in the power of God. This is exactly what this village needs after what just happened a few days ago. Why are you so against this? Aren't you glad that Jacob and Joshua can talk?"

"Of course I'm glad. But it's kind of out of nowhere, don't you think?"

Jill squared her eyes at Troy before uttering, "After the attacks, I was about to pack up and follow you home. But...this is a sign from God, Troy."

Troy stood with his hands on his hips, physically drained and out of words. He wanted to tell Jill about the dream he had of Chris, but something told him that whatever he had to say would have only fallen on deaf, disillusioned ears.

Jill then placed her hand on Troy's face and said, "Just try and believe, Troy. God is with us all."

Troy looked on as Jill turned and carried on back to the infirmary. There sat inside him a deep array of dismay, like there was absolutely nothing he could do or say. He felt completely helpless.

As he began to go about his daily duties, Troy paused for a second to watch Pastor Hudson and Finch bicker back and forth down by the start of the trail.

He couldn't hear exactly what they were talking about, but it was loud enough to make him want to take sharp notice. Troy hadn't seen Finch since he brought both him and Jill to the village, and his presence there, of all times, was all the more unsettling for some reason or another. It wasn't that Troy didn't trust the man, but Finch's timing was just a little too perfect for his liking.

Troy observed as Finch angrily stormed away from Hudson and down the trail that led to the pier. Hudson silently stood in the middle of the ground with his head bowed as if he were praying.

Troy then looked back and took notice that most of the crowd was gradually beginning to sift away from the infirmary's doorway. Though the once lively and welcoming emotion that circumvented through the village was long gone, the miracle from the night before had somewhat brought a vitality back to those who needed it the most. Troy walked back to the infirmary and stepped in to find both boys speaking back and forth with their parents.

Their speech was that of a long, drawn out gibberish, much like toddlers learning to speak for the first time. But the more they tried at it, the clearer their words became. Troy wanted ever so much to be happy, he wanted to share in the joy of the phenomenon that had occurred, but the sentiment just wasn't present inside of him. There was something holding him back, and that same something was shaking him violently.

Troy walked up to the boys, and with his own forced, gracious smile, he said, "Well, it looks like no more signing behind peoples backs anymore for you two."

Jacob opened his mouth and dragged out, "…Yeah."

"Now…we…can…sing…in…church." Joshua said.

"You can sing anywhere you want, my love." Josephine happily wept as she cradled both of her boys in her arms.

"I need my water, please!" An ailing male patient requested from a nearby corner.

Seeing that the other attendants were still waiting on the boys, Troy saw fit to see to the man's ardent plea. He went over and poured a cup of cold water from a pitcher into a glass before handing it to the gentleman.

Just as soon as Troy turned around, he saw Joshua and Jacob both standing over and staring down at an elderly Aborigine lady. The woman stared right back up at them with the most confounded glare on her wrinkled face.

Ardan, Josephine and the five other attendants were all gathered in a corner talking and totally ignoring the boys for a few moments.

Suddenly, a rancid odor shrouded the entire infirmary. The stench resembled human waste, but on a stronger, more dizzying level. Troy covered his nose while continuing to observe the boys and their staring duty.

The destitute woman laid there in her bed, her hands were shaking so much that it looked like her fingers would fall right off at any given moment. Neither the boys nor the woman parted lips to each other.

Troy slowly began to trek his rigid body out the door, all the while keeping a tight eye on the boys' out of character behavior that struck him so amazingly.

CHAPTER 18

Coming out of the church along with numerous Aborigine children, Pastor Hudson stirred amongst the crowd of little people who were all clamoring around the man like he were made of bronze.

For the past hour, Hudson, as he did every day, taught bible lessons to the children; trainings that only their youthful minds could comprehend and grasp. Tobias enjoyed it just as much as they seemed to. Teaching them various stories from the bible gave Tobias a sense of worth for the next generation that would come about. He was becoming an old man a lot quicker than he expected, training up the children, in his mind, slowed his aging process to a crawl.

Gathering the kids together, Hudson knelt down to their level. "Alright now, once more, what was today's teaching?"

"Hosea," the children all shouted in unison.

"Very good," Hudson beamed. "Remember, no matter how far we stray, God always brings us back, no matter what. Now, run along and tell your parents."

At once, the children all scattered into the village. Hudson stood back up and looked on as they melded into the fray of villagers and visitors before his eye caught a glimpse of both Jacob and Joshua sitting on the back steps of their house.

Hudson's legs at that moment felt rubbery, like they were too skittish to move a muscle. They were just sitting and staring down at the ground beneath their feet like they were either bored or in a daze.

Tobias shook off his timid demeanor before straitening his glasses and walking ever so slowly over into the yard.

Just before he stepped closer to the boys, Tobias took notice of the makeshift basketball hoop above him, and the ball that was lying aimlessly on the ground near the tree. The man reached down and picked up the ball before bouncing it in the hopes that the racket would awaken the boys.

"I see Brother Troy has gotten you two into playing basketball." Hudson said. "How good do you think you are?"

Neither boy raised their heads in response to the pastor. The children sat perfectly still with their dull faces hanging off their heads.

Realizing that a more pressured approach was in order, Tobias turned and shot the ball straight through the crate. He then sank another shot and three more after that before stopping and turning around to find Jacob and Joshua standing up.

It startled the man to where he lost his grip on the ball. Tobias stood and stared on at the boys for what seemed like minutes before he reached down and picked up the ball again.

Holding the ball out, Tobias asked, "Would you two like to play?"

Jacob was the first to step forward, while Joshua stood back with an odd pout on his face, as if he were hesitant in his tactic.

Tobias tossed the ball to Jacob and attempted to play defense, only to have Jacob throw the ball in the air. Tobias turned around and watched as the ball flew across and out of the yard.

Both Hudson and Jacob stood face to face. The pastor wanted to look the boy in the eye forever, but once more, his wary condition wouldn't allow for such a feat to take place. The boy's eyes were too sheltered to let anyone inside.

"We all missed you two at bible study today." Tobias calmly stated. "We studied on the book of Hosea."

"The…man…who…married…a…whore," Jacob questioned in a contemptuous manner.

Hudson stood inflexible against the child's remark. It sailed right past him. "Tell me, how are you two feeling?"

Joshua stepped forward and approached his brother's side. The twins stood by each other in an unyielding pose, like they were locked in an old west duel against the pastor.

Tobias stood defiant as well; the man's unwavering determination wouldn't permit him to be shook. "Yes, Jacob, the man who married a whore," Hudson said. "You see, the moral behind Hosea was—

"This…is…a…very…nice…place…you…have…here." Joshua spoke up.

Taken aback by the statement, Hudson blinked before saying, "Thank you, Joshua. But you've been here ever since you and your brother were born."

The silent stare down took precedence once more, expect now, Tobias was starting to lose his patience, not so much from the boys' stubborn remarks, but more from the abnormal state in which they seemed to be encased in.

"God...help them please." Tobias whispered ever so softly.

"Speak...up." Jacob's eyes opened wide.

Grinning from ear to ear, Tobias said, "I said, God, help them please."

"I...see." Jacob subtly commented.

"Tell me, does it hurt to speak? It would seem to me that all of that struggling would wear you two out. Perhaps you both should rest your vocals for a while until we are further able to discover why it happened so suddenly."

"But...we...like...to...talk." Joshua said.

Don't...you...want...us...to...talk...captain?" Jacob questioned.

Right there, Tobias' heart stopped beating for at least five seconds before it resumed its march, which in turn allowed the man to catch his breath.

"Shall...we...pray?" Joshua smiled before taking his brother by the hand and walking into the house behind them.

Pastor Hudson stood in the heat of the day, unable to stretch even a simple finger.

CHAPTER 19

"There it goes again," Troy shivered while standing next to the steps with a cloth bag in his hand, "that same sound that I heard last night."

Ardan stepped up beside Troy with a concerned look on his face and asked, "What exactly did it sound like again?"

"Like something or someone moaning." Troy replied. "Then it's usually followed by something falling to the floor."

Both men stood and listened patiently for any other noises that would possibly emanate from the above floor. After an entire two whole minutes, Troy shrugged his shoulders, turned to Ardan and said, "I guess it's all in my head. I could have sworn that I heard something falling to the floor up there, and then—

Out of nowhere, both Jacob and Joshua literally came stumbling into the living room like a couple of punch drunk fools, bumping into each other.

Ardan looked back and asked, "Are you two alright?"

At first, neither child said a word; Joshua then opened his mouth and slowly uttered, "Yes...papa...we...are...alright."

Troy stood back and watched as Ardan gathered his boys into his bosom, stroking their heads back and forth with a proud appearance on his face as though they had been born all over again.

Troy observed the distant, off-shoot look in the boys' eyes; physically they were present within the house, but judging by the star struck appearance on their faces, they were far away in another dimension.

Just as Troy was about to re-direct his attention back to the second floor, Jacob handed him a cold, belligerent stare that caused Troy to suddenly freeze up.

"Ohio…is…a…long…way…from…here…boy." Jacob spoke.

Ardan looked up and sternly said to the child, "You do not speak that way to adults, Jacob. Do you understand?"

Jacob eyeballed his father before saying, "Yes…papa."

With a blushing grin, Ardan said to Troy, "I must apologize for my son; I guess his newfound ability has made him quite the little big-headed one."

Troy handed the man a polite, yet, brief smile before diverting his attention back to the stairs. The longer he stood and looked up the more he could hear the racket that was beginning to jar his nerves.

"He's…coming," Joshua all of the sudden blurted out.

Troy looked back and all around the living room before hearing four knocks at the front door. Out of a sense of urgency, he immediately went for the door and swung it open with a powerful force.

"Good evening, Troy," Pastor Hudson pleasantly greeted. "May I come in?"

Caught in between the pastor's ultimately visit and the strange happening inside the house, Troy found it difficult to operate his own tongue at that moment.

"Pastor," Ardan smiled with an uncertain surprise. "Tonight is not your evening to dine with us."

Stepping past Troy on his way inside, Hudson replied, "I realize that, but I thought I would just stop by to see how the boys were getting along."

Troy shut the door and watched as both Jacob and Joshua ran up to the pastor and hugged the man's legs. Hudson only stood with a kindly smile attached to his face before stepping back.

"Pastor, we were not expecting you this evening." Josephine said as she rushed into the living room from the kitchen. "I can always make an extra pot of stew."

"Do not make a fuss over me, my dear. I only stopped by for a few moments to visit the boys." Hudson responded as he sat down on the couch.

Troy stood by and observed as the boys sat down on opposite sides of the pastor while Ardan and Josephine sat themselves down in two other wooden chairs.

While he was still leery of Hudson, Jacob and Joshua were more of a puzzle to Troy than anything else. Their behavior ever since receiving their speech had been uncanny at best, and so far, Troy seemed to be the only person in the village that had noticed.

Both of the boys sat and stared strongly at Hudson as though his every word was life altering. Their eyes never left his pious face.

"Jacob here seems to be developing a very impolite tongue." Ardan said. "He spoke quite disrespectfully to Troy just before you arrived, Pastor."

"I see," Hudson replied. "Just the rants of a zealous boy. You, too, were that way yourself, Ardan, my friend."

Right then, at all times, the racket from the above floor began all over again. Out of anxiety, Troy backed away from the stairs and held himself.

"We have been hearing these noises upstairs for the past few hours, Pastor." Josephine said. "But whenever we go up there, they just stop."

For a few seconds, Troy and the pastor's eyes connected before Hudson turned away and giggled, "Probably Ju Ju up to her old tricks again."

"But Ju Ju is outside in the back." Ardan said.

Once more, Troy and Hudson glanced at each other with a concerned look on their blushing faces.

Looking down at both boys, the pastor asked, "So, how have you two been feeling?"

Neither Jacob nor Joshua opened their mouths; they just sat and stared continually at the patient man without a single pause.

"I got an idea," Troy urgently stepped in, "how about we all go upstairs and see just what is making that noise?"

"Yes, that would be a good idea." Ardan said before getting up from out of his chair and heading towards the steps.

Both Josephine and Hudson followed before Troy joined in, leaving Jacob and Joshua behind on the couch.

The second Troy rounded the corner that led to the second floor he saw Ardan and Josephine's bedroom door hanging wide open. All four individuals cautiously stumbled in to find a porcelain statuette of Jesus lying on the floor in pieces.

"Oh no," Josephine openly wept as she knelt down to pick up the shards, "it's broken."

Pastor Hudson crouched down as well and helped her while Ardan began to skulk about the tiny bedroom. Troy stood and gawked all around but could see nothing else that looked broken or out of place.

"Mama gave this to me when I was a girl." Josephine sobbed. "Who could have done this?"

"I heard more crashing up here, maybe there's something broken in the boys' room." Troy said as he began for their bedroom.

"Troy," Hudson said, "do not bother, I have seen enough. Let's all go back down and pray."

"But no one has been up here since this morning, Pastor." Ardan urgently insisted. "I cannot understand what could have done this."

Hudson placed his consoling hand on Josephine's back and rubbed gently before helping her up and leading her out of the room.

Confused, Troy stood back and watched as all three walked back down the stairs. He wanted the pastor, of all people, to investigate the matter further, and he was shocked at how the man had just eluded the situation altogether.

"Come now," Hudson carried on, "we will see if Isabelle can piece it all back together."

Troy stood in the middle of the hallway perplexed at what was taking place. He wasn't as miffed by the destruction of the statuette as he was at Hudson's blatant dismissal of the odd occurrences that had all of the sudden besieged the home. At that point, Troy thought less of the man than he had earlier.

The very moment he reached the bottom floor, Troy saw both boys still seated on the couch, staring directly at the wall ahead of them as if they were watching something that wasn't there at all.

"Come on, you two," Ardan said with his arms outstretched, "we are going to pray."

Everyone, including a reluctant Troy, all knelt down to the floor, took each other's hands and closed their eyes while the pastor prayed for peace and solidarity to fall upon not only the village but also the house.

Choosing to listen rather than pray along with the others, Troy squinted open both his eyes to see Jacob and Joshua staring straight at Hudson like he were the most fascinating thing they had ever laid eyes upon.

Troy just happened to be holding Joshua's cold, hard hand. He could feel the boy's strong grip tighten around his sweaty palm.

Troy glanced over at the boy who never once took his face away from Hudson's. He looked down at the child's hand that was trembling with such a force that Troy had to release himself just to get the circulation running again in his appendage.

Once the pastor was done praying, the boys right away stood back up, and in unison, sat down on the couch, side by side, in perfect time.

"I must be going now," the pastor said. "I believe the ladies in the infirmary need me. I will see you all at supper tomorrow."

"The Lord be with you, pastor." Ardan added as he led Hudson to the front door.

With the ugliest sense of trepidation lurking inside of him, Troy looked on as Hudson walked right by him before handing him a quick, nonchalant glance and stepping out the door.

Troy wanted so badly to say something before he left, but he felt that whatever words he could pull out of his mouth would be nothing but so much rubbish, the ramblings of a paranoid American who had seen too many horror movies.

Once the door was closed, Troy looked back to see the boys still sitting and staring off into space as though nothing had just taken place within the recent span of time.

He wanted to retrieve his beloved diary and tell it all what had just transpired, but it was completely pointless at that stage.

CHAPTER 20

It was towards twilight the following day when Troy, Jill, the boys and Josephine were all gathered inside the house. All five individuals rummaged through an assortment of handmade baskets at the dining table.

The boys carried on between each other, as they usually did, picking and poking at each other like puppies while Troy and Jill glanced back and forth in a peculiar way, smirking and giggling at the various, multicolored baskets that they were charged with assorting in their proper places.

"Uh, Josephine," Jill looked up, "Troy and I were curious, just what do all these drawings on these baskets mean?"

Holding a basket in her hand, Josephine explained, "They usually tell stories, stories of our people from many ages ago, or from a time not too long past, when we were a more savage people." Holding one basket in her hand, Josephine continued, "This one tells the story of how Pastor Hudson first arrived here. The one Troy is holding tells the story of Ardan's father who was a drug dealer at one time. But when the pastor came here, he prayed for him to stop what he was doing, and he eventually changed his ways. Or so that's how the story was told to me."

Troy held up the basket that was lodged in his hands and eyed the while lines and curves that were drawn all over it in odd interest.

Jill picked up another basket from within the batch and asked, "What about this one?"

Josephine studied the markings closely and said, "Ahh, that one tells the story of Christ's crucifixion. Believe it or not, there were a lot of people who had never even heard of Jesus before Hudson came here."

With a patronizing tone that he had hoped would raise eyebrows, Troy said, "It's hard to believe that one man could change so many lives. The pastor, I mean."

"It wasn't just the pastor that did it," Josephine remarked, "there were others that crashed upon the shore that showed up with him. Tobias was once a smuggler. Both he and his crew were running away from the authorities when a storm forced them here to the village."

Both Troy and Jill's jaws hung wide open upon listening to the unbelievable. Their ears were stinging with what they were being allowed to hear come from the woman's mouth.

"At first, all Tobias and his crew wanted was to leave, but once they realized that they couldn't find their way out of the bay, they just settled here. His crew began to carouse and partake in all the evil that was taking place here, but I guess Tobias wanted nothing to do with it all. He, unlike his crew, changed his ways. He began reading the bible. He would be seen praying almost every hour. There was a lot of fighting amongst the crew, so much so that they all ended up leaving, but Tobias stayed behind. They left him with the evil that resided here. But the pastor once said that 'evil never livers forever. It wins momentarily, but eventually, it is destroyed.'" Of course, this all happened before I was even born."

Unlike all the sermons from the pastor and all the various testimonies from other visitors, Josephine's story seemed to captivate Troy like a bitter wind. The fable of a man that had perhaps spoken only two or three words to him ever since first arriving at the village suddenly caused Troy's perception of a crusty Pastor Hudson to sift away like grain through a strainer.

As Troy snapped back to his duty, he turned his head to see both boys staring at the wall in front of them. Once more, like in past days, his pulse began to race. He looked at the brown wall to see just what they could have been staring at, but in his eyes there was absolutely nothing there. They just stood side by side, gazing on as if they were locked in a powerful trance.

"Uh, are they okay?" Troy stuttered.

Josephine turned away from the baskets and frowned over at the boys before snapping, "You two turn around and stop all that foolishness!"

Simultaneously, Jacob and Joshua turned around and dropped their hands onto the table. Troy watched them a bit longer, waiting to see what they would end up doing next before taking another basket and examining it.

"Holding it up, he asked, "What's this one mean? It has the craziest shapes of any of these."

"It...tells...the...story...of...how...you... and... Amber... went... into... Mike's... house... and... fucked... all... night." Jacob said out loud.

At the snap of a finger, Troy stopped what he was doing. Then, with a head that was as heavy as a bowling ball, he turned to see Josephine staring daggers at Jacob. And there was Jill, with a confused contort on her face, looking back at him. He held his breath as long as he could, trying his best to divert his jittery eyes away from her.

"What did you say, young man?" Josephine asked with a cold tone in her speech.

Jacob didn't reply, instead he lowered his head in shame and stood still beside his brother who in turn sank his head as well.

Hearing whimpers come from Jill, Troy spun his head around and watched as tears began to flood from her eyes.

"I am so very sorry for that." Josephine urgently pleaded. "I cannot imagine what would possess Jacob to say such an ugly thing."

Ignoring Josephine's heartfelt apology, Troy looked on as Jill turned and ran out the front door. At the blink of an eye, he chased after her, hoping that he would be able to catch her before she reached her shack.

"Jill, wait," he frantically screamed while darting down the trail that led to the pier. "Jill, please stop!"

The moment Jill reached the edge of the pier she knelt down and right away vomited into the water. Troy ran up beside her and attempted to place his hands on her shoulders.

"Get off of me!" Jill snarled before getting back to her feet.

Troy jumped back and tried to catch his passing breath. He watched as Jill wiped her eyes with her blouse.

Stammering, Troy said, "You…you can't believe what some silly little boy says."

Without even looking in his direction, Jill whimpered, "Oh really? Then how did Jacob know about Mike and Amber? Did you write about them in your diary?"

"No, I don't know where he got that from!"

Troy watched as Jill paced back and forth, from him to the tall pole that stood next to the edge. Troy tried to recall in his head if he had accidentally left his diary out in the open before attempting to once more console Jill.

"Just stop, Troy," she snapped back. "I should have known, you always had a thing for Amber!"

"No I didn't; I can't stand her!"

"But you did go over to Mike's house before we left, didn't you?"

"Well, yes, but—

"And she was there, wasn't she?"

At first, Troy didn't know how to reply; he reached deep down to try and find the words to say, safe words.

"Don't lie, Troy." Jill firmly said with gritted teeth.

Once again, Troy struggled to find something to grab a hold of, but he realized that all of his so called lifelines were out to sea.

"Jill, Jacob is only ten years old. How are you gonna take his word over mine?"

Jill handed Troy a blasé expression, as to say that she wasn't impressed with his evasive skills. It cut Troy to the bone to see such an uncharacteristic look upon her face.

"Troy, unless you told both Jacob and Joshua about Mike and Amber, how else did he know? Did you do it because I wouldn't have sex with you?"

Troy stood back and turned up his face.

"You know I don't do that sort of thing before marriage."

"Jill, you have to understand—

"Understand what, Troy, that until the woman that you say you love gives it up, you'll go around and poke anyone you want to?"

"I wish for once you would let me fucking talk!" Troy furiously shouted back. "This is what I mean, you never let anyone have a say! It's always what you want, what you see is right! You treat me like

I'm some child!' 'You'll love it here, Troy!' 'It'll be the experience of a lifetime, Troy!' He furiously mocked.

Jill began to cry all over again, except now her tears weren't having the effect upon Troy that they usually carried. He was mad, not only at Jacob and his loose lips, but also at Jill. He had held his true feelings in for as long as he could possibly bear to.

"I've done everything you wanted me to do and more!"

"If you didn't want to come then why did you?"

"Did I ever have a choice?" Troy hollered back. "For God's sake, you practically cried before I said yes to it all!"

"So this is all my fault? If you didn't want to come then you should have been man enough to say so!"

"I told you months ago, but as usual you just kept blowing me off like everything I say is garbage!" Troy yelled before taking a pause to look at the dying sun out to sea. "I swear, Jill, I'd do almost anything for you, but it seems that the more I do, that's all the more my dreams get pushed to the back!"

"Your dreams?" she frowned strangely. "I know what this is. You're still upset about UCLA. I can't believe this. Troy, you flunked the entrance exam! Don't blame me because you chose not to study!"

At that instant, Troy turned his head in disgust and balled up his fists as tight as he could while trying to tune out Jill's loud voice which for a second was beginning to sound a bit like his dad's.

"All you had to say was no and I would have never brought up Australia ever again! You could have gone on about your life! But I'm so sorry for inconveniencing you! You were the one that said you were looking for something special in your life, something that made a difference. I figured maybe this is what you were in search of."

Gradually, Troy found the courage to turn his head around to at least see Jill's shoes stomping on the pier planks.

"So instead of me wasting any more of your time, I hereby free you. You are free to go home and live your life the way you want. I only hope you and Amber have a great life together. And you can write that down in your diary, too.

With a pair of flaming eyes, Troy watched as Jill stormed past him and back up the trail that led to the village. He could only recall one other time that he had ever been so angry at her, but that instance didn't even come close to what he was feeling at that particular moment.

There honestly wasn't a single muscle in his body that wanted to chase after her. He was beyond fed up with so much that his rage was somehow keeping him in place. Right then, just about anything or anyone would be able to set him off. The wrong word or a simple gesture of the eyes could possibly have him behave in such a ghastly manor that Sinai Village would have no alternative but to cast him out, post haste.

With legs full of fury, he marched back and forth on the dock, glancing every so often at the vanishing sun that was glimmering in and out of the soft, puffy clouds in the orange and red sky.

When he could no longer see Jill in the distance, Troy began to pick up rocks from off the ground and hurl them into the water with such force that his right arm felt as though it would rip right out of its socket.

It wasn't so much that a child had tattled on him that infuriated Troy as it was that in certain areas he knew Jill was right.

"Brother Troy," a young, blonde Swedish man said as he approached Troy from behind.

"What," Troy screamed as he spun around with a rock clutched in his hand.

With his hands up in a defensive manner, the man trembled, "Pastor Hudson needs your help bringing out some of the instruments from the basement."

Hardly giving the young man a simple glance, Troy dropped his rock to the ground before sighing heavily and storming past the fellow back to the village.

CHAPTER 21

Like a raging steam locomotive, Troy blasted his way right through the front door of the church before rampaging straight to the back where the basement door was located.

Once down there, he reached up for the bulb that had to be twisted in order for it come on. In the darkness, Troy stumbled and fumbled upon numerous boxes and other assorted items until he came directly under the bulb. With a simple twist of the wrist light exploded into the small room for only seconds before the bulb burst into tiny pieces, leaving the room completely black all over again.

Exasperated, Troy dropped his head and began to pick up and toss items from one end of the room to the other before stopping to listen to a dull, male voice that was speaking behind him.

"Hello," he stuttered, stopping right where he was standing to listen for a response. "Who's there?" Troy continued to ask before making a mad dash back to the door to open it for a sliver of light to come in.

When he looked back he saw nothing in the basement but what was usually there to begin with. As far as human beings were concerned, he was the only one present inside the stench ridden room.

When he spotted several cymbals and a flute, Troy immediately gathered them in his arms and stampeded out of the basement on his way to the pastor's study that was upstairs and down a long hallway. As much as he wanted to just barge his way in and just throw the instruments down in front of Hudson's face, Troy chose instead to keep at least one shred of decency with him. The young man sighed before knocking on the door like a storm trooper.

"Come in, please!"

Troy opened the door to find Pastor Hudson sitting behind his desk, thumbing through his bible. Without opening his mouth, Troy shut the door behind him and stood in place, waiting for the man to say something.

"Ahh," Hudson looked up, "thank you, Troy. You can place them over there in the corner, please."

Rolling his red eyes at the pastor, Troy went over and tucked the instruments away in the corner as he was told to. From there, he started for the door.

"Troy, can I speak with you for a moment, please?" Hudson all of the sudden asked.

Troy stopped moving at that moment. Once again, just on one hand he could count how many times he and the pastor had spoken since he first arrived. It was even the first time he had ever been inside Hudson's study.

The man that he could hardly even get to look in his direction was unexpectedly starting a conversation with him out of the blue, but at the worst possible time as far as Troy was concerned.

"I was wondering if I could have you do something for me." Hudson spoke in earnest.

It was like someone had fired off a gun. Right then, everything that Troy had held in since being at the village was beginning to boil up and funnel over.

"What do you need me to do?" Troy impatiently answered. "Do you need me to bring up some more instruments? Or do you need me to dig a few more ditches outside? Or better yet, do you need me to clean up everyone's dirty asses in the infirmary?"

"I'm sorry?" Pastor Hudson inhaled.

"Ever since I've been here it's been Brother Troy, do this, Brother Troy, do that, Brother Troy, fly to the moon and get some milk! I'm nothing but a damn slave here!" Troy irately waved his arms in the air.

At least a full minute passed before Hudson eventually pressed his lips and sighed, "I see."

Holding back tears and even more frustration, Troy said, "No, you don't see. I just lost my girlfriend, and now I think I'm losing my mind! Everything is going to hell and there's nothing I can do about it!"

Once more, a great silence breathed inside the small study. For a glimmer of a second, Troy actually felt bad for lashing out; the stale look on Hudson's face gave him the impression that he had emotionally broken the man in half.

Pastor Hudson got up from out of his seat before carrying himself around the desk and sitting on the edge. He then calmly said, "You and I haven't had much of a chance to talk, have we, my boy?"

All of the sudden, there came upon Troy a strong stillness that jolted his entire frame. He had no idea just how to cope with it.

"No...no we haven't." Troy reluctantly answered back.

"Troy, let me ask you a question. Do you know why I invited everyone from around the world here, of all places?"

"No," Troy mumbled, wanting so much to make a crass remark.

"Do you realize that I sent over five thousand invites to believers all over the globe, and only so few bothered to show up?"

Troy stood and tried to conjure the number in his head. All he could think was how grateful he was that more people didn't arrive.

"I truly do believe in God. Do you, Troy?"

Troy grinned for a second, like he was amused with the question." Yeah...yeah, I believe in God."

Troy watched as Hudson sat and stared fire into his eyes as though he were delving for more information that he was willing to give up.

With a more serious tone, Hudson once more asked, "Do you believe in God, Troy Gaston?"

Gone was the haughty grin from Troy's face, what remained was a hard glaze that he couldn't help but to point at Hudson.

"Before I first arrived here years earlier, I didn't believe in God, Satan, or heaven and hell." Hudson explained. "When I witnessed all the demonic devastation that resided here, that was when I needed God the most. So much evil prevailed here, and there was no one to combat it. What I am saying is, sometimes, we all need a...jolt, to either gain a belief in the Lord, or to reinforce it."

With a nervous giggle, Troy said, "Look, I believe that there is a force in the universe that...controls things. Is that force God? Who's to say?"

"You sound like a lot of Christians today sound. I know that the invitation was out of the ordinary for some. I realize that most people figured this to be another cult-like affair. Mr. Sollenberg was one individual that I wish I could have spoken to on a more personal basis."

"You knew that David was here to write a hit piece?"

Hudson gave a light-hearted chuckle before saying, "Yes, I was aware that David was here to, quote, unquote, bring me down. But the Lord told me to invite people from all over the world, and I am grateful for the ones that did arrive."

"There aren't that many Americans here, though."

"Well, I figure your countrymen have a great deal more to deal with at the current moment. You're Gipper seems to have given some a reason to celebrate." Hudson smirked.

"Yeah, I guess so. I don't keep up with polities that much." Troy said before sitting down in the armless chair that was placed in front of the pastor.

Pastor Hudson again stopped and stared at Troy for what seemed like an eternity before asking, "Troy, why did you come here?"

Seemingly unable to operate his tongue, Troy sat glued to his warm seat and scanned the walls until he came face to face with numerous newspaper clippings of dead animal reports from Japan and the state of Minnesota.

"Did you do it because of Jillian?"

Troy looked up at the man and meekly replied, "Maybe."

"So you climbed on board an airplane and flew around the world for the woman you love? I'm sure someone will write a love song about that one day, if they haven't already." Hudson kindly smiled.

Troy shook his head and said, "She seemed so happy to come, and I couldn't let her come here all alone."

"So you left everything behind just to make sure that Jill was safe?"

"I guess you could say that."

"But what about yourself, Troy," Hudson questioned. "What about your soul? Don't get me wrong, I believe it admirable that you are looking out for the woman you love, but, your eternal soul is just as important as Jill's."

Troy turned his head in angst and swallowed. "I don't know… maybe I was looking for something, too."

"Looking for what? Something you couldn't find back home?"

"I guess so," Troy modestly answered.

"You did attend church back home, didn't you?"

Troy rolled his eyes and smirked, "Yeah, for all it was worth."

"How do you mean?"

"Do you know what a ghetto is?"

"I do."

"Well, the church where Jill and I attended was smack dab right in the ghetto, and the pastor there wanted me to go house to house and ask people to come to church. I did exactly what the guy asked me to do before this black lady cusses me out. I didn't say anything wrong to her."

Pastor Hudson concealed his chuckling behind a blushing face. Troy looked up and was astonished to see the man actually entertained.

"Yeah, it's real funny, isn't it? The pastor back home thought it was, too."

"I'm not laughing at you, Troy; rather, I'm laughing at the situation."

Troy frowned, "Situation?"

"Do you realize how many Christians out there believe that it is their mission to go all over the world to serve? It is so easy to swoop down out of the sky like Superman with food, clothes and medicine for the poorest of those in the darkest realms of the earth. But ask them to make a difference in their own community, and they shy away. Now, you say that you are looking for something, but I also believe that the reason you came here was out of guilt, as well. You didn't want to disappoint Jillian. Don't get me wrong, I think Jillian is a very sweet and well-intentioned girl, but you have to come to God on your own terms, Troy."

Troy glanced down at his black t-shirt that had Bela Lugosi's *Dracula* image printed on the front before looking around the room as if he were lost. He was trying to take in Hudson's ardent words all at once. Suddenly, God didn't seem as distant and foreboding as he once perceived him to be.

"Yes, I experienced a lot of evil when I first arrived here. I was young and brash, full of malign arrogance. But it was ultimately my decision to follow Christ."

"I don't know," Troy sighed, "maybe it was a mistake to come here after all."

"It's kind of late to think that way now, my boy." Hudson grinned.

Troy sniggered, trying to buy himself more thinking time in between the pastor's words and his own ill-advised decisions that were pressing at his lungs.

"Tell me something, Troy, does your family attend church?"

Troy haughtily smiled before saying, "Let's just say that my dad doesn't see church as a place of refuge."

"Does your father believe in God?"

"He believes in God, he just doesn't believe that a man who works six days a week should have to get up bright and early every Sunday morning just to listen to some preacher tell him how sinful he is."

Pastor Hudson laughed out loud and said, "That's funny, I used to believe the same thing at one time. I once thought the whole notion of praising a fairy tale was mere piffle. That is…that is until the jolt."

"The jolt," Troy questioned with squinty eyes.

Troy watched as Hudson grew quiet and withdrawn. The man sulked on the edge of his desk while giving his study a scrupulous once over with his eyeglasses, like he had just left his own body behind. It appeared as though he was too afraid or disturbed to even answer the question.

Hudson then turned to Troy and grinned, "I see you are a Dracula fan."

Troy looked down at his shirt and said, "Oh yeah, I know the church looks down upon all that evil stuff, but I think it's cool."

"Is that your favorite movie?"

"Actually, my favorite movie is Nosteratu. Sure, it's not really scary anymore, but there's something about it that makes your skin crawl. I don't know, that's just my opinion." Troy carelessly shrugged.

Troy watched as Hudson sat back and observed him with a thoughtful glaze as though he were pleased before he inquired, "Troy, have you ever had someone or something pursue you?"

"You mean chase me down? Sure, way back in the seventh grade. There was this one kid that hated that I could shoot more three pointers than he could. The guy chased me all the way from school to my house like he was nuts."

The pastor giggled and said, "Well, something like that, I suppose. Let's just say that I've been running from something for quite some time, now. I will admit that I tend to carry an impetuous nature at times, and that same nature has gotten me into a lot of trouble over the years."

"Believe me, I know all about trouble." Troy's eyes rolled in angst.

"Do you, now?" Hudson said. "Do you write about your troubles in your diary?"

Troy sat back, and in a stunned manner asked, "You've seen me write in my diary?"

"My boy, I see a lot more than you know." Hudson replied with a hint of senior charm attached to his tenor. "Tell me, by any chance have you written anything about me in your diary?"

Troy blushed and turned his head. A shy grin came across his face at that instant.

"I am only fooling with you, my friend." Hudson smiled. "That is your business and yours alone. Tell me, what made you want to start keeping a diary in the first place?"

Troy paused momentarily; he knew the answer right off hand, but after all those years, Pastor Hudson was the very first person that had ever asked that question of him.

"My mom gave it to me." Troy solemnly answered, sounding like he was too embarrassed to speak. "For a while…my diary was the only person in the world I could talk to."

"What about your friends?"

"How do you mean?"

"Weren't you able to talk with them?"

"My parents divorced a long time ago. The friends I had then had to be left behind."

"I see," Hudson grunted. "Do you see your mother often?"

Troy relented at first, trying to conceal his fidgety eyes. "I haven't seen or heard from my mom since I was ten. You see, my mother was a nurse. She was having an affair with one of the doctors at the hospital where she worked. She ended up running off with the guy."

The pastor pressed his lips together as to say he was ashamed of the woman. Troy only withdrew even further away from the man's face, trying his hardest not to look the man in the eye.

"Do you miss her?"

"I can't exactly say that I miss her. I do think about her sometimes, though."

"Do you forgive her for doing what she did?"

Just then, a tidal wave of heat engulfed the young man to where he could hardly breathe at that uncomfortable second.

With a quaint grin wrapped around his face, Troy asked, "How can I forgive the woman who did so much to me?"

It was right there that Troy realized that he may have said something that he wished he hadn't said out loud.

"What did she do to you, Troy?" Hudson seriously probed.

Troy looked up at Hudson with contempt bubbling all over his blushing face. Unexpectedly, the peace that he thought he had gained with God was beginning to gradually break apart.

With a growl in his tone, Troy explained, "You wanna know what she did? Fine, I'll tell you. My mother got custody of me in the divorce. That meant that I had to live with her and her new boyfriend. You wanna know what my mom did? She let that son of a bitch... do things to me."

There wasn't a single pause in Troy's indignant diatribe; it was as if he were being driven to speak so cross.

"The bitch stood back and let that faggot do all sorts of things to me. So, one weekend when I was visiting my father, I accidentally left my diary out on the coffee table, and he ends up reading it. When he read all the things that I wrote in there about her new boyfriend, my dad tried to kill the guy. So my mom, wanting to protect this guy, packs up, and they both run away. I haven't seen them since."

At that, Troy sat back and watched as the pastor looked on as if he wanted to cry right in front of him. The man's trembling lips never parted.

"Where was God when I was going through all of that?" Troy snorted. "Where was God when all those people were eaten by those sharks? He couldn't even stop a storm."

Hudson shook his head from side to side in dismay before saying, "Troy, God was with you the whole time. It is by his grace that you are here now. It is by his mercy that you have endured all that you went through. As for the attacks, I was very upset when all of that took place. But I can assure you that God never forgets one of his own. I did not calm the storm, the Lord did that. I was only the tool in which he worked through. Always remember, my boy, God requires something from each of us at one point in our lives."

Troy sat for a moment and soaked in his own bitterness. The pastor's words didn't exactly comfort him, but for the time being, there came upon him solace to his violent storm.

Feeling a bit less overwhelmed, Troy sat up in his seat and chuckled some of the rage away before saying, "For my ninth birthday my mom got me some *Planet of the Apes* action figures, a new bike, and my diary. When I first opened it and saw that the pages were all blank, I looked at my mom like she had lost her mind. She eventually told me what its purpose was. I write almost everything down in it."

"It does help to get angry at times, Troy. Believe me, anger and I have been very good friends over the years."

"Well, soon after all that went down, my dad married this woman named Carla. I liked Carla a lot. She was really sweet. She tried so hard to make me love her, but what she didn't understand was that... she never really had to work at it. She and my dad had my little brother Chris."

"I bet he looks up to you, doesn't he?"

Troy blushed and humbly said, "I guess he does. I still feel guilty for leaving him."

"How do your parents feel about you coming here?"

"My dad thinks the whole thing is ridiculous. Carla, however, died five years ago from breast cancer."

Troy's eyes began to water, but no matter what, he would not allow one tear to drip. He clinched his body as tight as he could before watching the pastor lean forward and place his right hand on his shoulder.

"I know what happened between you and your birth mother was tragic, but Christ wants you to forgive her. Do not allow misfortune to keep your heart from finding his love. We all have—

Unexpectedly, a series of blistering scrapes and scratches from behind the door disrupted the dramatic conversation between the two men.

Troy looked back and shook his head, "It's probably Ju Ju. I swear, those boys can't keep an eye on that animal to save their lives. I think she was even down in the basement, too, it smells like she's been taking a big number two down there. I'll go and take her back."

Before Troy's backside could leave its seat, Pastor Hudson, with only two fingers pressed into his chest, kept the young man in his place. Tobias' face, however, never left the door that he was endlessly staring at.

Troy sat and looked up at the man as though he had lost his senses. He then noticed that Hudson's fingers were trembling.

As soon as the scratching racket ended, three steady knocks echoed behind the door. Troy once again stared down the pastor who would still not budge from his desk. His two fingers remained pressed firmly against his chest.

With his head pointed at the door, Hudson quietly said, "I believe it is time for you to leave now, Troy."

Feeling a bit alarmed, Troy gladly got up from his seat. He could tell that there was someone on the other end of the door, he could actually feel their presence linger about, but by then, the young man had no desire whatsoever to open to see who it was.

The pastor got up from the desk and faced Troy. He rested his cold hands on Troy's shoulders and asked, "Troy, have you noticed anything peculiar lately about Joshua and Jacob? Anything out of the ordinary, with the exception of the obvious, that is?"

The only thing that seemed to catch Troy's memory at that second was Jacob's blatant outburst earlier in the evening.

"Not really, they seem to be their usual goofball selves."

"I need for you to do something very important for me, my lad."

Usually, whenever someone at the village required his help, Troy would roll his eyes and sigh in disgust, but at that juncture, just looking into Tobias' suddenly pale face seemed to bring out a new kind of respect for his duties.

"I need you to watch both Jacob and Joshua very carefully. I believe in my heart of hearts that there is something very wrong. I only ask you because you are staying with them. But be very careful, no matter what, do not confront either of them."

"What do you think is wrong with them?" Troy mildly stammered.

Hudson hesitated, he then turned his head and responded, "I need you to keep what I am about to tell you a very tight secret. Next Friday, I am sending everyone that arrived from their respective countries back home; that includes both yourself and Jill. I am also going to relocate the villagers, as well. Both Joshua and Jacob, however, will remain here with me at Sinai."

Troy started to blink his eyes rapidly; he abruptly felt his chest cave in at what he had just been allowed to hear come from the pastor's mouth.

"Wait a minute," Troy gasped, trying to regain his breath, "you're sending everyone home? What...what's going on? Are they that dangerous, for God's sake?"

The pastor shot a blank stare at Troy as though he had momentarily lost the use of his tongue. The man then opened his mouth and said, "I haven't even told Ardan any of this yet, he is still too overwhelmed with the boys to listen to any indifference I have to say."

Troy's head began to spin, everything was rushing at him all at once and at full speed, and there wasn't anything he could do to stop any of it.

"I would send everyone home right away, but the cargo boat from Perth won't be arriving until next Friday morning, bright and early. I will inform everyone during Sunday evening service tomorrow."

"What are you going to do in the meantime?" Troy panted. "I mean, you and the boys, that is?"

With a frozen face, Tobias opened his mouth and uttered, "I am going to pray...simple as that, my friend."

Still too dazed to confront what the man was telling him, Troy clinched his fists and asked, "Don't you think people should know about—

"No," Hudson adamantly stepped in. "Everyone's spirits are high right now. I need these people praying and trusting in God, not fretting. Panic and hysteria is the last thing this village needs. Can I trust you, Troy?"

Troy reluctantly nodded his head yes before rubbing his clammy hands together and beginning for the door.

"No," Tobias said, "go out the other door, please. And, Troy, tonight, before you lay your head down to rest, I want you to say a very important prayer. Possibly the most important prayer you will ever utter in your life."

Troy steadied himself for what was about to come. Everything that had taken place within the last hour, from the fight with Jill, all the way to revealing his ill-fated childhood to Tobias had mysteriously been erased from his psyche.

"Repeat after me," Hudson said in stern tone. "Holy God Almighty, be our guide in battle. Be our shield against the darkness of our foe Satan. May thou rebuke him, shun him away. Cast that wicked beast into the flames of hell and all of his evil spirits along with him who dare wander the earth in search of souls to devour. Amen."

Without blinking, Troy diligently repeated every word Pastor Hudson told him to before starting for the adjacent backdoor. "Just one thing," he paused, "was that you down in the basement before I got here?"

The pastor stood in place and stared at Troy for seconds before finally saying in a dry tenor, "No, Troy…it was not me. And always remember something, my boy; everyone here is well aware of their salvation in Christ Jesus. No matter what, they know that their next destination is beyond the clouds. That is the understanding all believers possess. You, too, must learn to gain such an understanding. For without it, your walk is fruitless. Have a good night."

Troy opened the backdoor and stepped out into the darkness of the night. Even though the house was right across the way from the church, Troy had no desire to turn in quite yet that evening. He instead chose to stroll along the warm, calm trail where various campfires and prayer meetings were being conducted.

More than ever he wanted to see Jill; he also wanted to bathe in the balminess of the evening glow. As he passed shack after shack and one bonfire after another, there would be those that would invite Troy to join along in their cluster groups, and as usual, he would politely refuse. He chose his own company to console his shattered nerves that evening.

Troy continued walking until he reached the very edge of the village that overlooked the infinite desert ahead. Even the pitch blackness couldn't seem to mask the grazing wilderness that seemed to never end. He could smell faint whispers of burning wood and boiling cabbage emanate from behind him.

As jarring as it was to hear Hudson speak so mysteriously just moments earlier, Troy honestly just couldn't gather in his head that either Joshua or Jacob were capable of inflicting harm upon any living soul. Their spirited nature just wouldn't permit such rancor.

Then of course, there came Jill. The one thing left in the world that he thought he could hold on to. In his mind, he wanted to see her soft, lovely face; the way she would smile whenever he told one of his off color jokes caused his stomach to drop in a jubilant way. But for the life of him, Troy couldn't conjure her image; it was like he had forgotten what she looked like all of the sudden. Everything was a twenty car pileup and he was on the very bottom being suffocated.

Even though Bixby, Ohio and Sinai shared the same bright moon in the sky, nothing in the world could convince Troy that home was within arm's reach. He could grow a set of wings and still feel like he was a billion light years away.

Suddenly, the being known as God felt nearer than ever before.

Chapter 22

Tobias opened a drawer within his desk and pulled out a heavy red book. Then, with his book clutched tightly against his heaving chest, the pastor prayed until sweat began to trickle down his cheeks.

Kneeling down in front of his study's door, Hudson wept as his fervent dialogue to The Most High increased to a fever pitch with every uttered sentence. His sweaty hands couldn't let his book go for anything or anyone in the world. The same prayer he had told Troy to memorize was indelibly printed in his brain, so much so that he could recite it backwards if he chose to do so.

Within his mind, Tobias was surrounded, by whom or what was uncertain, but the man was well aware that he was not all alone inside the church that evening. There came upon him such an overwhelming sense of heaviness that he could hardly lift his own head.

With his eyes still closed, Hudson opened his mouth and urgently wept out loud, "Dear Lord, they have come. They have come for me at long last. Please grant me authority over the wicked. Grant me the strength I need in my hour of combat. Please spare these precious boys from harm, Lord. Protect them from all evil. Take me, a lowly, wicked sinner, instead. May my wretched life be a ransom. Banish my tormented soul to hell so that they may live. I beg of you, father, give me authority to purge this unspeakable evil. May the father of lies have no dominion here. May he be delivered into—

Before Tobias could say another word, the bulb that was swinging above his head unexpectedly exploded into a thousand pieces, sending its shards sprinkling to the floor. Unfazed by the bizarre disturbance, he continued on, in the darkness of his study, pleading with God.

The unrelenting sweat that was pouring down his face grew increasingly cold with every passing minute. His skin felt tight, like it were about to crack and peel right off his body.

"God…may my sins not fall upon these people!" he shouted to the ceiling. "Give me the wisdom, Savior! Save us, O Holy One!"

Tobias then opened his bloodshot eyes, and for one fleeting glimpse, remembered Troy. He couldn't explain to himself why the troubled young man had just suddenly appeared out of nowhere in his head, but Troy's humble naivety seemed to grant Hudson a fleeting, if not simple, breath of relief.

"Turn back the evil upon my foes; in your faithfulness destroy them. Freely I will offer you sacrifice; I will praise your name, Lord, for it is goodness. Because from all distress you have rescued me, and my eyes look down upon my enemies. Glory be to the Father."

At that, Pastor Tobias Hudson rose to his feet, wiped the sweat from his brow and opened the door. A bright light invaded the small hallway that led to the sanctuary. Hudson, with his red book in hand, boldly marched forward until he stepped right into the sanctuary.

He stood perfectly still inside the silent of the church while staring off down the dim aisle that led to the double doors ahead. Standing in the darkness were two completely naked white men who were drenched from their heads all the way down to their toes in blood. Neither of their faces could be seen, only their feet were visible.

The standoff between the three lasted for nearly five minutes before the pastor placed his book down onto the floor. He then took off his thin eyeglasses and straightened his collar. The man should have probably been scared, but fear was nowhere present inside of him. It was eagerness that was driving his soul. He wanted the entire ordeal to be over sooner than later.

"I never imagined you two would be here, but nonetheless, I have monitored your progress all over the world." He said. "You both are condemned to hell for an eternity. Christ commands it."

The two individuals at the doorway said absolutely nothing. They both stood side by side, intently staring back at the pastor.

"You have no business being here. You've no right to be in this house of worship. The God of grace forbids it. You are both guilty and you will be punished once more. I hereby command you, unclean spirits, by the power of God in heaven, to leave this place. Though

I once was a lowly sinner, myself, arrogant, lustful, greedy, I am a servant of The Most High, and I command you to leave."

When the two beings at the door refused to move, Hudson grew progressively impatient. Their silence only seemed to infuriate the man to the point where all he wanted to do was pick up something and hurl it at them both.

"You are both worthless!" He screamed out loud. "You do not know the Lord God! You are perverse, wicked and malicious! You have defiled the house of God! You have committed great sins in your time! You are ugly in his sight!"

As his loud voice echoed throughout the sanctuary, Tobias began to cough up blood. He touched his lips and wiped the blood on his shirt before continuing, "You are unworthy of mercy! You are to leave this place at once and—

Blood then began to seep out of his cheeks, but no matter how much of it flowed, the man utterly refused to relent, the physical pain was just a mere distraction.

"You have tried to use vessels to find your way back into this world, but Christ Almighty will have the victory over you! He is the one true God! He will humble you both! You both will bow before him and—

Like his bones had given away, Tobias collapsed to his knees. Still bleeding profusely from the face, he tarried on. "God…give me strength to overcome the forces of evil! Holy God Almighty, be our guide in battle—

Pastor Hudson kept on until he could no longer hear the sound come from out of his own mouth. He then dropped the floor, still trying to speak while swimming in his own pool of blood.

He could feel the nerves in his body shudder before the simple movement of a finger became an impossible task. Tobias then looked up to see two pairs of bloody, deformed feet stand over him.

Shivering and convulsing on the floor, Pastor Hudson looked on as all the lights in the sanctuary went out suddenly and simultaneously.

CHAPTER 23

It is May the tenth 1970

Mom said that I should write down all the stuff that happens to me in my day. Today for my birthday I got some planet of the apes toys and a brand new bike. It is red and blue and it has these paper things on the handles and they fly when I ride it. Trumaine wanted to ride it, I thought he would try and steal it from me because he said that if I didn't let him ride it he would beat me up. so I let him ride it for a little bit this morning after I ate breakfast but he didn't bring it back until it was time for dinner. When I got inside from playing with my toys, james said for me to come inside his den and talk to him. so I did go inside and he told me to put my tongue in his mouth again. I told him that I didn't want to and he said that he was going to go and hit me again. Then I said I was going to go and tell mom and he told me that he was going to cut my mom's throat if I told her. So I did not say anything to her about it. After I put my tongue in his mouth he told me to touch his wee wee again. The other night when he tried to put it up my but it hurt and he told me not to yell or he was going to kill dad. I hope god kills james one day so I can go and live somewhere else. I don't like living here anymore with james and mom. I wish I could turn into that vampire like the one from dracula has risen from the grave and kill james in his sleep. mom doesn't even care what james does to me, I think she's afraid of him. I hope mom lets me stay up to watch tv since it is my birthday today. The end.

August 22nd, 1982

I honestly don't know where to begin. I would have written last night, but I had a ton of shit all on my mind at once. Between eleven p.m. and five this morning I must have got at least thirty minutes of sleep. I can't believe all of this is happening. I don't know just how to feel right now, so forgive me if I ramble. I had a very serious talk last night with a guy I hardly even know, about a subject that I never imagined I would discuss with another human being. You know me, diary, I never was any good with one on one talks. I try my best to avoid the Dick Van Patton, "Eight is Enough", emotional moment of truth whenever possible.

I don't know what possessed me to discuss James with him. It just came out at a moment of weakness. But something very strange besides that happened. I don't hurt as much as I once did. Sure, I still hate James with a passion, but I'll admit that there's something inside of me that doesn't want to hate him anymore. I can't forgive the dickhead, but at least for now, I can move forward. I can't believe I'm talking like this.

Pastor Hudson is an alright guy. Talking to him last night felt like talking to an old friend. Perhaps that's what I needed all along. I loved talking to Chris all the time, but there's such an age gap between us both that him trying to relate to me is like me connecting to an alien. It just doesn't compute or feel right sometimes.

Right now I feel like a ton of wet cement. I can hardly keep my eyes open. I've been up all night crying and reading this stupid thing over and over again.

I can't seem to focus on just one thing; my mind keeps going round and round in pointless circles, from one thing to another. I did my best to steer clear of the boys last night, just like Hudson said to. Of course, with their crazy selves, they always seem to be in their own world. I hope to God that the old man is just plain paranoid. But even I have my reservations about them. There's an unsettling strangeness in this house all of the sudden, something I haven't felt before, and it goes far beyond the disturbance upstairs the other day. I just can't excuse the tension that I'm experiencing as I sit here.

What I have to say next may seem weird, but hey, it's been "Twilight Zone" central ever since I first arrived here, so nothing can sound anymore out of the ordinary. I have to say that after my talk with the pastor, I'm beginning to feel different about God. All that force in the universe crap I mentioned to him was just a cover-up. I was trying to avoid a philosophical discussion that I wasn't smart enough to talk my way through. I do believe in God, I just don't believe that the guy has much compassion. I'm still stuck on why he allows bad things to happen to good people. I can live to be a hundred and I'll never understand what the fuck James was for. Was I supposed to learn anything from that or what?

Sometimes I believe that we are pawns in his and the devil's little game, like Job; these two powerful beings playing with this poor guy as if he's a chess piece. If anyone can tell me face to face just what the meaning of all that was then I'll be satisfied.

I have to get out of this house, I feel like the walls are starting to cave in on me. We have a few days left before we leave; let's hope I can clear up some of this mess before I kiss American soil again.

Troy shut the pages of his diary and promptly wiped tears away from his face before sitting up on the couch and staring straight ahead at the porcelain statuette of the Virgin Mary that sat on the mantle.

There was so much he wanted to accomplish that day that he could hardly contain himself. Conspicuous by their absence, neither of the boys was around.

His body was full of energy, but his will was shiftless, without direction. He remained on the couch, and with a pair of lazy eyes, gazed from one corner of the compact downstairs to the other. It didn't have the softness of his house back in Ohio, the same warm glow that would bounce off his bedroom walls at sunset every summer evening, but he could always feel love amongst Ardan's family, a kind of compassion that Troy had imagined for himself ever since he was a child.

Troy lifted his body up from off the couch and began to wander over to a small mirror that was perched next to the front door. The young man stared endlessly at his sun-tanned reflection like he was searching methodically for something. When he had seen enough of his own face, Troy turned around began to root about in his duffle bag. The second he found an audio tape that was labeled, *Journey*, on both sides, he reached over, picked up his Walkman and inserted the tape inside. Once he pushed the play button, the song, *'Open Arms'* was nearing its final stanza.

Troy allowed himself to listen for only a few seconds before he snatched the tape out, got up, ripped out the long, stringy film, and tossed the thing into the trash can in the kitchen. Then, with as much gusto as he could gather, he barged his way out of the house and down the trail that led to the beach.

It was a cloudy, breezy morning; much appreciated by the visitors who hated the insufferable heat that they had been drowning in since being at Sinai.

The closer Troy approached the pier the more he could see a slender, female figure sitting on the ledge. When he saw the blowing blonde hair, he knew right off the bat who it was.

Troy's paced quickened a bit until he could see Jill wading her bare feet in the salt water that was splashing up against her. For a moment, he was too afraid to even approach her; he could sense just by the way she was hanging her head that he was the last person in the world that she wanted to see. But Troy was determined to recoup his losses at any cost nonetheless.

Troy kept on until he came within three feet of where she was seated. Jill never bothered to turn around, and that alone gave Troy reason to be suspicious.

He took a long breath before muttering, "I figured since the eighty-six that you wouldn't want to be so close to the water as you are."

Troy stood with his hands in his pockets and waited for a response. When he didn't receive one he turned his head and looked on at the raging, foamy water that seemed to grow more agitated with every passing moment.

"I threw our song away." He said. "I tried listening to it, but…it just wasn't in me."

Brushing her long hair to the side, Jill suddenly looked up and asked, "Was it something I did?"

A bit startled by the question, Troy frowned and said, "Something you did? What do you mean?"

"I mean, did I make you cheat?"

"No, Jill," Troy quickly exhaled. "I guess I did what I did out of… anger."

"Were you angry at me?"

"I was confused," he said as he sat down next to Jill on the pier. "I didn't know my right from my left."

Jill turned her head back to the water before saying, "I know sometimes I can be a little pushy. I prayed and prayed, thinking that maybe this would be the ideal place for you to get closer to God. But

I guess I should have known better by the way you kept stalling when I first mentioned it months ago."

"It's just that, it's so far away from home. I never imagined you would bring me all the way to Australia."

"Would it have made a difference if it were in Cincinnati?"

Troy turned his head away, trying not to look at Jill's despondent face staring directly at him. He already felt like a bag of crap just sitting there next to her.

"Did I really push you to come here?"

"It doesn't matter."

"It matters to me. I don't want you to think that I'm pulling you around on a leash. I mean, I do realize that you have to come to Christ on your own terms. And I'm sorry for forcing that on you, Troy. But do you want to come to Christ?"

Troy sat and contemplated for a few seconds before replying, "It's not that I don't want to, it's just that, I have a lot of stuff that's keeping me from doing so."

"And that's just it, Troy. There are times I can read you like a book, and then there are other times you're like a sealed tomb. You don't have to tell me everything about your life, but I want to be there for you, no matter what."

Troy bowed his head before looking over at Jill. Beyond the freckles and wild hair, he could see the one person that had his heart and soul within her own, and that fact broke him into pieces even more.

"I love you so much, Troy, I really do." Jill compassionately smirked. "I don't know, maybe I'm too big of an Ali McGraw fan, but I really do believe that you and I will be together forever. I've thought that ever since we first met."

"I believe in the same thing, Jill. God, I feel like I'm going through the ringer here." Troy moaned. "Jill, you don't know how much I love you. I'll admit that I had my doubts about this place, especially when it came to Hudson. But...last night I got a chance to deal with something that I haven't faced in a long time, and now I think I can finally put it to rest."

Jill began to wipe her eyes before asking, "Do you think I'm a ditz?"

Troy giggled and replied, "No, if anything you're further along than I am."

Jill, too, giggled and said, "I'll let you in on a little secret, I was scared to come here, too. But when I saw that you were more frightened than me, I knew that I had to man-up and be the strong one."

Troy laughed out loud before taking Jill by the hand. "Have I been that much of a scaredy cat?"

Jill amusingly rolled her eyes before turning back to the water and sighing, "Did you really throw our song away?"

"I'm afraid so," he murmured. "But when we get back next week, I'll go to the mall and by another one."

"Next week," Jill abruptly chocked.

"Oh yeah, I almost forgot." Troy caught himself. "I had a talk last night with the pastor. He thinks there's something very wrong with Josh and Jacob."

"You mean that thing from yesterday?"

"No, not that, he believes that it may go a lot deeper. You should have seen the look in this man's eyes, Jill; it was like he had seen a ghost or something."

"So what is this about us going home early? We weren't supposed to leave until the end of next month."

"Well, he feels so strongly about this that he's sending all of us away, including the villagers. Apparently there's a large boat that supposed to come next week to take us back to Perth."

"Does he really believe the villagers will want to leave their homes?"

"I don't know, all I know is that he wants everyone, expect the boys, to leave."

"Wait a minute, do Ardan and Josephine know that he wants to keep their kids here?"

"I don't think he's gonna tell them. And I need for you to keep tight-lipped about this, too. Hudson is going to announce it to everyone this evening at service."

Jill scratched her head and asked, "What could be so wrong with the boys that he wants to send everyone off the village?"

"C'mon, Jill, there's something going on with those two. Deep down you know it to be true, you just don't want to admit it out loud. Both Josh and Jacob have been mute since birth, and then out of nowhere they can speak? This is beyond bizarre, its downright spooky."

Jill's face took on a more demoralized appearance as she said, "I believe in miracles, but…you don't think that perhaps they're poss—

"Don't even say that word; you and I both have seen way too many movies on such things."

Jill then scooted close to Troy before nuzzling her head into his chest and moaning, "I'm scared, Troy. I don't like you staying in that house with them."

"You don't like it?" he grimaced. "Luckily for me I didn't see them last night." Troy gasped before looking up to hear a series of loud commotions emanate from the village.

"What is it," Jill asked.

Troy listened more intently before getting to his feet and staring towards the trail. "Stay here," he commanded in a troubled tone.

"I'm not staying here." Jill retaliated before getting up and putting on her sandals.

Both Troy and Jill raced off together down the trail at breakneck speeds. The instant they reached the village center, seemingly everyone in the community was gathered at the infirmary, some were crying while others were notably shaken and disturbed.

Holding Jill by the hand, Troy shoved his way past scores of people until he eventually made his way inside the sickbay to find Pastor Hudson lying in a bed with his eyes wide open to the ceiling above.

"What happened?" Troy asked Ardan who was standing next to Hudson.

"I do not know." Ardan desperately inhaled. "I went to see him this morning, and there he was on the floor in the sanctuary, bleeding. I tried to talk to him but he can't seem to speak."

Troy stared down at the pastor with the most urgent sense of fright that his face could form. Even though he couldn't seem to turn his head, he could sense that Tobias was aware of his presence.

With tears welling up in her eyes, Jill reached down and attempted to take the pastor's hand into her own.

"Oh, God," she cringed before dropping the man's hand.

"What's the matter?" Troy asked.

With trembling jaws, Jill replied, "His hand is stiff and freezing cold."

"His entire body is that way." One of the attendants said. "It is like he is paralyzed. We can hardly move any part of his body without breaking it."

"Look at his face," Ardan pointed. "It looks like something or someone had poked him with something sharp."

The longer Troy's paranoid eyes stared forever at the pastor, the more Tobias' attention appeared to wander over to him. For a brief moment both men's eyes connected before Hudson shut his eyelids and started to weep silently.

Troy couldn't watch anymore, he took Jill by the hand and began to once more shove past numerous people on his way out. But before he could leave the infirmary, on the wall was nailed a piece of paper. It caught his eye so vividly that he had no choice but to stop and read. 1st Samuel 2: 12.26.

"What is it," Jill asked.

At first Troy said nothing at all, he was trying ever so eagerly to soak in the writing that seemed to strike at him like an angry rattlesnake.

Troy pulled away from Jill before pushing towards Ardan who was still attending to the pastor. Once he was able to grab a hold of the man's thick arm, Troy took him to the side.

"I need to know something. I hear that there are exactly sixty-six books in the bible. Why is it that ever since we've been here Hudson keeps harping on 1st Samuel?"

Ardan glared deep into Troy's eyes and whispered, "Pastor Hudson has been having us all study 1st Samuel long before everyone arrived here. I know I shouldn't, but at times I often question him about it. All he tells me is that we all need to heed its message. I trust both him and the Lord on that much."

"I was with the pastor last night."

Ardan's eyes opened wide in shock before he asked, "You were? What happened to him, then?"

"I don't know for sure. He was fine when I left him. We were just sitting and talking. But there's obviously something scaring him to death."

Ardan carefully glanced back at the pastor before looking at Troy and saying softly, "I think this is the perfect time we all sit down and have a very serious talk, my friend."

Troy watched as Ardan left his side to be next to Tobias. Right beside him appeared Jill who was wearing the most distressed glare upon her red face.

"I wanna get out of here, Troy." She stuttered into Troy's ear.

Troy took Jill by the hand and led her out of the stuffy infirmary. Once they were outside, Troy pulled her close and murmured, "Gather some of your friends and meet me by the pier in about two hours. Ardan may know something we don't."

CHAPTER 24

"This was lying on the floor next to the pastor when I found him this morning." Ardan announced, holding up Hudson's red book in the air for the crowd of sixteen to see.

Gathered underneath a tree near the beach, Troy, Jill and the others all looked up at the renowned book. With a perturbed frown, Troy glanced over at Jill momentarily before redirecting his attention back to Ardan who was pacing back and forth in front of his anxious audience.

"Now, I realize that most of us are probably wondering why the pastor had been stuck on the book of 1st Samuel for as long as he has been. Unfortunately, I have no answer to such a question. But I am quite familiar with this book; it contains the rite of exorcism."

Everyone, including Troy, panted and chattered amongst each other as though they were flabbergasted at what they were hearing.

"Pastor Hudson allowed me to see this some years ago. I believe he knew that something dreadful was coming this way."

"Perhaps he was battling that same something last night inside the church." An Irishman spoke up.

"That is the only explanation," an Ethiopian man said. "Do you believe that the pastor was able to vanquish this demon, Deacon Ardan?"

"It is hard to say. If he was able to defeat it, then praise be to God. We can only pray that the pastor will recover from his ailment."

Troy wanted ever so much to say something at that juncture. He was listening to so much innuendo and speculation that his tongue found it difficult to move a muscle; he didn't know where to start.

"Wait a minute," a Japanese woman uttered, "how do we know that this demon is still not inside the church? How do we know for sure that the pastor destroyed it? Look at what happened days ago. Those people just ran to the water for no apparent reason other than to be eaten by sharks. Perhaps this evil is worse than any of us know."

Jill all of the sudden stood to her feet and said, "Maybe we should all just wait and see what happens next. Let's just continue to pray for God's wisdom on the matter."

"She is right," an Englishwoman said, "we must never stop praying. So much has taken place here, but we cannot give up trusting in the Lord. He is the one who will deliver us."

"Then it is settled," Ardan shrugged, "we will gather at the church and pray. We will continue to pray as if our very lives depended upon it. We don't know for sure that the pastor overcame this evil, and if it is still here then it is up to us to finish what the pastor began. Now, what is written in this book can only be recited by another pastor, but I happen to believe that as one, we will be able to accomplish the impossible, with the aid and power of God. We will not tarry or flee. We will not—

"So....were...not...going...to...leave...the...village...like.... the...pastor...said...so?" Jacob suddenly asked from behind his father.

Everyone turned to see both Jacob and his brother standing side by side with confused glares upon their faces. No one was more surprised than Troy, however. They just appeared seemingly out of nowhere and at the most inopportune moment. His body began to tremble the longer they stood there.

With a nervous sneer on his face, Ardan looked down and asked, "Who said that we were leaving, son?"

Jacob looked up at his father answered, "Pastor...Hudson...did... sir. That's...what...he...told...Troy...last...night."

Right then, every set of eyes that was gathered immediately pointed directly at Troy like guns ready to fire. Troy's entire body instantly broke out into a violent, freezing cold sweat.

"You saw the pastor last night?" The Irishman asked in an amazed tone.

"What is this about us leaving the village?" Ardan choked.

Troy still couldn't speak; by then he had swallowed his tongue and hoped that there would be something or someone else that would interrupt the moment he was drowning in.

"Speak up, man!" The Ethiopian man yelled. "What happened last night inside that church?"

Troy stood to his feet and slowly began to back away from the crowd with Jill close to his side. He wanted to turn and run away, but his legs were too flimsy to even make a vaunted dash in the opposite direction.

"Troy, what is this about us leaving?" Ardan desperately questioned. "Is what the boy said true?"

"Forget what the boy said." The Irishman grunted. "I want to know what Gaston was doing with the pastor last night. Why were you there, lad?"

"I…he needed some instruments from the basement." Troy foamed at the mouth. "All we did was talk, after that I left."

"What about us leaving the village?" The Englishwoman pleaded. "Is something going to happen here?"

Troy didn't have the nerve to answer, all he could do was continue to slowly back away until his body eventually hit another tree behind him.

Pointing directly at Troy, the irate Irishman said, "How do we know you didn't have anything to do with the pastor's sickness? You never were too fond of the man. You never join any of us in prayers. You always keep yourself isolated from the rest of us."

"Wait a minute!" Jill forcefully shot back, waving her skinny arms in the air. "Troy had nothing to do with the pastor's condition!"

"Troy, is there a danger here in the village?" Ardan asked. "Is that why Hudson wants everyone to leave? We need to know, man!"

Shaking, Troy said, "Look, all I know is that Hudson seemed real scared last night. It has something to do with the boys and—

"My boys," Ardan jumped back wide-eyed. "We need to get Joshua, Jacob and everyone else down to the church to pray at once!"

Troy stood and watched as the small, agitated group, with the boys in tow, took off down the trail towards the church. For a brief moment the young man breathed a heavy sigh of relief at his own expense.

Jill gawked oddly at Troy before asking, "Troy, why didn't you tell them what you told me about the boys' strange behavior?"

Pacing from one tree to the next, Troy blurted out, "What did you want me to say, Jill, Pastor Hudson wants everyone but Jacob and Joshua to leave the village? Ardan and Josephine would both have an aneurism! I didn't ask for any of this shit! Not one bit of it!" Troy screamed at the top of his lungs.

Jill quickly grabbed a hold of Troy's neck before hugging the life out of him and kissing his cheeks from side to side.

"Troy began to cry, "This is all fucking crazy! I feel like I'm in a nightmare!"

"Listen to me," Jill adamantly said straight into Troy's face, "were gonna get through this. Now, the pastor said that this boat will be here in a few days, right?"

Troy shook his head yes before asking, "What does that have to do with anything? No matter what, everyone here is gonna think I had something to do with what happened to Hudson."

"If we can only survive till then, then we can get on that boat and leave this place behind."

"Survive," Troy swallowed. "What is there to survive, for God's sake? That mad mob will only grow angrier by the day."

Jill exhaled and said, "Pastor Hudson obviously sensed a grave danger here, that's why he had that book. Now, what you and I need to do is sit down and read 1st Samuel from start to finish, except this time, we dissect its true meaning. If you didn't tell the boys about what you did with Amber or about your talk with Hudson last night, then there's something very wrong with those two, and the pastor knew it."

Troy stared deeply into Jill's frazzled eyes, hoping that she was as solid as she sounded. He then followed her back to the village square where upon entering found the entire congregation gathered around the church, in a formed chain, praying and weeping before the Lord to not only heal Pastor Hudson but to also destroy the evil presence that they believed had infiltrated the community.

With Jill dragging Troy into the crowd, both individuals knelt to the ground and began to pray alongside their fellow Christians. Troy listened as Jill prayed the prayer of the determined. Sweat dripped from off her forehead and onto her folded hands. He couldn't quite exactly make out the words that she was saying, she was speaking so fast, be he could tell that it was a passionate plea to the Almighty for both mercy and answers.

Troy on the other hand glanced around at the rest of the congregation as they prayed their hearts out. He, too, wanted to join in, but his own fear kept him distracted and confused. He didn't know just where or how to start a prayer, he couldn't even remember the prayer that Hudson had told him to memorize from the night before. All he could do there on his knees was fold his hands, close his eyes as tight as he could and think of the softness of his home back in Ohio.

"Oh my God in heaven," a woman horrifically screamed out.

Troy opened his eyes and gawked around to see an Aborigine women bleeding profusely from her face, as if someone had stabbed her repeatedly. Her terrifying squeals were followed by a white man who was suffering the same fate, except his bleeding was so intense that it funneled all over his own hands.

There were some others that yelled out in horror while others continued to unceasingly pray as though nothing were happening at all.

Jill buried her face into Troy's chest at that second while crying her eyes out. Troy held her close while watching the macabre frenzy take place all around him. Never before had his eyes witnessed such terror that was only reserved for last night movie pleasure.

From side to side Troy gawked at every hysterical member until his eyes locked onto Ardan, Josephine and their boys, all standing side by side together near the church. Ardan and Josephine wept in each other's arms while Jacob and Joshua kept their heads pointed to the ground beneath their feet in what appeared to be a shameful pose.

CHAPTER 25

August 23, 1982

I got half the village and its visitors ready to attack me at a moment's notice, a pastor who all of the sudden can't speak or move a muscle, two kids who have completely lost their minds, and, oh yeah, I almost forgot, two people were pouring blood from their own faces.

I want to say something sarcastic, anything that will take the weight off, but I can hardly write anymore, my hands just can't stop shaking.

I wish to God I could remember that damn prayer Hudson told me to memorize.

*   *   *

David's body laid there in the ever moving water, bobbing up and down. His lifeless face watched as the colossal great white, with its sharp dorsal fin cutting the water in two, came hurtling at him until its teeth, along with the rest of its body, leapt out of the water.

Its teeth wouldn't stop tearing the poor, unbelieving man apart. Much like a ravenous wolf, its powerful jaws whipped David from side to side before its entire mouth managed to encapsulate half of the man and take him under completely. From there, blood bubbled up, making it seem like the water were boiling red.

The entire ocean had turned a deep red for endless miles. From one city to the next the evil red took over until the water's hue began to reflect off the once blue skies, which in turn caused the sky to enflame with such rage and ugliness that it spat back down to the earth.

Troy abruptly awoke from his nightmare, biting his own tongue in the process. He squawked before rising up off the couch and wiping the sweat from off his face.

Breathing heavily, he looked around at the blackened downstairs of Ardan's house before getting up and stumbling out the front door to the dunny.

Troy closed the door behind him and pulled down his Fruit of the Loom underwear to relieve himself standing up. When he was through, he spat out the remainder of blood that was continuing to foam up from his injured tongue.

The moment he was done he let himself out and started back for the house. But before he could reach the front door, something quite startling caught his sleepy attention.

Troy stood there in the warm early morning air, gazing about at the eerie quiet darkness that he was trapped in. He could feel a dense presence surround him, like something or someone was standing right there next to him.

The more he gawked around the more he could hear nothing but loud crickets and dingoes howling off in the ever so distant wilderness beyond the village. But there was the heavy existence that was still amongst him that kept Troy planted directly in place.

Whenever he turned he could feel the eerie existence move alongside him in unison. When he stopped turning, so did the presence. He stared towards the house in front of him and then to his back only to see nothing but trees facing him. His hands were already clammy, and his heart was beating twice its required rate, all that was left was for him to begin shaking from fright.

Still sensing the weight of his unwanted companion, Troy began to spin around and around like a dog wildly chasing after its own tail until he became lightheaded enough to stop. Once he was through spinning, Troy immediately grabbed a hold of the front door handle and bolted right back into the house.

He shut the door behind him loud enough to where everyone inside could possibly hear. Troy stood up against the door, heaving in and out as though he had left his breath back outside, while sweat drizzled down his face.

As soon as he was able to regain the use of his wonky legs, Troy started for the couch, but right before he could even reach the arm, the faint sounds of deep voices from the kitchen seized his already frazzled attention.

His faltering nerves couldn't take another unexpected journey down the dark road that he was traveling upon. The voices he was hearing were unfamiliar to him. He couldn't quite make out just what they were saying or who they could possibly be talking to; their dialect seemed both foreign and distraught.

To the right of the couch sat Troy's duffle bag. Ever so silently he stepped over and unzipped it; from within he took out both a flashlight and a switchblade before carrying himself towards the kitchen.

He shined his light all around while listening to the voices carry on back and forth like they were arguing. But just as soon as Troy reached the kitchen's threshold, instantly, the voices ceased.

Troy raised his right hand with the knife in it before shining the flashlight to find Jacob and Joshua standing side by side in the middle of the kitchen floor. Seeing that it was only the boys didn't settle Troy's pulsating heart one bit, he was still curious just where the men that were speaking seconds ago had ran off to.

"Hey, guys," Troy stammered while carefully approaching the children from behind, "who else is in here?"

When the boys wouldn't reply, Troy used his flashlight to illuminate the entire tiny kitchen, only to find absolutely nothing but the children still huddled against one another like they were concealing something.

Troy shined his light above and over Jacob and Joshua's heads and down to the floor to find what appeared to be a bloody mess quivering from side to side. When Troy's eyes were able to examine the specimen even closer, he noticed a set of claws that were followed by a paw and a furry, severed head.

Out of fear, Troy dropped both his flashlight and switchblade to the floor before stumbling back to the wall. Troy then reached down and swiped up the flashlight; he shined it at the boys who were still immobile over their butchered carcass.

Troy dropped to his knees and spun both boys around before frantically asking, "What the fuck, you two?"

He looked into their sullen, withdrawn eyes that appeared like they were still asleep. There was no life on their faces whatsoever, and definitely no remorse for what was lying on the floor.

"Did you two do that?" Troy trembled, trying not to bite his tongue all over again.

Joshua's mouth opened, but for at least an entire minute, no sound came out. But after so long, the child muttered, "They…told…us…to…do…it."

"Who told you," Troy gasped for air.

"They…did," Jacob answered in a morose tone.

Troy shined his light all over the kitchen, but could see nothing or no else around. He then glared the light into the boys' faces and asked, "Guys…why did you kill Ju Ju?"

"They…said…it…was…a…sacrifice." Joshua replied. "They…said…it…was…a…sin…sacrifice.   Don't…tell…our…father…please. Tell…him…we…won't…do…it…again…please. Tell…Yahweh…we…are…sorry…please."

Troy gathered the boys into his sweaty bosom and hugged the life out of them before taking them back into the living room and washing their bloody hands in the basin that sat next to the couch.

Joshua asked that his father not be told, but Troy could hardly believe it himself, therefore, telling another person of such an unspeakable atrocity would have left him completely speechless.

As much as he didn't want to be anywhere near the boys, Troy felt it proper that they remained with him for the rest of the evening.

All three persons sat down on the couch, Joshua and Jacob on both sides of Troy.

Troy kept his flashlight on for the remainder of the night, not wanting any darkness to invade.

Chapter 26

Dear Troy,

Hey how is it going? Not too bad here I guess. I got a real punk for a teacher, his name is mister Brooks. He teaches english. he makes us read all these stupid books about nature and this guy called john steinbeck. You wont believe what happened on the dukes of hazard, the guys who play bo and luke aren't there anymore, they got these two new guys and I don't like them, I won't watch the show anymore. they got this brand new show on nbc now, its about this talking black trans am and this guy he drives around and solves crimes, dad said that it's the dumbest thing he has ever seen. dad said that he misses you and hopes you come back home soon. he keeps talking about when you come back we are all going to go and move to a new house, I sure hope so because its getting real bad in this neighborhood, some black guy busted out dad's windows in his car last night. I sure do wish you come back soon so we can play basketball again, I got these new pictures I drew about these naked women, I hope dad doesn't find them. See you soon. Love Chris.

Sitting on a stool underneath a eucalyptus tree with a fond smirk across his face, Troy wrapped up Chris' letter and slipped it in his back pocket as the rain steadily fell on his dirty pair of Pony's. In his head he could hear Chris speaking like he was sitting right next to him. There was such a hungering inside of the young man to hold his little brother in his arms that Troy found himself wanting to jump into the ocean and swim all the way back home.

Never before in his entire life did he long for something so strongly; to go home and shut himself off from the rest of the world, just the very image consumed him to the point where at times he would shake.

Troy should have been sleepy, his body felt like one hundred and ninety-one pounds of stale meat that had been left out for weeks. The event from just a few hours earlier still stung at him. In his hands he could still smell the blood from the koala corpse that he buried, he had been trying to rub it out for hours.

Troy recalled Pastor Hudson's statement of the famed 'jolt', wondering if the boys mutilating their own pet was the experience he was eluding to; the very last thing he wanted was for things to become even worse than they already were. He wanted the entire excursion to end, even if it meant running back home.

He dropped his head and rubbed his hair from front to back as though he were completely spent.

"Hey," Jill sighed as she came and sat down next to Troy underneath the same tree. In one hand was her bible, while in the other was clutched a small, silver crucifix.

Troy looked at the young lady with a syrupy sympathy, as if he felt sorry for her. Jill's once blushing, freckled face had become insipid and frail over the past few days. The faithful exuberance that she brought with her from America was all but a distant memory.

"I got a letter from Chris this morning." Troy glumly stated.

Jill glanced over and polity smiled before asking, "How is he doing?"

"He's okay. He said that dad is going to move to a new house once I get back."

Jill just pressed her lips as to say that his news was nice before cracking open her bible and saying, "I think what we're searching for is found in 1st Samuel, chapter two, starting at verse twelve."

Troy scooted close to Jill and braced himself for whatever clues she had to offer. He listened hard as she read word for word out of the King James Version. As she read, certain words seeped through his thick skull while others bounced right off like the rain from the eucalyptus tree he was seated under.

When Jill was done reading Troy sat up in his stool and scratched his head. "So…does all of that have something to do with sacrificing meat correctly?"

"I don't think so, Troy." Jill impatiently replied. "I hate to speculate on these things, but I just saw two people bleed out of nowhere, so anything at this point is possible. I think this may have something to do with Eli's sons, Hophni and Phinehas."

"Why them?"

"Who knows," Jill shrugged. "What they did at the temple was pretty nasty. Maybe they're looking for revenge."

Troy rooted around in his head for a moment before saying, "So they decide to take control of two boys? C'mon, Jill, I think that's just a little too far-fetched."

"How can you sit here and deny all of this, Troy?" Jill yelled. "We all just saw blood pour out of two peoples faces, and you're gonna just sit here and play like it's some sort of stupid mind trick?"

Troy turned his head and waited for Jill to calm down before he muttered, "They killed Ju Ju last night."

"What," Jill's jaw dropped.

"That's right; they both took that animal and cut it up like a fucking science experiment."

Jill stood to her feet and asked, "Troy…why did they do that?"

Troy looked up at Jill with sullen eyes and responded, "They said that they wanted them to sacrifice Ju Ju for them."

"Wait a minute," Jill froze, "who's them?"

Troy got to his feet and faced Jill. "I heard voices in the kitchen last night. Voices I've never heard before since being here. When I found Josh and Jacob they were both standing over Ju Ju and just staring. They carved up their own pet and they didn't even seem to care."

"Troy, how can you stand there and continue to deny all of this?" Jill desperately asked.

"Because, I don't wanna have to deal with it!" he hollered. "I'm not stupid, Jill, I can see things with my own two eyes! I saw people get eaten by sharks; others bleed from the face, and now this! If I can keep on denying, then hopefully it'll all go away!"

"It won't just go away, Troy! This evil is here to stay!" She fired back before stepping out from under the tree and into the rain to pace the ground.

"When I was with Hudson the other night, there was someone at the door. Maybe it was them. How else did they know about Tobias wanting everyone to leave?"

Jill stepped back under the tree before looking Troy dead in the eye and saying, "This isn't some stupid coincidence. You can stand there and deny this all you want, Troy, inside your heart you know this isn't right. I don't want you in that house anymore." She began to cry.

Troy pulled Jill close to him and hugged her shaking body as tight as he could. If he could hold onto her for hours and never let go, then that alone would make up for all the hell that he had experienced at Sinai.

Jill pulled away from Troy and said with a wet face, "Please, Troy, don't stay in that house another night. Come and stay with me in my shelter. I'm sure the girls in there won't mind, considering the circumstances."

Troy exhaled, "Everyone here would go ape if I stayed with you."

"But this is a special emergency, though!" Jill pleaded.

"I know, but at least—

Right then, Troy's entire body was spun around before a fist came hurtling straight at his face, sending him crashing to the muddy ground.

Troy could hear Jill screaming bloody murder before he was able to look up and see Ardan standing over him with his fists balled up and a disgruntled, almost evil frown on his wet face.

"You did it, didn't you?" He furiously yelled. "You did it to them, damn you!"

Trying to wipe the blood that was gushing out of his nose away from his face, Troy struggled to get to his feet, but not before Ardan's strong hand snatched him up from off the ground and began dragging his along.

"Stoppit," Jill screamed, following in behind the melee. "He didn't do anything!"

All Troy could do was hold on while attempting to free himself from the enraged man's clutches. As he was being pulled along, he could feel his legs take on mud while both of his shoes came right off of his feet. The rain that was slow and tepid earlier had turned ferocious and cold as it nearly drowned the young man that could hardly do anything to shield his face.

Once Troy was able to notice where he was he immediately grabbed a hold of the doorway and held on for dear life. Ardan was a big man, so it didn't take much energy for him to snatch Troy's hands off the door before continuing to drag him into the living room.

With fury burning all over his insane looking face, Ardan pointed, "Look at them! Why did you do that to them," he growled.

Slumped against the couch while being coddled by Jill, Troy looked over at Jacob and Joshua to see both of their faces bruised and bludgeoned, like they had been beaten.

Troy stared up in amazement at Ardan who began to advance towards him like an enraged, hungry bear.

Ardan grabbed Troy by the collar of his shirt and yelled, "I found your knife in the kitchen! Why... why, damn you?"

"Troy didn't do that to them!" Jill screamed while trying to pull Ardan off of the young man.

"Let him go, Ardan!" Josephine begged from behind her husband.

Troy struggled to free himself, but Ardan's hold was both powerful and angry; in that split second he realized that freeing himself from the man would require all of his strength and some more after that.

"Stop this, Ardan!" Josephine beseeched, trying to pull Ardan's arms away from Troy.

Ardan suddenly released Troy before spinning around and wrapping his livid hands around his wife's neck where he proceeded to shake her within an inch of her life.

Not taking even a single second to catch his breath, Troy jumped up and attacked Ardan from behind before wrestling him from one end of the room to the other, knocking over tables, books and even the boys in the process.

As hard of a fight as Troy was putting up, he was no match for the larger than life deacon. Ardan simply flung the young man to the floor like he was a measly child.

"You beat my boys!" Ardan screamed with his hands waving in the air. "It's you and that girl! You two are always whispering and hiding out here and there! What are you hiding?"

Every inch of Troy's body and soul was completely fed up. Ignoring whatever pain he was in, he leapt up from off the floor and used his reserve energy to grab Ardan by the shirt before pulling him out the door and to the backyard.

From there, Troy began to dig into the muddy ground before reaching in and snatching out the mutilated remains of Ju Ju and presenting it to Ardan.

"This is what your boys did last night!" Troy roared while holding up Ju Ju's decapitated head in the rain. "They did this! I never laid a fucking hand on them!"

Ardan's face went from brazen fury to complete repulsion at what he was seeing. Within a matter of seconds he had become a totally different man.

"There's something wrong with your boys!" Troy persisted. "Pastor Hudson knew that! That's why he's sending everyone but them away!"

"What," Josephine cried out in shock.

"Hudson told me not to say anything! He was gonna keep the boys here so he could cure them!"

"You don't even believe in God!" Ardan shot back. "I've never even seen you pray!"

"I do fucking believe in God with all my heart and soul! And I believe that if he loves us then he will end all of this shit! Ardan… something terrible has your sons!"

As though he were knocked down, Ardan dropped to his knees and began to weep in the filthy mud.

Troy stood over the man while allowing the giant raindrops to pelt onto his skin. He flung Ju Ju's head to the side before taking Jill into his arms and holding her tight.

With both boys in front of her, Josephine boldly proclaimed, "We are not leaving our sons behind. Their father and I will stay here, with the pastor. We will defeat this evil."

Troy glanced down at Ardan who was still sobbing. He then looked over at Jacob and Joshua who were wearing the most miserable expressions on their beaten faces. Never before had he felt so much pity for another human being, even Chris at that point seemed like the most fortunate person in the world.

"This evil has done this to my babies!" Ardan cried as he approached Troy. "And yes…we will defeat it."

At that, Ardan wrapped his hulking arms around Troy, Troy responded in kind. Holding both Jill and Ardan's broken bodies in his arms only made Troy realize that his time in Australia was far from over.

The entire experience, from first arriving in the country, to fighting a man twice his girth came rushing at him all at once.

"Mama…I…am…tired." Joshua grunted.

Troy looked over and watched as Josephine escorted both children back to the house. Once they were out of sight, he stared down at the severed head of the koala bear.

He was at last familiar with evil.

CHAPTER 27

August 24ᵗʰ, 1982

I was never into poetry, it just wasn't my thing, but this whole experience has me feeling out of character, so forgive me if my Edgar Allen Poe starts emerging out of nowhere. If the mood here at Sinai was demoralized back when the shark attacks took place, then it's near purgatory now.

Ardan gathered everyone and told them that they would be leaving the village come early Friday morning. Don't ask me how he convinced the villagers to leave, but he did. He and his family, however, are staying behind with Pastor Hudson. I don't know how they plan on helping Jacob and Joshua without Hudson's assistance, but Ardan seems confident, in his own troubled way, that it can be accomplished.

The boys are now limping around like two cripples. They both woke up this morning and neither of them could hardly even move. It's as if their bones had just given out on them. They're now in the infirmary. For the past couple of nights they have been complaining about having nightmares. Poor Josephine won't leave their side; she sleeps with them in the infirmary.

People around the village know that there is something wrong with them. Some actually do their best to stay away from them, like they had a disease. Most believe that it is a dark omen of bad things to happen, while others see it as a medical condition, considering the out of nowhere bruises that have shown up all over their bodies. Either way, I'm hearing murmurs among the gathering that some are ready to pack up and leave right away. I feel so bad for Josh and Jacob. They remind me so much of Chris, innocent and unassuming. I hate seeing them like this, so shattered and helpless. It kills my heart to know that I can't do a damn thing for them.

An old village lady died yesterday. Granted, she was 99 years old, but the last thing this gathering needs is more tragedy. It's like pouring a gallon of gasoline on an already raging inferno.

Then there's Jill. She's behaving worse than when the shark attacks took place. She won't eat, she won't sleep, and she even misses daily services. For the most part, she mainly keeps to herself. For the past few days she could be seen down at the pier, just staring away at the water. I have to keep a close eye on her just to make sure she doesn't do something crazy like jump in.

She keeps on apologizing for bringing me here. What she doesn't realize is that I would have followed her to hell if she asked me to. But I will admit that there is distance between us. As much as I love and adore Jill, now, whenever I look at her, I don't get that tingle in my stomach anymore. Whenever we do speak its only for perhaps ten minutes before she takes off for the pier for hours on in.

It kills me to know that we are drifting apart, but it pains me even more to see her pull away from God. That was the one thing I never wanted. I didn't want that for anyone here. It frightens me to wonder just what will happen when she and I get back to Bixby. I know things between us won't ever be the same again, but I also see an eventual break-up in our relationship as well. We're not the same people we once were before all of this took place. I just hope and pray that no matter what we can still be friends. Above all else, I hope that Jill will be able to overcome this ordeal.

Right now, I don't know what to believe. I can deny to myself that there is no such thing as demons and spirits till my hair falls out, when right around the corner there's more proof that demons do exist. I can sit and recall all the strange occurrences that have happened since being here, from the sharks, all the way to the pastor being shut down and the boys killing their pet, and in the end, I'll still do my best to cast it all off as coincidence, or a simple brain fart.

Perhaps I'm doing something stupid like waiting for more proof, something that will increase my belief. But I know better, something has taken control of Joshua and Jacob, and if Ardan believes that he can expel whatever it is, then he is in way over his head.

Friday is only three days away. If I can keep Jill from cracking up, then maybe I can still salvage what is left of both her traumatized faith and my patience with everything that I've had to put up with so far.

Three days.

* * *

Like he was sneaking, Troy crept into the infirmary to find seven sleeping villagers all lying in their own separate cots. The young man weaved his way in between each bed until he reached Pastor Hudson who was lying motionless with his eyes wide open, staring straight up at the grimy, metal ceiling above his head.

Troy glanced over at Jacob and Joshua who were both sleeping on opposite ends of their mother in one bed before he took a stool and placed it beside Hudson's bed. He sat down and reared as close as he could to the comatose man.

Troy found it difficult and downright disturbing to look at the pastor. His blue eyes were still, while his stone face appeared as if he were caught in a sudden state of utter shock. The man had left so many blazing questions behind that night during their discussion that it plagued Troy to no end. It was like Hudson had given Troy the key to the city, but he couldn't find the doorway.

Troy looked out the window at the starry sky before staring down at the pastor with a pair of glassy eyes and whispering into his face, "I know you were always a man of few words, but I need something from you. I need you to tell me that prayer you told me to memorize the other night. I totally forgot it."

The pastor's immobile facial gesture never budged, the man couldn't even blink. Troy decided to keep pressing on, however, hoping that by some miracle Hudson would somehow open his mouth and speak.

"I'm sure you know that everything here is going straight down the toilet. Jill is a mess. I don't think she'll make it to Friday in one piece. I've never seen her like this before." Troy began to stammer. "I never did tell you about my dream I had last month. It was about my little brother. I dreamt that my mute brother could talk. It was really strange because he got his voice back the same way…the boys did. He said something to me, but I can't remember what it was. I wish I had told you that the other night. I wish I had told you a lot of things."

Troy wanted to cry, he felt that Hudson was the only person in the world that could truly understand him without criticizing him at the same time.

"I feel like everywhere I look my lifelines keep falling away. I do believe in evil. My mom's fiancée was evil. What happened to the eighty-six was evil. I don't think it can get any worse. I feel like like the world is closing in on me. None of this makes any sense, and I—

Out of nowhere, Pastor Hudson began a violent coughing tirade which caused him to gag up blood from the mouth. Troy shot up from off of his stool and tried to calm the man. He could tell that Tobias wanted so desperately to say something, but his constant coughs were stifling whatever words he needed to utter.

Every so often Troy could make out what sounded like words coming from the man's mouth, but in his ears it was all a garbled mess that made no sense.

Before he could get any louder, a nurse came up beside Hudson and attended to him by handing him a cup of water. Almost instantly both the coughing and bleeding ceased. Sensing that he may have been causing more harm than good, Troy silently stepped away from the bed and let himself out of the infirmary.

Troy was restless, more so than ever before. Usually, his nighttime strolls along the trail were the only thing that seemed to keep his sanity at bay, but he was finding that even his walking had become more of a trial rather than a relief.

He aimlessly blundered past one shack after another; some were lit inside, while others were pitch black. When he had come upon Jill's shack, Troy paused and studied the one light that was still on. Jill shared her accommodations with three other females, so there was no way for him to know whether or not she was the one that was still awake. And even if she were up, he didn't think it wise to disturb whatever mood she could have possibly been in at that moment. The last thing he wanted was to see her gloomy, colorless face stare longingly into space.

Troy resumed his twilight ramble until he came face to face with the edge of the village. It wasn't exactly his ideal spot, gazing out at the desert land ahead; it was vast and unforgiving, and yet, all he could do was imagine what could be out there waiting for any unassuming individual that dared cross it.

"Nice night there, mate." A strong voice said in an English accent.

Troy spun around in the darkness before looking downwind to see a cigarette being lit and a round shape behind it shining its pearly white teeth.

"Oh, I didn't see you there, sir." Troy caught his breath.

"Didn't mean to scare you," the man sincerely said. "You're Troy, right?"

"Yeah," Troy nodded before looking back at the desert.

"Yeah, you're a real famous bloke around here."

Troy grunted before asking in a humorous tone, "Oh really? How do you mean?"

"Practically everyone around here wants your bloody head on a silver platter."

"Would you happen to be one of those people, too?"

The man laughed, "No, I'm just an innocent bystander. The name's Cliff. Cliff Regal."

"Do you come out here often, Cliff?"

"Almost every night," Cliff replied, taking another drag from his cigarette. "It's perfect just right here. At the right time a person can see almost every star in the sky."

Troy gazed up at the black heavens and took notice of the countless stars that seemed to dance about in their own kind of routine display. It was the one thing that he hadn't bothered to take notice of since arriving at the village.

"I don't think I've ever seen so many stars before." Troy mumbled.

Troy looked down at Cliff and suddenly realized that the man was smoking. He saw the cigarette seconds earlier, it just never really registered in his brain.

"Where'd you get that thing at?" Troy pointed.

Cliff took the cigarette from between his lips and replied, "The chap that was here a while ago, the Finch fellow. He let me buy a pack off of him. I've given up a lot of my vices over the years, but I'm afraid that the bloody smokes have me beaten for life."

"My dad used to smoke years ago, that is until he found out that he was in danger of getting cancer."

"Now you're starting to sound like my ex-wife."

Moments of quiet hung about between the two men before Cliff asked, "Do you ever think about just racing out there?"

"Racing out where?"

"There," Cliff pointed to the desert. "The villagers call it the badlands. I've grown up hearing all kinds of wild stories about Australia's bush. Had an uncle who came here back in the fifties, he said that it's full of all kinds of hell; from rattlers to cannibals, and the sort."

Troy smirked and sarcastically said, "That's all I need to know, cannibals just a few yards away from me. Now I can sleep real well at night."

"I'm surprised you get any sleep at all in that house you're staying at."

Troy looked down at Cliff's dark outline in a strange manner, wondering in his head just where he was planning on taking the conversation next.

"How do you mean," he grunted.

Cliff chuckled, sounding as though he were tickled before saying, "I think you know what I mean, mate."

Sensing that he was being challenged, Troy turned to Cliff and said in a cross tone, "Why don't you explain it to me, mate?"

Keeping his face towards the desert, Cliff slowly uttered, "You know there's something terribly wrong with those kids. Their daffed in the head."

Troy rolled his eyes before kicking at the dirt on the ground and asking, "What do you think is wrong with them?"

Cliff cleared his throat and replied, "I hear whispers around this place. Those two behaving like a couple of cheeky little buzzards. Some say they saw them both swimming down at the pier in the middle of the night. Others say they hear a wild animal roaming around the village before sunrise. Whatever happened to that little bear of theirs, Troy?"

Troy turned his head, practically refusing to speak a word.

"That's alright, sometimes we all have to see things in a different light."

Troy looked down at Cliff and asked in an ominous sort of way, "How do you mean?"

Cliff dashed his cigarette under his shoe before gently saying, "I wasn't always a Christian. There was time when I, too, led a very different life."

"Uh oh," Troy grimaced, "you have a life changing story, too?"

Cliff paused, "Yeah, I sure do. You see, way back in '62, I murdered twelve people. I broke into their homes and carved them up like Christmas birds. Don't know why I did it. I guess it gave me a rush."

Right then, Troy began to ever so slowly back away from Cliff's vicinity. All of the sudden, in Troy's eyes, the cool darkness that the man was sitting in became more like a veil of evil that was concealing his face.

"Don't fret, my boy, I'm long cured now. Being on the run, you meet certain people who end up changing you for the better. I almost slit the throat of a nun, that is before she told me about Jesus. Sure, I knew of Jesus, but I never worshiped the bloke. That woman sat with me for three whole days, trying to convince me of his love for me."

Exasperated and flat out scared, Troy sighed, "So what does any of this have to do with Jacob and Joshua?"

Cliff took a moment before answering, "Well…seven years after I was saved, I got to see something very remarkable. There was this one chap, old man, I'd say around seventy or so. He was the janitor at our vicarage. Nice old fellow, wouldn't hurt a fly. Then one day, he started behaving strangely. He'd say things that wouldn't make any sense, words that have no business being said inside a house of God. Soon, something happened to his eyes. They just weren't his eyes anymore. They changed from brown to…to something else."

Troy stood and swallowed. As much as he wanted to turn and run away, he just couldn't tear himself apart from Cliff. It was as if he was drawn to the man's mysterious aura like a bumbling insect to a flame.

"His voice changed completely, too. Like there was someone else talking behind him. Sometimes during service, the lights would flash off and on. We would hear the damndest sounds come from out of nowhere, sounds we've never heard before in this world."

Troy tried his hardest to tune Cliff out, be he found that the man's words were too penetrating to be shut down. He didn't want to carry any of what he was hearing back home with him.

"This whole thing went on for almost an entire month before… before the vicar himself took things into his own hands. I've seen most of your country's movies, my boy, but nothing compares to seeing the actual episode in person. It's like you're in a whole other world, separate from this one. You're standing there watching it all, and you still can't believe that it's happening. The vicar fought and fought for two straight days before he had to bring in two more vicars to assist him. You would have thought all three of those blokes had just run a blooming marathon after it was all over. It kind of made what I did years earlier seem like child's play. I've never seen anything like it before or after. I don't think I got a decent night's sleep for two straight weeks following that ordeal."

Melting inside of his own body, Troy gazed down at Cliff and curiously stuttered, "What happened to the old man?"

Cliff amusingly grunted before saying, "No one talks about dear old Richard, the poor, wretched bastard. I couldn't sleep for two weeks. Or did I already mention that?"

Troy looked away and began to fidget with his fingers. Once more, as he did in past instances, he tried to expel what he had heard out of his memory banks completely.

Troy then watched as Cliff stood to his feet. He was sure that he had seen the man before in the village, but with all of the daily commotion, he couldn't recall all too well. Cliff appeared taller than Troy, and far more bulky. Standing there beside the man, he was surprised that he never noticed him after all the time he had been there.

"Friday can't get here quick enough, my friend." Cliff said. "But then again, I've never been one to wait on others. Watch your back, boy."

Troy stood there at the edge of the village and watched as Cliff started down the steep hill that led out to the desert. He stared on as the man trekked across the land until his dark image vanished completely out of sight.

CHAPTER 28

Pastor Tobias Hudson lay immobile in his bed while his attendant covered his body with a thin blanket. She then placed a cup of water next to his bed and said a standing prayer before him. Once she was through meditating, the woman cut off the light switch and exited into another room within the infirmary.

There drew upon the entire room an uncanny silence. As if he had a choice, Tobias remained still while reminiscing upon Troy's visit earlier in the evening. He could still hear the stifling fear in the young man's voice ringing in his cold ears. To him, it didn't really matter if Troy had forgotten the prayer, all that seemed to race through Hudson's mind was the fact that certain danger was afoot, and there was absolutely nothing he could do about it.

The man felt like a prisoner inside his own body that wouldn't budge an inch. Every time he attempted the feat of moving his fingers, a painful surge of what felt like burning electricity ripped through his entire body, exhausting all of his energy in the process.

He felt like crying at the defeat that had befallen both the village and its inhabitants. Daily, he would pray to God for more time, or, as absurd as it was, the ability to reverse time altogether.

Tobias closed his eyes momentarily before re-opening them at the sound of a scraping racket that was moving towards him.

He wanted to lift his head, but common sense reminded him that such a task was impossible at the moment. Instead, he succumbed to his condition and allowed only his ears to be his guide for the time being.

The closer the scratching clamor drew, the more Tobias could almost immediately feel a presence hover over him. Soon, another heavy existence approached him from his left side. Hudson's eyes couldn't have grown any wider at that second. He could feel both entities breathe down on him like two snorting bulls.

Out of the corner of his right eye appeared a dark outline that judging by its size, could have possibly been a child. Hudson then shifted his eyes to the left to see another profile of the same dimension.

With the exception of a couple of snoring individuals, it was completely quite inside the infirmary. The silence that was standing over the pastor felt angry and ominous. Their weight was heavy, like someone was preparing to inflict some sort of physical harm down upon him.

Both persons stood over the man for what seemed like an hour before one of them held up what looked like a book in the air. They then placed it neatly on Tobias' chest and stood back.

Even though it was too dark for him to see, Tobias could tell just by the hefty bulk that it was his red book. He wanted to move so badly, so much in fact that blood began to drizzle from out of the side of his mouth.

"Do you hear the angels calling you, Captain?" A man's voice grunted in a European accent inside of Hudson's head.

The pastor's eyes shifted rapidly from side to side, his mind was trying to figure out just what in the world was happening at that instant. At first, he thought dementia was at last beginning to settle in on him.

"You thought you could get rid of us, sir?" Another European voice echoed inside his mind.

Pastor Hudson continued to stare up at the two persons standing over him. He could hear them speak, but he could tell that their lips weren't even moving.

"You thought we'd forget about you? You, of all people," one of the hateful voices said. *"We've searched all over the world looking for you."*

"You should have killed us better, Captain."

"Now, look at you, a shaman, preaching to these fucking animals. We found you at last, Captain."

"We found you at last, Captain!"

"You're time is drawing to a close, my dear Captain. You won't know the time, or the day."

One of the individuals turned around and pointed directly at Josephine who was fast asleep in her cot. "*I want her,*" the menacing voice hissed.

Hudson started to writhe about in his bed, coughing up more blood while attempting to speak out.

One of the person's hovering over him took their index finger and used it to scrape some of the blood off of Tobias' chin before wiping it all over their own face.

"*You should have killed us better, Captain.*"

"*I want to fuck every last one of these fuckers!*"

"*You should have killed us better, Captain!*"

"*Hell is a lot bigger than you believe it to be, Captain!*"

"*After we're through fucking every woman here, we're gonna fuck you next, Captain!*"

"*Call God,*" One of the voices dared. "*Call God and beg him to save you!*"

Tobias coughed louder and more vigorous until the attendant cut on the light to reveal both Joshua and Jacob standing over him. Jacob had inscribed a sloppy looking cross of blood across his face, while Joshua wore a dull grin that hung to the floor.

"What are you two doing?" Josephine asked, rising up out of her bed.

Hudson watched as both boys stood at attention, seemingly stunned to be caught in such an uncompromising position.

Josephine walked over and examined Jacob's messy face before asking, "What is this?"

Without saying a word, Jacob slapped his mother's hand away and stood back. Josephine stood and gawked at the boy as though he had lost his senses.

She snatched Jacob by his left arm before spanking his backside and yelling, "You know better than that, young man!"

Jacob didn't even wince; instead, he stood directly in the middle of the floor and eyeballed Josephine from head to toe like he had never laid eyes on her before.

"You...won't...touch...me...again...you...black...cow." He boldly said without batting a single eyelash.

Right then, Josephine's face took on a more disgruntled appearance before she reared back and slapped Jacob across the face so hard that it caused the child to stumble backwards.

Joshua got down on his knees, and like a cat, he scurried underneath Pastor Hudson's bed to hide. Tobias could feel the boy bumping up into his back from beneath him.

Jacob, however, stood defiantly in front of his mother before cracking a vindictive smirk and sitting Indian style on the floor right in front of Hudson's bed.

"Get up from there, the both of you!" Josephine hollered, pulling at Jacob while trying to grab a hold of Joshua who was doing his best to evade his mother.

"What is happening in here?" Ardan bellowed as he came blundering into the infirmary.

Hudson couldn't see the boys, but he could very well tell that they were readying themselves for an attack of some sorts. He realized that it was opposition that they hated the most.

He wanted to speak, to yell out and warn the world, but as hard as he tried, nothing audible could come out of his bleeding mouth.

As Ardan came storming towards Hudson's bed, Tobias could see Joshua stand up beside him before the cot began to move all by itself, sending him flipping onto the floor face first.

All the pastor could hear were women screaming and the boys hollering 'bloody murder' as their father beat them within an inch of their lives.

Soon, Tobias could see himself being lifted from off the dusty floor and back onto his cot. Tears flowed from his eyes as the attendant began cleaning blood away from his mouth and chin.

"It will be alright, pastor," she tried to reassure the man. "They are gone now."

Tobias shut his eyes and braced himself for whatever impact was sure to approach. All he could think of was his precious gathering, nothing or no else in the world mattered.

The instant he opened his eyes, the light bulb that dangled in the center of the ceiling exploded into tiny pieces all over the floor, causing the entire infirmary to vanish into absolute darkness.

Everyone inside grew eerily quiet.

Chapter 29

August 25ʰ, 1982

Well, it's Wednesday, and I just got through packing my bags. I know it's early, but from what I've been told, the boat arrives sharp at five a.m., and I definitely don't want to be left behind because the boat was over packed. I plan on being second in line on that thing, right behind Jill, of course.

All morning I just took a stroll around the village all by myself. The mood here is still salty, there's a real, 'you don't fuck with me, and I won't fuck with you', vibe in the air. It's like everyone is suspicious of the next person. We've all managed to get on each other's nerves. Me, on the other hand, I actually feel kind of good. I guess it's because I know that I'm going home soon. Just over the sea, across the desert and back on the plane again. It's that damn simple. I can feel it as if it were right in front of me within reach. Chris waiting outside in the driveway with the basketball, dad screaming my ear off, telling me to pull my head out of my ass like a drill sergeant. Yep, it's that's close.

I can't believe I'm about to say this, but despite all the hell that they put me through, I'm actually going to miss Josh and Jacob. I'll miss their spirited ways when I first arrived here. I still laugh at the time they found out I could sign; the look on their faces is almost worth coming all the way here. Sure, they snitched on me not once, but twice, but I can't hate them, they're both going through some serious shit right now. I'd rather not explain what that shit is, I want to leave here believing that they are going through early puberty rather than wrestling with otherworldly forces.

I wanted to shoot a few hoops with them this morning, but I heard that there was an incident last night in the infirmary involving them right after I left. Both Ardan and Josephine are tight-lipped on the situation altogether, which suits me just fine.

Both of the boys seemed so fascinated with my Magic Johnson and Kareem Abdul Jabbar sweat bands, so I'll let them have them as a parting gift. I wish that whole family all the best, even Ardan after punching me square in the nose. He's a good man with a big heart, and he's lucky to have such a wonderful wife as Josephine. What they're all going through right now shouldn't be happening to them. I'm still trying to wrap my brain around the fact that the four of them and Pastor Hudson are all staying behind. Once the boat takes off, Sinai will be a ghost town.

I wish I could have got to know Hudson a little better. Behind that passive mask hid an everyman, the kind of guy that once and a while enjoyed a beer or two with his mates. I don't know for sure what happened to him inside that church after we talked, and I probably will never know, but I do know that Tobias believed enough to risk a fate worse than death; that alone is enough to make the most hardcore atheist believe. No offense, David.

When I get home, I plan on doing some real soul searching. Sure, dad can be a real "Archie Bunker" whenever the mood strikes him, but the man makes a great point here and there. I do have to pull my head out of my rear end and do something with my life. Ever since high school, I've been racing from one endeavor to the other, the only constant has been Jill, and even that seems fractured for the time being.

I never had the nerve to admit it to myself, but my basketball days are over. So are the days of me hanging with the guys. God knows I don't want to work in the construction field for the rest of my life, but there has to be something out there for a six foot three white kid from Bixby, Ohio to do. I don't want to be another aimless sports washout. Great, now I'm getting depressed all over again.

Tomorrow night will be our last worship service. I'll actually be glad to attend it.

With a hull of self-pity welling up inside of him, Troy closed his diary before finding the strength to sit up on the couch and look out the window at the various people that were walking about the village in their usual daily fashion.

He then unzipped his duffle bag and took out a pair of Los Angeles Lakers sweatbands. Just as he was about to get up and take them to the boys' room, a knock at the front door diverted his movement.

Troy stepped over and opened the door saying, "Hey, babe."

Jill immediately slid inside and hugged Troy's neck as hard as she could before kissing his cheek and wandering about the living room.

Troy blushed as he shut the door. He looked on with inquisitive eyes as Jill drifted from one end of the room to another as though she had lost all control of her own body. Troy was well aware that she hadn't been herself lately, but the last thing he wanted was to bring that same person back home with him.

Troy stepped over beside Jill, but even before he could reach her, she dropped her lazy body onto the couch and asked, "How it goin'?"

Troy took a moment before sitting down next to her and examining her doleful eyes that looked like they were ready to fall right asleep at any moment.

"It's going okay," he cringed. "How is it going with you, honey?"

Jill flung her head back in a sort of sensual way before saying, "Okay, I guess." She then looked down at Troy's bag and asked, "Why did you pack so soon?"

"Because, I wanna be ready when that boat comes Friday morning at five," Troy cracked a grin. "Do you have your bags packed yet? You know it's gonna be a mad rush to the boat."

"Not yet," her tongue dragged. "I have all night to do that."

Troy continued his hard gaze at Jill who seemed more lethargic than usual, like she were tripping off on some drug.

"So…is there gonna be anything you'll miss when we leave?" He asked.

Jill slouched into the couch and replied, "Not really. There's really not much here to miss, I guess. I just wanna go home and sleep."

"I know what you mean. But I will admit that I'm gonna miss listening to the sea at night. There's one thing you don't get in Ohio."

Troy stared on and on at Jill, who by then was wearing a sultry, cleaver smirk across her sunburnt face. It unsettled the man enough to where he shot up from off the couch and stepped over to the miniature wooden cross that was nailed to the wall in front of him.

"Yep, the next few hours are gonna move like sludge down a mountain, all because we wanna get out of here so bad." Troy rambled on.

He then glanced back to see Jill smiling from ear to ear. He realized that his attempt to conjure frivolous small talk didn't seem to snap the woman from out of her heated trance.

"Tell me, have you ever heard of a guy by the name of Cliff Regal?"

Jill rolled her eyes and sighed before replying, "Yeah, he helps serve food at suppertime. How can you miss the guy, Troy? He's bigger than you."

"I know that now," he blushed. "He and I were talking last night. Let's just say that he had some pretty interesting things to say. One moment we were talking, the next thing you know, he just up and walks out into the dessert. I was just wondering if you happened to see him this morning."

Troy turned around to see Jill get up out of her seat and stroll towards him. He could actually feel her body heat radiate off of her as though she had just stepped out of a sauna. The sensation was robust enough to cause Troy to stumble back into the cross on the wall.

She then wrapped her warm arms around Troy's sweaty neck and whispered directly into his face, "Nobody's here, now. It's just you and me."

Troy reluctantly placed his shaky hands on Jill's hips before looking into her eyes and seeing a far off glare swimming within.

Jill then unwrapped herself from Troy and began to fondle her breasts. Troy couldn't step back anymore, he was trapped. In all the years in which he had known Jill, he had never seen her behave in such an unrefined manner. All he could conjure in his brain were the boys' behavior and wonder if it were contagious.

Breathing erratically, Jill said, "I need something, Troy. I need something so bad."

Troy watched in utter anxiety as his girlfriend began to lift up her sweat soaked t-shirt to reveal her teacup sized breasts to him for the very first time. It wasn't what he had expected, and that made it all the more bizarre to him.

"I want...I want you to fuck me." She groaned. "I want you to fuck me, then I want you to come all over my tits and face."

Out of a sense of urgency, Troy strongly grabbed a hold of Jill and said, "Honey, what's the matter with you?"

With a carnal grin, she said, "It's just you and me in here. The others won't be back until service time. We have at least three hours, still."

"That's not the point," Troy panted. "Jill...we can't do this here."

"Why not," Jill scrunched up her face before taking off her shirt and tossing it behind her like a filthy rag. "Do you know what this fucking heat can do to a person?"

He couldn't explain it, but Troy's heart was actually breaking at that second. He was not only frightened of Jill, he also pitied her as well.

"C'mon…let's go to Ardan and Josephine's bed and fuck!" She excitedly ranted. "I'll suck your dick so good and hard!"

"Jillian," Troy roared before restraining her all over again.

With a look of absolute disgust, Jill stood back and screamed, "Oh, I see, you won't fuck me, but you'll fuck some trailer park trash cunt that gets passed around like a fucking joint! Did she let you come all over her fucking face?"

Troy couldn't believe what was taking place. Jill's entire face had turned apple red right before him. Her eyes were bulging out of their sockets while she sucked in air through her teeth.

All both of them could do was stand in the middle of the floor and stare on for what seemed like countless minutes before Jill turned around, snatched up her shirt from off the floor and ripped right out the front door without speaking a parting word.

There stood Troy, all alone and scared to death. There wasn't a single bone in his body that wasn't shaking at that point. All he could gather was her outraged face that looked back at him with such hatred and bitterness.

He couldn't move, it was like someone had planted him directly in the middle of the floor and dared him to make one step. Still, no matter how hard he tried, Troy couldn't get her face out of his head, it was stuck there permanently.

When he was at last able to budge, Troy stumbled his way over to the couch where his beloved diary was lying. Shivering, he reached for it and opened its pages wide. With his pen shaking in his right hand he began to write.

August 25th,
Never mind…

CHAPTER 30

Weak rumbles of thunder scaled the black, starless sky that night as both Jacob and Joshua, hand in hand, limped across the forbidden embankment that led down to the desert that they, much like the other children in the village, were strictly told not to cross into.

The darkness that they were walking in seemed to be more of a beloved calm rather than something to dread, especially when a storm was approaching. Their composed faces wore a tranquil smile that didn't seem to want to go away.

They walked on until they reached what appeared to be the midpoint between the village and the opening of the desert; about two hundred yards separated both areas.

Joshua and Jacob then sat down in front of one another Indian style and stared endlessly into each other's blank eyes. They did so for at least an entire hour before they began touching the other's faces with their warm hands as though they were examining something that neither of them had ever experienced before in their young lives.

The feeling out stage lasted for about fifteen minutes before they stopped what they were doing and sat back to stare each other down once again. Soon, from out of the oblivion of the desert came a prowling dingo that was whining along the way.

Jacob and Joshua paid the lowly creature no attention; they continued to stare until right beside them, a human hand from out of the dry, cracked ground protruded. It remained stationary until Joshua got up from his position on the ground and took a hold of the dingo's neck. Then, without even the slightest grunt, he snapped the animal's neck before standing back and watching it collapse to the ground in a heap.

Jacob soon got to his feet and stood beside his brother before the hand opened its palm to reveal several shiny gold coins. Joshua reached down and retrieved the coins before standing beside his twin brother. The boys stood at full attention like two on duty soldiers. Their stale looking faces never moved from their original positions.

The thunder in the sky grew a scant more intense as the boys took each other by the hand and turned back towards their unsuspecting village.

The desolate quiet in the vast desert seemed more like something that Jacob and Joshua wanted to stay amongst more that evening; but planted inside their individual heads were orders, orders that they and they alone could only possibly comprehend.

They were handed their sufficient payment; it was time to go back home, hand in hand. Neither boy looked back once at the hand that was slowly sinking back into the tough ground from which it emerged, or at the dead dingo.

In their static minds, there was no looking back at that point. They were paid in full.

CHAPTER 31

Thursday evening,

Troy sat and listened to the loud chorus of singing and clapping to the tune of, 'When we all get heaven', coming from the church as he pulled his diary from out of his hip pocket. He wanted to write about the incident with Jill from the day before, as well as his final few hours at Sinai, but the longer he sat and stared at the book, the more he began to realize that words couldn't quite explain how he was feeling at that particular time.

He could replay it a million times in his head and still never understand what happened with Jill. It absolutely demoralized him to no end to know that he had cheated on her, and that she had possibly had never forgiven him in her heart. There were words that he wanted to jot down, words that would express his sorrow for his sin against the woman he loved so dearly, but he couldn't pull them out; they were lodged inside his brain like a festering corpse that was waiting to be buried.

But rather than write down pointless, rambling words, Troy instead slipped his diary back into his pocket, as well as his pen, and sat there and listened to the boisterous crowd over in the church. She was over there; whether or not she was praising the Lord was another matter that he would have to see with his own two eyes.

Troy sat for a few moments before gathering the will to lift his sluggish frame up off the couch. As soon as he began for the front door, he heard Josephine, along with Jacob and Joshua coming down the steps.

"We were on our way over, too," Josephine smiled, standing behind the boys. "Well," she sighed, "I guess this is it. By the time service is over this evening everyone will be too tired to do anything but sleep tonight."

"Yeah," Troy amiably grinned. "It's just hard to believe that this is our last night."

Josephine looked down at her sons and asked, "Aren't you two going to thank Troy for visiting us here and for giving you those basketball bands?"

Joshua and Jacob both gazed upwards at Troy with dual blasé-type expressions in their bloodshot eyes, like the tall man in front of them were completely worthless to them. Then, without so much as a simple goodbye, Joshua snatched himself away from his mother before turning and walking out the front door, slamming it shut behind him.

Well," Josephine humbly pressed her lips, "I am sorry for that."

"Don't apologize, I understand."

Josephine then stepped away from Jacob and approached Troy with the most earnest appearance on her small face. She scanned the young man up and down before saying, "I never told you this, but I always believed that there was something weighing heavily upon your soul, like you have been wrestling with something very powerful."

Troy looked down at Josephine and all of the sudden took notice of a completely different woman before him. She was always a warm spirit, but never had he seen such compassion in her eyes as he did at that instant.

"Did you ever find what you were in search of?"

Troy exhaled before responding, "There's an expression we use back in the states, kinda, sorta. I've made a lot of bad decisions in my life, and I've wasted a lot of time. But my time here has opened my eyes to things that I've never seen before. I've got a lot of soul searching to do once I get home…a log of growing up to do. I'm just concerned about you guys staying here all by yourselves."

Blushing, Josephine softly stated, "Do not worry about us. If Pastor Hudson believes in what he has been teaching us all these years, then God will deliver us, no matter what. Paradise is right around the corner." Josephine then stepped into the kitchen for a second before coming back with one of her baskets in her arm. She handed the blue and yellow basket to Troy and happily said, "This is for you. The writing on the side says that you will never be alone. God will always be with you, everywhere."

Feeling the urge to want to cry, Troy immediately took the basket and hugged Josephine before allowing one tear to drip from his eyes.

The second he let her go, Troy looked over to see Jacob sit his bored self on the steps as the singing at the church grew louder by the minute.

"Oh," Josephine snapped, "I almost forgot the hymnals for the balcony crowd."

Troy watched as Josephine took off for the kitchen before sitting himself down onto the couch and examining his basket from side to side, as well as several, shiny gold coins that were placed mysteriously on the small table next to the couch.

Out of the corner of his eye he could see Jacob staring back into the kitchen at his busy mother with the most lurid manifestation on his dull face. It was like he was ogling a gorgeous fantasy woman that he had finally got the opportunity to meet for the very first time.

It disturbed Troy enough to want to look away and re-direct his full attention back to his basket. It was such a jarring sight to witness.

When Josephine made her way back into the living room with five hymnals gathered in her arms Troy immediately got up and attempted to help her along the way.

"Oh, thank you," Josephine huffed before spinning around to find her son pawing at her skirt. "What are you doing, child?" She nearly chocked.

Jacob continued to tug at his mother's skirt before actually having the audacity to lift it up to reveal her panties to the world. Out of a complete state of astonishment, Josephine immediately dropped the two hymnals that were in her hand and popped the boy right across the face as hard as she could.

Troy stood and looked on in downright amazement at the child. He realized that both he and his brother weren't well, but at that second, their septic condition was going to a place that he never imagined it would end up.

Turning the other check, Jacob gawked up at his mother with a wicked glare, and in a completely different sounding voice yelled, **"You black whore!"**

Right then, with impossible strength, Jacob tackled his own mother to the floor and began ravaging her helpless body.

Before Troy could even set one rescuing foot forward, he felt a force shove him backwards into the couch. The second he tried to get up, a man's strong arm ripped out of the couch and held him down by the waist. The arm was so powerful that Troy could hardly slip out from its unearthly grip.

Sounding like a grown man with a case of laryngitis, Jacob ripped away at his mother's clothes while cursing her and slapping her across the face. Josephine screamed for help, but all her pleas seemed to go by the wayside while her body was being destroyed by her son.

Troy helplessly watched as Jacob flipped her body over onto her stomach and ripped off her underwear before attempting to enter her from behind. But Josephine was as willful as her insane son. She scratched away at the boy's face before trying to get to her feet.

From one end of the room to the other they fought, but Jacob proved to be the stronger of the two as he pushed his mother back down to the floor and clawed away at her top to expose her bra.

Troy wrestled and tussled with the arm that was restraining him while unfortunately watching an unspeakable act play out just a few feet in front of him.

It was such a devilish experience to be locked in to that the young man didn't know what to focus on more, the rape scene or the phantom that had him locked down.

And then the screams from out of nowhere; shrill, collective hollers from the church that caused Troy to nearly break his neck just looking over at the window. All he could hear was Jill, nothing or no else inside the building even mattered at that point.

"Jill!" he yelled with all his might.

But his loud voice, along with those of the others in the church and inside the house that he was trapped in was completely drowned out to a simple whisper. He had no other alternative but to continue to fight while watching a woman succumb to her demonic son's evil impulses.

Josephine was as defenseless as a little girl. Jacob repeatedly slapped her across the face to the point where blood began to splatter left and right, spotting the Virgin Mary statuette that was beginning to shed a lone tear down its face.

"God…please help us!" Troy hollered before the crucifix that was nailed to the wall collapsed to the floor and twisted itself like a withered branch.

Jacob suddenly halted his vicious attack long enough to look up at Troy with a pair of black eyes; his pupils were all but gone. With pulsating eyes, Troy watched as the boy smiled hatefully at him before he resumed his attack on the woman by kissing all over her face like a raving lunatic.

Troy kicked and tossed before watching Josephine claw the floor with her fingernails, trying to hold on for dear life before being dragged along by her hair.

"Is this not what you wanted, you fucking mongrel?" The angry voice inside Jacob said before stepping away from Josephine completely.

Just as it seemed as though the monstrous attack had ended, Josephine's weak body was unexpectedly lifted into the air by an invisible force. For seconds she levitated above the floor before her spine was snapped in two. Just like that, she was dropped back down to the floor in a bloody heap; her opened eyes stared ever so blankly at Troy.

Troy couldn't help but to look at the dead woman that was spread out before him, it was all his crying eyes could seem to focus on for the time being.

The screaming noises from the church soon grew silent, but at the second, inside the house, what was taking place across the way at the church had become secondary. There in front of Troy stood Jacob's body, but the black eyes that were staring back at him were those of someone else, someone not of the world Troy Gaston knew.

Still restrained by his captor, Troy had no choice but to sit and watch as the ghastly demon glared his teeth at him before Jacob's body momentarily stood still.

Troy could sense that it was preparing for something even more horrible; the threatening, drooling gaze in its eyes sent the dreadful message loud and clear, like it were waiting for Troy to scream some more.

Then, Jacob's body did something that Troy never imagined was even humanly possible. The child's neck protruded outwards before his entire body collapsed upon itself, sending him down on all fours.

Troy could not only hear the gut-wrenching cracks and twists of the child's bones, but also faint cries from Jacob, sounding as if the entire, hellacious experience was hurting him beyond belief.

The demon looked up at Troy like a smiling animal before crawling about on all fours towards him. Troy once more began to wrestle about on the couch, kicking at the beast that was nearing him.

"**Do you know who we are, boy?**" The demon snarled in a gruff, European accent.

Troy was too scared to answer, but he was finding that his fear was making him all the stronger. Before the demon could climb onto the couch next to him, with every muscle in his body, Troy pushed against the hand that had him bound as hard as he possibly could while gritting his teeth in the painful process.

"**He should have killed us better!**" The demon raged on. "**Your God is no more!**" It snapped before turning and crashing through the window.

The very instant the demon was out of sight, the hand that had Troy simply released him. Giving no attention to where the hand had vanished to, Troy raced past Josephine's dead body on his way out the front door. The one and only person he could see in front of him was Jill. Even though her screams blended in with the rest of the terrifying yells and screams of the gathering, in Troy's head all he could hear was her and no one else; if it wasn't about Jill then it wasn't worth the effort.

Troy sweated profusely as he struck across the grassy trail that led to the church's backdoor, nearly running into the door itself.

Like a marauding soldier, Troy flung open the backdoor before ripping through the hallway that led to the sanctuary.

In front of him, inside the unnervingly silent church, was a wasted menagerie of bloody carnage that Troy's frazzled eyes couldn't take in all at once.

From atop the balcony were draped dead, blood drenched bodies that all hung over the wooden barrier. On the bottom floor, more bloody corpses lay; people of all ages, dead within the span of ten minutes.

Troy's body shook so hard that his eyesight was beginning to go blurry. As pertinent as Jill's well-being was to him, he honestly didn't have the nerve to turn around.

Everywhere his eyes stared was nothing but death upon death; every set of eyes were left wide open to view their final stages of horror before leaving the world behind forever.

The more his eyes criss-crossed from one end of the sanctuary to the other, the more he could see other carcasses lying about, broken and bleeding. Down in front of the pulpit was Ardan, who had a long candlestick that was used to light the church during Sunday evening service sticking straight through his chest. Right beside him laid Pastor Hudson's headless body. His own decapitated head was placed ever so neatly beside his feet.

Troy all of the sudden turned a blatant three hundred and sixty degrees to see none other than Jill. Though he wanted to find her first among all the evil, she was the last person he wanted to see. Somehow, whatever demonic force that had invaded the church just moments earlier managed to use the tall, gold cross to impale her through the back, just a few feet away from the pulpit.

Troy could hardly move. In his head, Jill was still alive, and everything that had just taken place was all part of a ridiculous dream. There was no way in the world any of what he was looking at could be real, he thought to himself.

He stood before Jillian's immobile body and examined the cross that stuck strong in the air through her back.

There were tears waiting to flow, as well as screams of agony and anger, but shock had overwhelmed him to the point where all he could do was stand there and ponder on the first time they had met years ago.

Then, without any warning whatsoever, all the lights in the church went out at once, leaving Troy completely in the dark. He raced over to the window, tripping over dead bodies along the way, to see both Joshua and Jacob outside, giggling and running back and forth like a couple of happy jackals. Their demonic laughter was soon followed by a series of distant howls and barks.

Troy gazed on and on outside at the black night. He realized that he was trapped inside the church with nowhere to go.

Just then, behind him grew a sudden spark that was followed by a burst of fire. From above in the balcony, another fire exploded, as did down below, behind the pulpit.

Like a trapped rat, Troy breathlessly ran to the front of the church and all the way to the back before fire eventually engulfed his every step.

Outside, the howling became louder, while inside, the fire blazed out of control to the point where Troy could hardly breathe.

"Come out here, boy," one of the demons gaily shouted. **"We want you!"**

Troy turned and gave Jill one final, heartbroken look. He wanted ever so much to at least free her body of the cross that had destroyed it, but the fire was entirely too relentless. He ran towards the nearest window, and without any regard for his own body, Troy jumped straight through the glass before landing on the grass.

Troy wasted no time getting to his feet. He ran directly to the side of the church that faced the pier, only to come face to face with Jacob, Joshua and a legion of bright-eyed dingoes, all seemingly blocking his path.

The animals shining night eyes, along with the two possessed boys standing in front of him let Troy know that his time on earth, much like those inside the church a while ago, was drawing to a close. Every shack, as well as the infirmary, caught fire at that instant. Ardan and Josephine's home exploded into flames right behind him before the church's roof collapsed upon itself.

As the demons and their feral army started to lurch forward, Troy somehow found it within himself to shut off his brain completely before allowing his legs to turn and run in the opposite direction.

He couldn't even hear the dingoes behind him howling and barking while chasing him down. He couldn't see the black desert in front of him as he jumped over the steep embankment and darted out into the vast darkness that was forbidden land to Sinai Village residents.

Troy left the world behind him that evening.

CHAPTER 32

Like a mad roadrunner, Troy ripped through the scorched desert at breakneck speeds. His continual, rampant fear kept his narrow feet racing nonstop. His brain was still a blank muddle of nothingness. In his eyes he saw only a never ending vortex, nothing or no one else beside him. It was like he was the only person left in the entire world. Even Jill had left his memory by then; just the limitless maelstrom that wouldn't allow him to stop no matter what.

The longer he ran the more he started to loose whatever coordination his numb body could maintain. As though it deliberately stepped out in front of him, Troy trampled on and tripped over a rock on the ground, which in turn caused the man to fall directly onto the right side of his face.

Without opening his mouth to yell, Troy looked back. The vortex that he was seeing in front of him was gradually diminishing. Second by second a violent brightness came into view the longer he stared off into what looked like a distance.

Once his eyes were able to gather their surroundings, Troy saw nothing around him but a wide open stretch of barren land. The only sounds his hot ears could gather were of the bleak wind that whistled throughout the desert he appeared to be all alone in.

From side to side, and front to back, Troy could neither see nor hear howling dingoes or the two little boys that were once chasing him. It was daytime, and Troy somehow couldn't comprehend that he had been running for hours unceasingly.

He could hardly catch his breath in the stifling heat. He was breathing so hard and fast that he was shivering. He could feel his blistering skin boil the longer he lay on the scorching ground.

Troy's mouth was dry and hollow, he couldn't even squeak out a simple gasp. His stomach grumbled and bubbled before eventually unloading upwards and out through his mouth.

He wiped his parched lips clean before gazing from left to right at the infinite desert plain that supported various small and withered tree-like plants, as well as red dirt that had gathered all over his face and hands. To the east he could see a somewhat large mountain range, but from where he was seated, it might as well have been clear on the other side of the planet.

The second Troy gathered the nerve to stand, right away his wobbly legs collapsed underneath him, sending the disheveled man back to the ground.

Just touching his legs felt like touching petrified wood, both appendages felt completely worthless.

Troy laid upon the cracked earth whimpering and drowning in his own sweat. He looked over at his skin that had turned a deep red from sunburn. As he laid on his back and glared upwards into the blue sky, his thoughts started to drift further and further away from the world, and back to Jill.

He didn't want to recall her face; it would have only reminded him of what she last looked like back at the burning church. All he wanted was for his parched mouth to say her name out loud just one time.

After lying down for what seemed like an hour at most, Troy eventually rolled over, reached into his back pocket and pulled out his diary. Surprising to him, neither the book itself nor his pen had fallen out during the events of the night before or his staggering run.

September 5th, 1976

Today was my first day of high school. I got homeroom with both Trumaine and Mike and I'm glad too, because I don't know anyone else here. I can't wait for AC/DC's new album to come out sometime this month, I read in a magazine that it may be their best one ever.

I got this one new teacher, he's a real dick. His name is Mr. Ford. He's the algebra teacher. I can't even understand algebra, but on the very first day he gives us homework. What do all the letters have to do with math? It'll take me the next four years just to understand this stuff.

Dad got on me the very second I walked through the door. He went nuts all because I forgot to take out the stupid trash. That guy is crazy. He'd probably lose his mind if I forgot to flush the toilet after I take a dump.

But all of that can wait. Today in homeroom I saw the most beautiful girl I think I've ever seen. The teacher said her name was Jillian. She's got blonde hair, freckles and she smiles so nice and pretty. I can't take my eyes off of her. I sure hope Steve or Scott don't try to get with her before I do.

She actually talked to me today while I was at my locker. She came and asked me if I had an extra pencil. When I gave her one of my pencils I got a chance to touch her hand, it was so soft. I don't think I've ever seen anyone so pretty in all my life. She looks like she's really shy, just like me, so I hope I get the chance to be her boyfriend, and if I do then I'll do anything for her. I'll go anywhere in the world she wants me to and I'll never, ever break her heart.

I think I'm in love, diary.

Troy shut his eyes and wept incessantly into the pages of his diary. The macabre image of a cross protruding through Jill's body caused a great physical pain to rush up his spine. It hurt so bad that he had to grind his teeth back and forth and grunt out loud just to bear it.

With the sun biting away at his neck, Troy, with his pen shaking in his hand, began to frantically scribble away on a blank section of his diary while tears continued to fall.

August ? 1982

I can't believe that I'm actually writing at all times. I don't know what day it is, all I know is that the sun is up. I'm going to die; I know this for a fact, so this will be my final entry. The last thing I want is to sound like a poet on his final leg. All I have to say before it all ends is that I wish to God that I was dead so I wouldn't have to recall any of what I saw and went through. I really do wish I was dead right now. Please, God, just kill me.

I have to get all of this out, I have to get it out before I leave this world. I don't want to carry any of this to the next life with me. They killed them all, every last one of them. Jacob raped and murdered his own mother. He ravaged her like she was some whore off the street. He ripped her clothes apart and just fucking raped her.

Then there was Joshua. I know it was him that killed everyone in the church, even Jill. The fucker put a cross right through her body like she

185

were made of clay. He killed every last person in that damn church within minutes. Pastor Hudson got his head cut off; Josh made sure to place the man's head next to his body, like he wanted the world to remember what he did.

I keep on saying Jacob and Joshua, but I know better, neither of those boys had anything to do with what happened. I heard their voices, the voices of grown men laughing like it was a fucking game to them. Jacob's eyes, I can't get those eyes out of my head. I keep hearing their voices, those ugly voices inside those little boys' bodies. Why did they take the boys? What did they ever do to anyone?

I can still feel that hand holding me down. I think I even saw that Mary statue in the house cry over whole thing.

Troy stopped writing to sob even more. The desert heard his excruciating cries echo from one stretch to the other. His moans remained agonizingly strong, keeping silent every living creature that may have inhabited the vast land mass.

All those dead bodies in that church, of all places; I can still hear them all scream. I just wish I could hear Jill one more time. I wish I could have been there with her. I've never known a sweeter soul than hers. Now, she's just burned to death, with the rest of the dead.

Ever since coming to this continent I've been robbed, and now I have experienced firsthand demonic spirits. Thomas Hutter, Nosferatu. The villagers told him not to go to the country of thieves and ghosts, but he wouldn't listen. He had to encounter evil eye to eye in order to believe. I thought I knew evil a long time ago with James, but now I know better. I could deny it as long as I want to, but it does exist, it is very much real. James was just mischievous; everything from a few hours earlier was from hell.

Please, God, bring Jill back to me. Please, don't let her be dead. Please, bring her back to life and—

"Please, God, bring Jill back to me!" One of the demonic voices echoed throughout the desert all of the sudden.

Stunned, Troy dropped both his diary and pen to the ground before jumping to his feet and spinning around like a top to see just where the voice was emanating.

"I fucked your girlfriend, boy!" The voice mocked, sounding as though he was pleased with the evil he did. **"I fucked her good before I killed her fucking ass!"**

In a state of sheer panic, Troy continued to spin around like a crazed man, but all he could see from all sides was nothing but land upon more land. There wasn't a single soul in sight.

"Why are you here, boy?" Another voice asked, sounding like he was angry. **"You should be dead along with the others."**

"God, please help me!" Troy screamed with all his might.

"No God here in the country of thieves and ghosts, boy," the other voice ghoulishly sniggered.

Troy began to run in the opposite direction as fast and hard as he could, trying not to trip over anymore rocks along the way.

"Why do you run, boy? You know we will find you."

Troy persisted in his race, forcing himself to block out the voices that seemed to follow him step by step.

"Troy, come back, please!" Jill's voice shrieked out in the sky.

Troy suddenly stopped on a dime in the hopes of hearing her voice cry out once more. He looked up at the bubbly clouds before weeping all over again.

"You left her to die! You should have been there with her to die!"

Too wound up to stand any longer, Troy dropped to his knees before ripping his t-shirt off of his sweaty body, picking up a sharp-edged rock from off the ground and pointing it directly at his stomach.

"Do it, kill yourself, now!"

Troy closed his eyes and held his breath, trying his hardest to insert the rock straight through his gut.

"Kill yourself, or we will!" The voice irately threatened.

Troy tried and tried, but no matter what he just couldn't stop crying, and the more he cried that was all the less of a grip he seemed to have on the piece of rock that he was clutching in his hands.

The rock simply dropped out of his palms and onto the ground. Troy then did something he never imagined he would end up doing at that moment. He bowed his head and began to pray. He prayed that the voices would go away and that Jill would somehow still be alive. It was such a fast and fierce prayer that he actually had to slobber in order to get the whole thing out.

Both of the voices, however, just laughed at the young man's urgency like it was the most entertaining sort of frivolity they had ever witnessed.

'**God, please help me!**' One voice flippantly mocked. "**You're God murdered us both! Now, we will murder you!**"

"Please, go away," Troy hollered.

"**God won't even be able to pull us off of you! Kill yourself, now!**"

Before Troy could scream another word, he immediately heard the sound of barking dingoes approaching from the distance behind him.

Without wasting another moment on prayer, he got up and used his unstable legs to carry him off further into the desert. At that point, east, west, north and south were all the same, all that was ahead of him was desert; as long as there was great space between him and the beasts then he was content for the time being.

The faster he ran, the more he found himself losing his footing until his own worn out tennis shoes fumbled across a sharp rock.

Troy hit the ground, face first...the desert was gone, it was darkness that he had stumbled in to.

CHAPTER 33

Dressed in all black, three piece suits, both Troy and his father walked hand in hand along the jagged terrain of the brutally hot desert and towards an isolated saloon that was ahead of them.

Upon their sweaty faces were ear to ear smiles, like they had just won the lottery. Neither man wanted to stop; they kept on pushing forward towards their most desired destination. The ever so pitiless heat felt more like a sweet kiss against their bodies after coming in from a freezing cold winter. The hotness didn't seem to bother either of them in the least bit.

Troy allowed his dad to enter the saloon before him. Once Troy closed the door behind him, he right away smelled the sharp aromas of hard liquor, along with the pungent stench of underarm funk before seeing the stuffed thirty-foot great white shark that was mounted on the wall above the barkeep's head.

Every man that inhabited the establishment appeared upset over their sudden arrival, like Troy and his father were the last people on earth they ever wanted to see. Their black eyes stared poisonous daggers at the Gaston's to the point where even the barkeep was becoming antsy.

Troy and his dad sat themselves down on separate stools in front of the bar, and without opening their mouths they waited as the bartender handed them both their own mugs of beer.

Troy sat and smiled at his father as though the happiness was painted on his face. He stared while his father sipped away at his mug before taking a slug of his own and asking, "I sure hope Chris doesn't find us here."

Sitting his mug down on the counter, Troy's father smiled, "Don't worry, he's still at Jason's house drawing."

Troy continued to slurp away at his cold beer as if it were the first drink he had in months. For some reason, he couldn't take his eyes off of his dad; he all of the sudden seemed totally mesmerized by the man that he had known for all his life.

"So tell me, how did you get here?" Troy's father continued to cheese.

Troy shrugged before saying, "Jill asked me to come here. She said that it would do me good. We took a plane, a bus and a boat. We saw a lot of sharks, too. They even killed some people."

"Really," the man's eyes stretched open.

"Yeah, they tore up about eighty-six people all in one day. I had to clean them up, of course."

"Well," Troy's father shrunk his shoulders, "you win some, and you lose some. Did you and Jill ever have sex?"

"No," Troy shamefully shook his head," she wanted to, but I didn't. I would have really fucked her brains out, too."

"Hey," one of the black-eyed brutes from the other end of the bar yelled, "what the hell are you two doing here?"

Still smiling, Troy and his father turned around in their seats and gazed directly at the man and his fellow cohorts who were slowly following their leader from behind.

"You know we don't allow your kind in here! Now, get out before we feed you to the fucking sharks!"

Troy suddenly looked up at the stuffed fish above the bar that was wiggling its tail-fin back and forth.

Without muttering a word, Troy and his dad jumped up from out of their seats and immediately instigated a brawl with just about every man in the bar. Fists went flying, as well as chairs and mugs. The great white roared like a raging lion as the fury of the Gaston men lit up the saloon with their strong, American bravado, until every man fell to the floor in an unconscious heap.

Once the dust had settled, Troy and his father sat back down in their stools and resumed their drinking detail; their heavenly smiles were still attached to their warm faces.

"We sure do miss you, son." Troy's father earnestly said.

Troy blushed at that second before he opened his mouth and replied, "I sure hope you do. I'll be home before Thanksgiving."

"Really," the old man responded with shock in his eyes.

"Sure, it won't be too long. I hope Carla will be okay so we can all have dinner together. Oh, and don't forget, the next Star Wars movie comes out next year, too."

"Is this where Han Solo is freed from carbon freeze?"

"I hope so," Troy sighed. "I know Chris will wanna see it."

Without a pause in their conversation, Troy's dad suddenly said, "Son, I want you to know that I'm happy that you've found something to do with your miserable life. I knew you could do it."

Troy nodded his head as if to say that he himself were proud. He then asked, "Do you know who Joshua and Jacob are?"

Taking a long sip from his mug, the man confidently grinned, "Yep, I sure do. Alphonse and Gregor are going to kill you next. They're going to rip out your guts and piss on your face. Then they'll fuck Jill up the ass."

"I know they'll kill me." Troy assuredly said. "As long as they don't feed me to the kangaroos, I'll be happy."

Troy's father laughed out loud before he remarked, "I remember a prayer that someone once told me years ago. I can't quite remember how it goes, though."

Troy excitedly snapped his fingers and said out loud, "I know a prayer, too, but for the life of me it's slipped my mind."

Both men sat in their stools and pondered on their individual thoughts to themselves. For what seemed like endless hours, the two appeared as though they were posing for a painting with their still-selves.

"If I remember it then I'll let you know." Troy's dad said before drinking the rest of his beer.

"Dad, do you think Jill will come back to life, again?"

"Who knows," he nonchalantly shrugged. "Maybe she will, maybe she won't. Until then, you just get ready to die, and then we'll see what happens with Jill."

Troy grinned before downing the remainder of his beer and slamming the mug down onto the counter. Just as soon as he was done swallowing, he could feel something tickle the back of his throat, like a feather was caught in his windpipe.

When he wasn't able to breathe any longer, he coughed and coughed until spurts of phlegm flew out of his mouth and onto the floor. But all that seemed to do was aggravate the tickle all the more.

Troy then stood to his feet and let out a heaving cough that was soon followed by a torrent of blood that came shooting out of his mouth. He watched as his father kept on smiling, no words came out of the man's mouth.

Troy then looked around at the suddenly empty saloon before turning back to his dad who by then had his own set of black eyes to see with.

Troy coughed and gagged before opening his stinging eyelids to see a wild-haired black man standing over him with what appeared to be a twig in between his fingers. When he saw the man proceed to stick the twig back into his mouth, out of a sense of startled urgency, Troy rolled over onto the ground before trying to scamper to his feet like a spooked horse.

From left to right all Troy's hysterical eyes could gather was one Aborigine after another, all standing back staring eagerly at him as if the crazed white man were in the midst of a violent fit.

When Troy saw that the people didn't have black eyes, ever so gradually he began to calm down. Out of pure exhaustion, he dropped back down to the ground. Every muscle in his stiff body felt as though it were trying to rip out of his own skin.

The second his foggy eyes could open wide, Troy saw in front of him a tranquil fire, as well as a shabby looking dingo that seemed just as frightened as he was. Troy looked all around him at the partially clothed Aborigine's. Their faces were painted with various white and red markings, while most of the men held sharp spears in defense.

Behind the fire, marked on a piece of oxen skin, was Aboriginal art that Troy right away recognized; he recalled it from the village.

Troy watched as the five half-dressed men with weapons slowly lowered their protection while a scantily clad woman with a plate in her hand kneeled down next to him. Troy peeked into the plate to see pieces of meat and what looked to be shreds of leaves. He was familiar with the leaves, but the meat was something he was skeptical of, given the variety of animal that resided in the desert bush.

With her hands, the woman demonstrated to Troy how to ingest the food. Scratching his sore nose, Troy picked up the meat, not wanting to take a guess as to what creature it once was, and stuffed it directly into his mouth.

Everyone in the tent looked so happy to see him eat that Troy himself found it somewhat amusing, so much so that his appetite that he never thought he would get back suddenly came roaring to life with an unholy vengeance.

Soon, the dingy dingo that was so afraid earlier had somehow gathered enough courage to blunder over to Troy and lick his face like it had known him for years. Troy's body began to shiver at that second before he carefully slid away from the animal while continuing to eat away at his meal.

Every curious person inside the tent stared on at him as though he were an alien. Troy understood that he was possibly the first and only white man they had ever laid eyes on, which was why he didn't bother to give their shock much attention.

The instant he was through eating, the woman that fed him got to her feet before carrying herself out of the tent, which left Troy and the five other tribesmen all alone. Troy swallowed as the men drew close to him and began speaking in their native tongue as if he was supposed to understand what they were saying. But thanks to his visit to Sinai, Troy could gather some of their dialect, in bits and pieces. Even though ninety-eight percent of the Aborigines at Sinai could speak English, most of them, however, would revert back to their native speech every so often, like they were using it as a form of code amongst their visitors.

From what Troy could gather from the men, it sounded as if they were re-telling the story of how they found him out in the desert and how they managed to mend his bleeding nose. Troy wanted to ask them if they had seen two little boys or a rogue pack of dingoes ripping through the area, but the last thing he desired was to find out the harsh answer. What was burning in his head was just where he was and how he could make it back to the mainland in one piece.

At first, Troy thought of using sign language to communicate with the men, but he remembered that they weren't mute or deaf, just foreign. He figured and contemplated until he recalled some of the language he learned from the village.

With as much broken dialect as he could speak, Troy tried to convey his ardent message to the men, but as much as he spoke to them and they spoke back, it seemed that the translation was completely out of focus.

Frustrated, he got up from off the ground and began to pace back and forth within the tent. One of the men then stood up and tried to get Troy to come outside with him. Not quite knowing what to expect, Troy reluctantly followed in behind the zealous man outside to where other natives were milling about. They all stopped dead in their tracks to look at the strange white man that had invaded their tiny village, even the children stood back in awe at what they were seeing before them.

Walking beside the five men, Troy gawked all around at the people, hoping not to see one pair of black eyes amongst the gathering.

Once they made it to the foot of the settlement, one of the men pointed out to the desert and began to speak. Troy listened carefully, trying to pick up on whatever words he could understand from the man's mouth. By that point, though, it was all just gibberish. All he could do was stand and gaze forever at the stunning red sky that was becoming darker by the minute.

Troy closed his eyes and realized that home had become just a metaphor, an imaginary place, much like something from out of a children's storybook.

CHAPTER 34

The sun came up the very next day, and that was all Troy could register inside his fried brain as he trailed in behind a group of natives out into the baking desert to hunt.

He had spent hours trying to convey his message to them. Earnestly pressing the question of where the nearest point of civilization was located, but no matter how hard he spoke or signed, their two languages were a galaxy apart.

He dragged his heavy, sweating carcass across the scorched bush, watching the men in front of him, twelve in all, and one little boy, carry their spears and wait for the perfect opportunity to strike.

The sweat oozed off of Troy's face like drenching warm water. The summers in Ohio were hot, he thought to himself, but never were they as searing as they were in the desert that morning.

When he was running away from the two demons and their dingoes, the last thing on his mind was the overbearing heat, but just then, while wandering the terrain like a nomad, he could feel his own body practically being weighed down as though something or someone were squeezing his head like a grape.

Suddenly, one of the men began babbling to two other men beside him. Troy awoke from his dazed ramble to see the man point to a nearby crag up ahead in the hazy distance. It wasn't an impressive looking mound of rock, a child could have ascended it and not have been overwhelmed, but to the obstinate native, it might as well have reached all the way to heaven.

Without warning, all twelve males took off down towards the mountain, one of the little boys that tagged along stood and waited for Troy to follow in suit. Troy took a long pause to consider his next course of action. Even though he had only known the natives for a few hours at best, it was what beyond the mountain that caused his apprehensive feet to shuffle at a snail's pace.

With a giddy excitement all over his face, the little boy took Troy by the hand and dragged him along, like it were life and death. Troy's feet were both sore and dry, much like the rest of his body, running a step further would have possibly crippled him for life.

The closer they drew to the small mountain, the more Troy could tell that their so called peak was really nothing more than a simple tall rock, more like an oversized jungle gym. The entire group of men climbed the jagged rock, and with their spears in combat position, poised themselves for an attack.

Tired, but curious, Troy, too, ascended the other side of the rock before standing behind the men and looking over to see a mob of kangaroos all bouncing about, unaware of their impending doom.

Troy watched carefully as the twelve hunters snuck down the rock as quietly as they could; the kangaroos were ripe for the kill, it was almost too easy. Then, without shrieking a battle cry, the natives, with their sharp spears, attacked the animals with such ferocity that it caused Troy's body to shudder.

The men struck down as many kangaroos as they could, but there were some that rather than run, chose instead to stay behind and fight. With their razor-like claws, the animals swiped and kicked at their killers like bold warriors, refusing to yield without laying down a descent scrap along the way.

It was such a maddening piece of turmoil to be locked in that Troy found it difficult to watch. He tried to turn his head, but no matter where he turned all he saw was one dead church member after another. Severed heads left and right, bloodied carcasses strewn all over. Troy then covered his ears and closed his eyes, hoping to block out the gruesome scene that was tearing him apart all over again.

The high-pitched squeals of the kangaroos were transformed into yells that sounded like Jill's voice, screaming for someone to save her from the evil that was devouring her.

Tears then began to drip down from Troy's eyes, so much so that they were mixing in with the sweat that was already saturating his sunburnt face.

A tug at Troy's torn pants caused the young man to jump suddenly before opening his eyes to see the little boy motioning for him to join the rest of the clan at the bottom of the rock.

Hesitantly, Troy climbed over one jagged rock after another until he ended up on the ground near where the remaining kangaroos were laying. The stench of dead meat was already hanging heavy in the humid air around him. It didn't take long for the vultures to smell the carnage; one by one a swarm of large, black wings circled around the scene like helicopters, awaiting their turn to feast.

Troy bowed his head to the ground and began to sob out loud. Their vile screams played repeatedly in his brain. He couldn't see a single kangaroo in sight, instead, all that lay before him was a throng of dead human beings for as long as the desert stretched.

"There'll all dead," he mumbled to himself while allowing a steady stream of drool to creep down from his bottom lip.

The others carried on as though they had all just stumbled upon a goldmine. The natives cheered and laughed for joy at the booty they had captured.

Troy looked up and saw nothing but Joshua and Jacob giggling and carrying on as if every atrocity they had dealt had pleased them to no end. Suddenly, every emotion that Troy had kept bottled up inside started to spill over and seep right out of his boiling body.

"What the fuck are you people laughing at?" He screamed with all his might while flapping his arms in the air. "Is that all you people can do is laugh, for God's sake? There'll all dead! There'll all dead and they're not coming back, ever again!"

Every one of the natives stopped what they were doing to look on at the young man with the most perplexed glares on their painted faces. They all appeared more frightened than anything else.

"They killed them all!" he continued to holler. "They killed every last one of them! They killed Jill!" After so much yelling and fist pumping, Troy broke down to his knees and cried out even louder, "Dad...please help me! Please...come and get me before they kill us all!"

Once Troy had seemingly exhausted himself to the point where his mouth was too sore to blurt out another word, an ominous silence whispered amongst the crowd. No words of any sort were spoken for at least two whole minutes. His eyes were closed; he didn't want to open them for the fear of seeing the dead bodies surrounding him.

Then, softly, a warm hand touched his hard, scratchy skin. Troy opened his eyes to see the little boy standing over him with an awkward, almost kindly look on his brown face, like he could feel Troy's pain.

The child then patted Troy on the back before handing him his own water satchel to drink from. Troy guzzled down the amazingly cool water before taking the boy by the hand and squeezing as tight as he could.

Trembling from head to toe, Troy stammered, "They're coming for us. I can hear them. I can hear them in the sky…like thunder."

The rest of the group assembled around Troy while the vultures continued to swing and swirl about in the air above.

CHAPTER 35

"Has anyone seen a diary lying around anywhere?" Troy's lazy tongue dragged as he sat Indian style by a tent while tracing aimless lines in the dirt.

It was early evening; the bright, orange sun was sluggishly melting into the clouds. In its faltering absence a blissful breeze whistled into the tiny village, making the nighttime a pleasant, if not tolerable experience from the severe heat of the day.

Miniscule goose bumps formed upon Troy's bare arms as he doodled in the dirt like a child at play. The other natives, though sympathetic to his plight, chose to keep their distance from the strange man. Most were dancing and singing around a roaring fire, while others, mainly children, played "spear wars" with sharp sticks that they had fashioned themselves.

Troy could smell the gamey stench of the kangaroo meat burning in the air. The tribe seemed grateful for the meal, so much that they just couldn't seem to stop laughing over it.

As he traced in the dirt with his index finger, Troy noticed that certain lines were beginning to take form. The lines seemed to take on a life all their own, much like words or sentences forming completely out of nowhere.

August the…I don't know the date.

All I know is that I feel so tired and worn down, and I haven't hardly done anything today but hunt kangaroo. I didn't eat any of it, but I did eat some kind of soup that this woman gave me a few hours ago. If I didn't know any better, I'd swear I've been poisoned. I can hardly keep my eyes open.

Every now and then, that same woman will glance at me from the bonfire that she's dancing at. Her eyes look deceitful, like she's waiting for me to pass out.

I can't stop thinking of Jill. I've accepted the fact that she's dead; I don't have any other choice but to accept it. She's not here with me, and that's death enough. I haven't heard Josh or Jacob since being lost back in the desert. I just hope to God that they've moved on.

Everywhere I look I see black eyes staring at me. I also keep hearing water all around me, too, like I'm near an ocean or something. I've never heard it since I've been here, but perhaps in the morning, some of the villagers can lead me to it so I can signal for help.

I can't keep my eyes open much longer. My arms feel like led weights. I'm going to pass out. God, please help.

Troy stopped scribbling long enough to look up and see a young, bald-headed aborigine woman staring back at him with the most devious stupor on her painted face from the bonfire where she was dancing at. He couldn't take his lethargic eyes off of her no matter how hard he tried to. It was like they were both locked in a staring duel neither wanted to surrender to.

Troy's eyes glanced beyond her face to catch most of the others still dancing and eating away, while the children pretended to kill one another with their make-believe spears. It was then that the young, long-suffering man chose to retreat into the tent he was seated in front of.

Like a slug, he hauled his three ton body across the dirt and inside the smelly shelter which bared the aroma of rotting flesh. From there, he crept up underneath a brown blanket and shut his glassy eyes. The crashing water that had invaded his ears became louder by the second, like it was right outside the tent.

Every so often he would open his eyes and shut them all over again. His eyelids were too heavy to keep open for an extended amount of time, and he found that the more he fought, that was all the faster he seemed to lose whatever strength he had left inside his limp body.

He realized that he had been poisoned, the look in the woman's eyes was entirely too sinister to be trusted. Therefore, Troy was aware that his time was drawing to a bitter close. With what little brain power he had left, he shoved aside the water racket and tried to recall Chris and Jill's faces one last time before departing the world that he knew.

For a final moment, he saw himself and his little brother playing basketball in their driveway. Troy allowing Chris to score on him was just one of the many things that for him, made coming home from work all the more bearable.

From Chris, Troy's fond memories diverted to Jill. It made his eyes water at how much she truly loved and adored him. How she went out of her way to bring him to a closer relationship with Christ. His brief affair with Amber cut right through him like fifty arrows through the heart when it all first took place, but lying on the ground, rifling through his sore remembrances, he wished that he hadn't met Jill in the first place; anything that would have spared her feelings from his malevolent desires.

A tear dribbled out of Troy's left eye as he lay on the hard ground. Minute by minute, he could feel his once flowing blood start to creep to a slow crawl. He would try to lift his arms, only to realize that they had become twice their original weight, he couldn't raise either of them to save his very life.

He attempted to raise his head, but that as well was an impossible feat to undertake, as was trying to bend his knees or even wiggle his toes. His entire body had become immobile.

Rather than fight, Troy chose to succumb to the fateful plight that had overtaken him. His warm ears could still hear the commotion outside the tent, as well as the water that sounded as though it were all around him. He wanted to pray to God, but even trying to pull words out seemed more like an arduous task; his mouth was completely numb.

At that second, from out of nowhere, the sound of feet scraping across the ground entered into the tent. Troy opened his sluggish eyes to see a dark silhouette standing over him. He braced himself as tight as he could before seeing a flash appear from his right side. It was fire, a small flame that was used primarily for cooking. The entire tent at that moment exploded into an array of glorious orange light.

Troy looked up to see the same woman that had fed him earlier kneeling down in front of him. Her red and white painted face concealed her mischievous eyes. Troy had no idea what she was up to, all he knew was that it was her that handed him the bowl of soup, that was all the proof he needed that he wasn't wanted there amongst the tribe.

The woman, who at first glance reminded him of a dark-skinned Josephine, all the sudden crawled over and began to kiss Troy all over his neck and face. Troy's body started to shake and squirm, like a poisonous snake was slithering over him.

The woman licked Troy's face up and down before she pulled back and stopped. Troy watched with bated anticipation at just what she was going to possibly do next. No matter what, he just wanted his existence to end right then and there.

He looked on as she slipped off the red and brown cloth that was covering her body to reveal her sagging breasts to him. The woman sat before him with a calm smirk on her colorful face, like she was telepathically telling him that everything was going to be okay.

As if he had a choice in doing so, Troy stared on at the ominous, naked individual before him before a long jaw struck up behind the woman and bit right into her neck.

It was a dingo, and the cruel animal had no mercy upon the person that it was ravenously tearing limb from limb.

Troy listened as she screamed out in holy terror before her body was eventually drug out of the tent. That was motivation enough to get the young man to lift his cumbersome carcass from off the dirt.

With every ounce of miniscule energy he had left in his body, Troy got up from where was lying an attempted to crawl over to the tent's opening. Before he could even look outside, he could hear the blood-curdling shrieks of men, women and children screaming for their lives.

He poked his head out to see the natives being mauled and mutilated by the ungodly pack of dingoes that had seized the camp. Never before in his life had Troy witnessed such brutal ferocity from an animal, but then again, he realized that they weren't just any animals, they belonged to a certain duo that couldn't have been too far behind.

Without watching any further, Troy struggled to turn back around and crawl over to where the fire was blazing. Perched beside a black cooking pot was a sharp spear. Troy pulled himself towards the weapon as hard as he could, bleeding from the mouth along the way. When he was able to grab a hold of the spear, Troy used the butt end to propel himself to his feet for a better fighting chance.

He stood against the spear and waited for the screaming to end. It took just about every bit of raw nerve to get up; Troy was beyond hope, it was all but a gutless dream, but as far as he was concerned, there wasn't anything in the rule book that said that he couldn't put up one last scuffle before departing his earthly realm.

As painful as it was to his body, he wanted to fight; he wanted to lash out at everyone and everything that his mother, her boyfriend, his father, and most of all, Pastor Hudson, had him endure. Troy felt as though it was Tobias that had put him smack dab in the situation that he was encountering, beyond that, he had no other explanation as to why the demons were chasing him down.

Once the yelling outside ceased altogether, there came a deafening silence. The dingoes couldn't be heard, nor could any other nighttime creatures for that matter, it had gone completely quiet.

Troy picked up the spear and wrapped his sweaty hands around it as tight as he could, prepared to thrash whatever was about to come his way with evil intentions swimming in their black souls.

He waited endlessly, bobbing his head up and down and from side to side, trying to see or hear anyone or anything that could have been outside the tent. To Troy, the minutes that passed by might as well have been hours.

After so much gut-wrenching waiting, Troy decided to limp his pain-stricken body towards the tent's entrance until he could hear a scraping racket scale across the rugged ground; it sounded like a multitude of snakes all slithering at once.

With the sharp end of the spear pointed straight ahead, Troy defiantly held his ground as he watched both Joshua and Jacob's bodies just casually stroll right into the tent.

Their faces were ash white, like they had been dead for months. Their treacherous grins suggested that the devils that had taken control of their little souls were happy to see Troy, just so they could impose whatever evil they had up their sleeves for one final time.

"Come to us, boy," Joshua ordered.

Like that, an unseen force snatched the spear that was secured in Troy's hand away from him before being tossed to the ground. Then, as though someone had pushed him, Troy went flying back until his body hit one of the poles of the tent. Before he could even attempt to get up, strings that were lying on the ground began to wrap themselves around his wrists until they fastened together, keeping the young man at bay.

Troy struggled to free himself but the restraints were too strong, add to the fact that his body was still in a state of complete pain from the poison he consumed earlier.

As he fought to free himself from the ties, he helplessly watched as both wicked entities advanced towards him like a couple of prowling lions, their black eyes never once blinking.

Just then, a blazing ring of fire encircled all three individuals within the small tent. Troy began to kick away from the fire as both devils started towards him.

Thrashing and screaming, Troy tried with every bit of power inside of him to keep the evil away. On one side, Jacob approached, rubbing his fingers through Troy's dusty hair, while Joshua stood directly in front of the young man, as if he were prepping to do something.

"Your father is fucking Chris up the ass right now, boy." Jacob cooed into Troy's right ear.

"No," Troy hollered. "Get away from me!"

Both demons snickered, seemingly delighted at the carnage that were putting down. All Troy could see were their black eyes that stared endlessly back at him. Their rotting breath seared into his face like hot steam as they laughed gleefully.

"God, please help me!" Troy cried out.

Joshua laughed, **God…your God couldn't even save our Captain! Your God is a failure!"**

Right then, Jacob slapped Troy across the face hard enough to where blood shot out and onto the ground. Joshua began screeching like a large bird before going down on his hands and knees and crawling about, poking his tongue in and out of his mouth.

"Please, let me go!"

Jacob stepped around to face Troy eye to eye and said, **"Call him again, call your God again and see where he takes you. You will die in our arms, just as the others did. Hell is your home now, child."**

From there, Jacob, too, went down on all fours before vomiting blood onto the ground beneath him. Troy closed his eyes and began to pray to himself the single hardest, from the heart prayer he could utter at that very second.

"I can see your thoughts, boy!" Joshua said out loud. **"We will never die. Nothing can kill us, ever again!"**

"Pray as hard as you can, Gaston. Tobias did the same thing and he lost his head." Jacob sneered.

"Get away from me!" Troy roared.

Still, both demons laughed and carried on, unfazed by Troy's incessant agony. When Troy was bold enough to open his eyes, he saw both individuals crawling about in an unorderly fashion. He was well aware that they were toying with him.

From one end of the fiery tent to the other they rambled on, looking like they were contemplating what they were going to do next. Meanwhile, Troy fought and tussled with the sharp ties that were beginning to cut off the circulation to his hands. It was a frail cloth that had his wrists bound, but they were tied as tight as possible, as to not allow the captive to escape.

From out of the corner of his eye Troy scanned around, trying to find an opening within the tent, anything that could possibly give him a hint of elusion from his jailers.

Just then, both demonic forces stopped right in the middle of the ground and stared at Troy for a few minutes before a lone dingo blundered into the tent and right through the ring of fire unscathed. Troy watched as the animal stepped up beside the demons before it opened wide its jaws and said in a European dialect, **"You will go to hell with Yahweh, child."**

Troy once more turned his head before looking back to see Joshua and Jacob's bodies begin to fuse into each other's until they appeared much like conjoined twins. From their two heads that were side by side, to their arms and legs, the amalgamated abomination crept about on the ground, behaving much like a rabid animal before approaching Troy and snapping at him with their teeth.

"God…where are you?" Troy cried out as loud as he could to the heavens above.

CHAPTER 36

Troy opened his blurry, stinging eyes to see both demons sitting Indian style on opposite ends of the tent. Cluttered behind them were the dead bodies of the tribe that they had slaughtered earlier in the evening. Each bloody carcass, from the men and women, all the way to the children, was neatly stacked upon one another in various rows.

The jarring sight caused Troy's eyes to spring wide open. The claustrophobic, stinking heat inside the tent caused him to fall asleep momentarily. He was still too weak from the poison to mount an escape, and the hotness only seemed to pile on the grief by eighty degrees. His own skin felt as though it were about to drip right off of his bones; from head to toe he felt like a sponge of sweat.

From right to left, Troy viewed all the dead persons that had taken him in and cared for him. The more he looked, the more he just wanted to break down and cry for their poor souls. It was happening all over again, just like back at Sinai.

Not once did he imagine that his own existence would come crumbling down on his head. It was no dream; everything that stared back at him, from the dead people, to the demonic individuals that held him prisoner was as real as the fire that was suffocating his lungs.

Suddenly, from out of the corner of his eye, Troy spotted Jacob's body stumble towards him. There was a blank expression plastered all over his pale face, like the entity that inhabited the boy's soul was totally confused.

Troy had no idea just how to respond to such a paralyzing force that was the two devils. There were absolutely no words he could conjure that could possibly garner his own freedom. He didn't know where to start.

The demon stood before Troy before kneeling down and eyeing him as close as he could. Troy tried his hardest not to look into Jacob's black, empty eyes that resembled a dolls eyes, but it was impossible, the creature just wouldn't relent.

Troy then happened to look up at the demon that was fidgeting with his hands as if they were agitating him. He fiddled and wringed with them so much that Troy became even more frightened at just what he was going to do next.

Then, just like that, Jacob's hands dropped to his side. A few seconds passed before the demon stood to his feet and lifted his hands in the air to sign the words, 'Save my soul, Troy.'

Troy's eyes opened with brilliant excitement at that instant. For a brief glimpse, he could sense the child's innocent presence in the tent along with him. Troy wanted to reach out, he wanted to say something, but still, his tongue was trapped in place.

"Do you like the dead, boy?" The other demon asked from behind.

Troy looked past Jacob's body and asked, "Why don't you let them go? They didn't do anything to anyone!"

"They want to come out, Troy. They want to be free."

"Then let them go!" Troy angrily screamed.

"We like being here. Soon, others will join us. It is his will. Look at all the dead around you, child. Even in their despair they long for life once more. We are now gods."

Then, Jacob's body dropped to the ground in a heap before going into a series of convulsions. Troy sat and watched with horrified eyes as the startling scene captivated him. At first sight, he figured that the force that had the child was beginning to lose its potency, but after so many minutes of nonstop seizures, the entity stopped before slowly sitting up and staring back at Troy once more.

Joshua got up and walked over to Troy where he proceeded to rub and caress the man's head and face. Soon, he forcefully grabbed Troy by the chin and calmly uttered in another man's voice, "Your mom is gone now, Troy. It's time for you and me to go to bed."

At that very moment, Troy froze up the second he heard the all too familiar voice. It was like someone had struck him across the face with a hammer.

Joshua's face grinned before he said, "We have to do it again, Troy. We have to before your mom gets back home. You want to make me happy, don't you?"

Troy squirmed and fought his way out of the demon's strong grip, but no matter what, the beast was too powerful to be withstood.

"Take off your pants, Troy. Take them off, now!"

"No," Troy yelled out like a madman. "Leave me alone!" he kicked.

"Put my pee, pee in your mouth, or I'll slice your mom's throat!"

"No…no, let me go!" Troy continued to holler until his mouth became sore.

From left to right he fought until the demon at last relinquished its grip and stood back away from the young man, still wearing his evil grin.

"Why, God," Troy wept. "Why is this happening?"

Joshua's entire body at that stage began to levitate above the ground before he said, **"Cry to him, boy! Cry out to God!"**

Troy wrestled about in his restraints, not so much thinking about freeing himself, but rather wanting to tear both devils apart with his bare hands.

"We will take you now, Troy." Jacob said before stepping over and picking up the spear that was lying beside Troy. **"Soon, we all will be one. That is why we came back. Our Captain took our lives; you will make us whole again."**

Still, Troy's flaming rage could not be quenched. He persisted in trying to kick and grab at both beings. Soon, his entire mind drew a complete blank. Everything he had experienced since arriving in Australia had been ostensibly erased from his memory.

His vicious tirade went on and on before he opened his parched mouth and mindlessly began saying the first thing that came to mind. "Holy God Almighty, be our guide in battle. Be our shield against the darkness of our foe Satan!"

Just then, something startling began to take shape within the tent. Joshua's floating body began to slowly descend back to earth. Jacob backed away in an almost alarmed sort of manner.

"May thou rebuke him, shun him away! Cast that wicked beast into the flames of hell and all of his evil spirits along with him who dare wander the earth in search of souls to devour! Amen!"

With sputtering fury, Troy repeated the prayer that Pastor Hudson had taught him three more times. The same prayer that he had forgotten the night the man had first recited to him.

"**Stop this,**" Jacob screamed in a frightened tone. "**God is not here! He is in hell!**"

A fourth time Troy uttered his prayer, it was that same fourth round that ended up sending both devils to their knees, wailing out in agonizing pain before vomiting all over the ground.

"**Help us, master,**" Joshua cried out. "**Save us in our time of despair!**"

"**Fuck you, you motherfucker,**" Jacob spat at Troy.

Both demons began to roar and snarl like a couple of wild animals before getting to their feet and advancing towards Troy, grabbing him by the legs. Troy, however, didn't stop praying, he kept on as though he himself were the possessed one.

"**Take him, take him now!**" Jacob desperately screamed into Troy's face.

"**Enter him now, before it is too late!**" Joshua snapped as he opened Troy's praying mouth wide. "**Make him ours!**"

Unbeknownst to Troy, thanks in part to all the tussling that he had been putting up over the course of the night, the restrains that had his bleeding wrists bound were gradually loosening. Without even looking up to see if he was free or not, he snapped the cords apart and bolted past both demons on his way out of the tent.

Whatever insufferable pain he was in hours earlier became at that instant mere rubbish. Troy Gaston had the sudden energy of an Olympic sprinter in second place, dying to reach his opponent before he raced past the finish line. Like a man on fire, Troy bolted out into the pitch black desert, while behind him, barking dingoes hounded him down like he was their last meal on earth.

"**Come here, Troy!**"

"**You will never go home!**"

The evil voices that ricocheted into the night sky were ever so gradually beginning to sound like someone or something even more sinister, something bigger and louder. All it did was make Troy run even harder.

There wasn't a single pause or misstep in his glorious, uncoordinated dash. The more he ran, the more Troy could hear what sounded like rushing water, as well as the ravenous dingoes behind him that felt as though they were only inches off his heels.

In front of him was nothing but endless darkness, even the moon was absent that ominous evening. Troy didn't have the wherewithal to turn around to see who or what was behind him, as far as he was concerned, if he had turned around then everything would have ended in the blink of an eye.

"I will kill you, Troy!"

In his brain was the same prayer that Troy had repeated back inside the tent, he couldn't get it out of his head. Soon, he couldn't even feel his own two legs that seemed to take on a life of their own.

Before he could race another step, Troy's legs, without warning, collapsed beneath him. Suddenly, he felt his entire body go weightless as he plunged countless feet straight down into the water.

It took a while before Troy could gather where he was, but as soon as he realized that he wasn't under attack any longer, he held his breath and started to swim upwards until he reached the surface. Scraping for their lives were two dingoes that had followed Troy off the cliff and into the salty sea. They yelped and howled until their bodies succumbed to the swallowing of the vast water.

Troy then looked up to see the great cliff from which he had dropped. From where he was in the water it looked as if he had descended at least a hundred feet or more. At the very top of the cliff stood both demons side by side, screeching and screaming like two irate vultures.

"Come back, boy!"

The overpowering current steadily carried Troy further out into the abyss, putting more distance between both him and his captors. He couldn't take his eyes off of them; at that point, he would have rather drowned than to gaze on any longer.

The further Troy drifted, the less he could see Jacob and Joshua's controlled bodies, until at long last, they were gone, the voices had ceased. The prayer that he had been saying out loud was starting to fade away to the back of his mind; the words were becoming more and more forgettable. All that was left was the sea that saw fit to carry him as far away from civilization as possible.

Soon, all that he could see surrounding him was nothing but boundless and deep water. In the distance, Troy could hear a mighty humpback whale sing its sad, wailing song for anyone that was willing to listen.

CHAPTER 37

The dark night seemed to drag on infinitely. Troy, at that point, wasn't even attempting to swim, his body was entirely too weak to budge. Instead, he chose to allow the current to carry him to wherever.

He still had the sense enough to realize that he was about as far away from the two demons as he could possibly be; if they wanted him that bad then they knew where to find him.

Earlier, just floating in the sea with nothing underneath him made his body feel completely weightless, but at that second, the numbness had begun to settle in. The cold water had already paralyzed his nerves to where he couldn't even feel himself urinate. The bitter salt that carelessly splashed into his mouth and face had all but dried out his skin.

As he was coasting along, much to his chagrin, Troy couldn't help but to reminisce on Joshua and Jacob. They were both trapped forever in a hellish exile, their souls to die inside the purgatory that was inexplicably thrust upon their innocent lives. He wanted ever much to pray for them, to ask God for his mercy to rain down upon their poor souls, but it just wasn't in him to pray any further. Troy was exhausted beyond all belief; all he wanted was to close his eyes and forget for an eternity. And close his eyes he did. The stifling cold gripped his body so tight that even the water that he was in began to lose its touch.

As he started to lose conciseness, an abrupt bump scraped across his left foot causing Troy to reawaken from his sliding sleep. It startled him only for a moment, until another bump rubbed past his foot. Troy opened his eyes wide, he was too weak to dive under and see just what was beneath him.

For at least two or three minutes the scraping had ceased before yet another bump caressed his bare feet. There was something large underneath him, he could tell because as it was passing along the length of its body never seemed to end. It felt like coarse rubber sliding across the bottom of his feet.

Troy suddenly snapped awake from his drowsy stupor. Around him he could feel something swirl about in the water. Seeing was impossible in the dark, but then again, he didn't have to see anything to know what was happening. On just about every side his hands could feel something smooth swim past one by one. They sailed by with such gracefulness that at first Troy took them for dolphins, curious and unassuming.

The circling rampage went on continuously until something that looked like a mammoth head calmly surfaced from out of the water right next to Troy. The young man slightly shuddered at first, not wanting to make any sudden, jerking movements.

He, much like his unwanted companions, was curious, but not enough to where he wanted to swim under and investigate. Soon, after so much swirling about, there came an abrupt quiet in the water. The swimming had stopped all of the sudden. Troy could no longer feel anything pass him underneath. He was wide awake and as stiff as a piece of steel, but for the time being he felt a serene composure breathe upon him; it would last for only a few minutes before something huge jumped right out of the water and back down again, nearly drowning Troy in the process.

Troy screamed out loud before another great beast leapt out and nearly landed on top of his head on its way back underwater. On one side Troy could feel something razor sharp, like teeth grating across his skin. He could smell such a rank odor that resembled old, rotting tires emanate from out of their gaping mouths as water scaled through their gills, causing them to make a sort of roaring racket as they surfaced.

Little by little Troy could feel his skin being lacerated by the sharp fins that just casually swam past him. All the man could do was float and cry as the underwater beasts encircled him, just waiting for the perfect opportunity to swallow him whole.

Beneath him he could feel a deep, powerful suction embrace his legs, like a vacuum sucking him under. Troy hollered at the top of his voice as sharp teeth yanked him below momentarily before spitting him back out. The second Troy resurfaced he yelled awfully loud, trying to regain his breath. For a few fleeting seconds he found himself halfway inside a shark's black mouth.

"Please, God," he stuttered with a trembling jaw, "help me, please. Please help me, Lord. Please don't let this happen."

One by one, the sharks struck in and out of the water around him; their sharp gills and fins bumping against his body as though they were sniffing him out, trying to make sure whether or not he was truly worthy of a late night meal. From side to side Troy heard the snapping of their teeth like someone repeatedly slamming a door shut in his ears.

He had been waiting to die ever since Sinai burnt to the ground; ever since Jill's precious life was snuffed out, but suddenly, Troy Gaston's existence meant more to him at that instant than ever before. He couldn't explain why he wanted to survive; he honestly had nothing else left to look forward to. All he wanted was one last chance, one final rung on a ladder to hold on to, at least one more year. He didn't know why it had to be just one year, all he knew was that he desired to hold it in his arms as tight as he could and never let it go.

Soon, the rain began to fall; hard, penetrating rain that blinded the eyes, which in turn caused the waves to jostle Troy's clinched body up and down like a bottle that was tossed out to sea.

The sharks that were still swarming saw fit to only leap higher and more aggressively. They were seemingly unfazed by the hostile water that they were swimming in.

Troy held on as the rain pelted his face, making it feel as though he were being slapped around. He then relaxed his muscles and allowed his body to be tossed about without any restriction, there was no other alternative.

CHAPTER 38

Troy opened his sore, misty eyes to see nothing but bright fog all around him. The once raging waters were more calm and peaceful. He started to wiggle his feet as he wiped the salty crust away from his eyelids and gazed around at the seemingly endless fog that surrounded him.

From just about every direction he turned the fog was just as thick; it was so dense that he could hardly see two feet in front of him without running into even more fog. He couldn't tell if he was still amongst his aquatic companions from the night before, but one thing was for certain, it was at long last daytime. Troy couldn't see the sun due to all the fog, but he could tell that the next day was upon him, and that alone was all he needed to hold on to.

Troy made a continuous three hundred and sixty degree turn before eventually coming face to face with the barrel of a shotgun that was pointed straight at his face. Troy looked up and tried to see the individual that was holding the weapon so vigilantly.

Behind the gun appeared an older, white, bald man with a handlebar mustache and a malevolent look that made Troy believe that perhaps his shark friends weren't so dangerous after all.

With such a wicked appearance on the man's forceful face, all Troy could think of doing right then and there was hold up his hands, but he found that his arms were too weak to even pull out of the water.

"Wait," a man's somewhat familiar voice said as he suddenly appeared from behind the bald man, "I know this one."

Troy squeezed his eyes as hard as could, trying to see the pudgy man clearly. Once his eyes could focus, Troy saw Finch extend his arm to him.

"What if he's just like those other bastards?" The bald man angrily spoke up in an Australian accent. "He's liable to have been taken, too!"

Finch hesitated at first, looking as if he were mulling over his partner's ardent words before resuming his earlier course of action.

Still too feeble to reach out, Troy held fast as Finch grabbed a hold of his neck before pulling him towards the boat and taking his emaciated body on board.

Shivering from head to toe, Troy watched as Finch took a black blanket from off a shelf and draped it across his body before he stepped back and looked down upon him like he was the most shocking sight that he had ever witnessed.

Ever so carefully, the bald man placed his gun down onto the floor before saying in a dry tone, "How the bloody hell did he survive that?"

Finch paused and then replied in a stunned voice, "Only God knows, mate. Only God knows."

Troy gawked all around at the boat that housed numerous guns and knives before looking back up at Finch who himself was still wearing his baffled expression all over his blushing face. The man then knelt down and examined Troy's swollen wrists, as well as the various lacerations that were all over his legs and torso.

Finch then drew close to Troy's ear and said, "God truly is on your side, boy-o. Do you know where you are? This is Satan's Kennel. This is where the world's biggest and most dangerous great whites reside. And yet...here you are."

Troy couldn't even open his mouth, he had nothing to say. In his head was nothing but a jumbled mess, like yards of yarn that no one could untangle.

Finch turned his head in a shameful fashion before looking back at Troy and muttering, "What happened to everyone else, son? Everyone at Sinai, that is?"

Just the very mention of Sinai evoked an image of Jill for a brief second before it eventually vanished away like a gentle breeze.

Finch once more stared down at Troy with his troubled, confounded glare, like he were trying to conjure the right words to say without sounding offensive at the same time.

215

"We know who they are, boy-o."

Troy couldn't help but to glance upwards at Finch at that second, trying his hardest to focus on the man's pitiable face.

"They're all gone, aren't they, Troy?" Finch asked with an admirable sorrow in his throat.

Troy turned his head briefly before re-directing his waning attention back to Finch. At that juncture, there honestly wasn't anything left to explain.

Finch exhaled, "I tried for years to warn him, but no matter what, he just wouldn't listen to reason. He was a man of strong convictions. His faith kept him strong here in this world, and it will be his faith that will carry him home."

Troy lay like a dead man on the wood floor and listened with ringing ears to the man, who with only his tongue was opening a brand new book right before his very eyes.

"He had a vision, and it came true." Finch went on before lowering his head as to say that he was trying so hard to cope with everything all at once. "Alphonse and Gregor were their accursed names." He growled. "They were two of a perverse nature; too bloody perverse, if you ask me. They had to be destroyed like the mad dogs they were…there was no other alternative. But, my brother once said that, 'evil never lives forever, it prevails momentarily, but eventually, it is destroyed'. "He believed it, and so do I."

Troy studied Finch as he got up and began for the door, but not before stopping midway. At that second, he wanted to ask Finch so many questions, even though he was afraid to hear whatever answers would come out.

"Judging by all this fog, I'm quite sure they're on their way to us next. That's why we have to get you home as soon as possible, my friend."

As if someone had lit a match underneath him, Troy all of the sudden opened his sore mouth and blurted out, "No…I don't wanna go home. We gotta go back to the village."

Finch's face turned a dreadful new shade of white at that second as the man stood perfectly still, appearing too afraid to even move.

Shaking, Finch said, "Son, there can't be anything left there. For God's sake, you made your way out here, somehow," he said astonished. "What else is there? They chased you all the way to the other side of the bay, Troy. This isn't one your movies, this is pure, real evil we have here."

Troy swallowed before cutting his eyes away from Finch. He could hear the man walk out the door before listening to him and his mate argue about having to go back to Sinai.

With his blanket wrapped around his frail body, Troy's crusty eyes wandered from one end of the small cabin to the other in a fashion that was both confused and aggravated, like he had forgotten what planet he was on.

His staring routine carried on for what felt like hours until he caught sight of a pen tied to a piece of white string, and a notepad that were both hooked to a nail on a cabinet beside a large fishing net. Ignoring the deep, blistering lacerations that coursed his ribs, Troy crawled over and snatched down the pencil and pad before leaning up against the cabinet.

There rested upon his pale, gaunt face a lifeless expression, a look that would have a person wondering if Troy Gaston was still inside his own body. Without even looking down at the paper, Troy began to scribble on the pad while his eyes remained stuck on the stuffed swordfish that was mounted on the wall ahead of him.

It's August, I know that much for sure. I can hear the boat starting up now. It sounds like dad's old Nova trying to turn over on a winter morning.

I think I got away from Josh and Jacob, I don't see their eyes anymore; I don't hear those scary voices in my head.

I think I'm running now. I see an island up ahead; it's so blue and beautiful, like something from out of one of those calendars that teases a person with its tantalizing images of tropical scenery while your digging yourself out of three feet of snow in the middle of January. Jill and I are walking hand in hand to the island.

The water is so blue and warm; the sand feels so nice and crumbly as my feet walk across it. We can see the goldfish swimming to and fro as we reach the beach. The tall palm trees hang low as Jill frees herself from my hand and takes off down the beach in her blue one piece that she's afraid to wear even to the Westside pool. She looks so gorgeous in the sun; her spirit is as pure and innocent as the strip of land that we've landed on.

I'm watching her soul dance against the calm waves that look like they're too afraid to touch land. I soon take off after her and start to dance alongside her, but she won't have anything to do with me. She won't talk to me or even look in my direction. She likes to play like that sometimes, (hard to get). I just laugh it off and try again to catch her, but she still runs like a scared little girl.

There I am, running like a crazy man after this lovely woman who just keeps on slipping out of my hands like water, until she finally stops halfway down the beach. Jill's back is turned; all I can see are the pink flowers that I could never pronounce which are printed on the rear end of her bikini. She won't turn around; she just stands there as the waves keep on and on ticking her feet back and forth.

I stop running, just to make sure she is okay. Then, just like clockwork, she turns around, her and those black eyes. She smiles and waves at me before turning back around and walking away down the beach until I can no longer see her.

And that's exactly how it ends; no matter what, whether it be from infidelity, death, or just a stupid dream, Jill Carter ends up leaving me, leaving me to find God all by myself.

I guess Tobias was right. Now I see it all too clear. The jolt.

I can feel the boat moving now.

Goodbye, Jill, I will always love you, just like I always have...

CHAPTER 39

For Troy, his return to Sinai was not only foreboding, but also quicker than he expected. He never realized just how far out into the wilderness he had escaped, or how deep into the ocean he had drifted. But there was something there at the village, a presence that he had to face one on one, no matter how much Finch and his crewmate urgently protested.

For the first time since evading the demons, Troy wasn't concerned about evil; in fact, he wasn't even the slightest bit scared or apprehensive. Growing inside his feeble body was an burning sense of determination, like he had to go back the village at all costs.

Once the boat docked at the pier, Troy stepped outside the cabin and stood perfectly still at the edge of the stern, like he was waiting for something to happen.

Stepping up beside him, Finch stuttered, "We don't have to do this, son. There can't be anyone else left."

Troy couldn't find the will to open his mouth to explain his actions; in fact, he really didn't know what he was doing at all. At that point, every movement was made out of gut instinct.

"This is insane," the first mate griped. "This little fart can hardly even walk! What if those Godforsaken monsters are here?"

Troy glanced over at the visibly upset man. He was already weary of the sailor's incessant grumpiness and skepticism, but not even that deterred the young man as he stepped down off of the boat's ramp and onto the pier.

"Troy," Finch hollered, running up beside him with a shotgun in both hands. "We're in hell now, boy," he frowned. "But there's no reason we have to die here."

Troy eyeballed the fretful man before taking the shotgun that was handed to him and carrying on down the fog-burdened trail that led to the village. He had no idea how to even cock and load a gun, not to mention the fact that he had never even fired one, but if it made Finch feel more secure then he wouldn't bother with putting up a fuss.

As all three men plodded down the trail, all they could see from front to back and side to side was nothing but thick fog, the same fog that had been with them all the way out in the open water. They were all very aware of where the fog came from. It was both ominous and frigid, but far from unexpected.

The usual animal noises that were commonly heard within the area were absent, all that seemed to remain were the sounds of bugs creaking and whining.

Once they cleared the trail and made their way into the courtyard, their every step then became meticulous, like soldiers touring a war torn section of the planet. Their individual weapons all pointed to the front, anticipating the first thing that would dare to jump out at them.

Troy stood still beside the tree where both he and Jill would at times sit and converse on the curious happenings at the village. Everywhere he could see was nothing but the charred remains of a once vibrant community that most called home. From the infirmary, to the shacks, all the way to Ardan and Josephine's home was nothing more than burnt, smoldering sticks that were ready to crumble to the ground at any moment.

The very second he began to walk, a lone dingo came trotting out of the fog in front of the three men. It stopped for a moment and stared them down with a pair of threatening eyes, as though it was trying to figure out who to attack first before growling like a mad fiend.

Without hesitation, both Finch and his partner raised their shotguns and unloaded on the animal until it went flying back to the ground in a bloody heap.

Unfazed by the brutal murder, Troy didn't even bother to look back at the men who were cursing the two demons that they were so deathly afraid of.

As they continued to rant on, Troy didn't waste another second standing around, he turned and headed straight for the charred remains that was once the church.

As soon as he stepped over what used to be the threshold, Troy right away saw the gold cross where Jill's burnt body was still perched. Right away, a piercing groan ripped through his gut, more scathing than the shark's fins that had frayed his skin overnight.

All around him, the rancid stench of burnt flesh and scorched wood prevailed as if the building were still on fire.

Stepping on broken remains of the roof, Troy stumbled towards the pulpit until he came face to face with Jill's body. Her face was so black and scalded that he couldn't even make out where her mouth was. As a breeze blew through the wide open church, the more body parts chipped off the cross and onto the floor. Soon, all that was left was what looked like a head.

He thought viewing such a ghastly image would cause him to crumble to pieces, but all Troy could think of doing at that point was cut his eyes and continue to move forward until he came face to face with the one item that somehow miraculously survived the carnage.

In front of the pastor's pulpit was the small cross that had Christ nailed to it. It, much like the golden cross, was untouched by the fire, still intact, not one single blemish had seared its wood frame.

Clothed only in his torn pair of shorts and shirt, Troy stood, his entire body trembled uncontrollably from head to toe. There wasn't a person alive that could move him at that moment. With his wobbly knees ready to buckle underneath him, he stared the object down for what felt like endless minutes before tears began to drip down from his eyes. He thought he had used up all of his crying after the events over the past few days, but low and behold, there was still something left.

"My brother died for this?" Finch spitefully frowned. "What kind of God allows such a thing to happen to innocent people? Where was he when all of this shit went down?"

"Yeah," Finch's mate chimed in, "we need to get the fuck outta here before they come for us!"

Troy could hear the man's ardent pleas for retreat, but no matter what, he couldn't budge an inch. Even if the demons were returning to finish him off, there wouldn't be one thing he could do to retaliate at that point.

Using every muscle he had in his jaws, Troy opened his mouth, and with a jittery tongue and a pair of eyes that wouldn't leave the crucified Savior, he stammered a question that he never imagined he would live to utter.

"What...what do you...require of me...my Lord?"

Captain's Log:
November 5th 1942,

Getting out of the accursed fog bank and away from that fucking Commander King was a trial from purgatory, but we made it. These waters are becoming more and more treacherous, even for the likes of us. The Mediterranean isn't like I remember it at all. Despite their recent turnaround, the Germans have managed to keep their stronghold on most of these waters with their U-boats, but we were able to somehow sneak past them without being noticed.

We docked portside this morning at Heraklion, Crete. Just dropping off and picking up. Our contact that was supposed to meet us there never bothered to show up; I figure the stories he heard about Finch scared him enough to want to stay as far away as possible. No matter, the crew and I dropped off our cargo and laid over for a few hours. The men are thirsty for something more than held over wine from France; they desire something more pungent to whet their appetite.

We went into a bar called Zeus' Bolt. The entire place was filled with all sorts of wretched scoundrels and miscreants. We knew we couldn't stay long on account of King and his crew; the bastards nearly caught us two days earlier along the Isles, and I'm not going back to prison. I'd rather go to perdition's gate.

While in the bar, we met this Gypsy woman by the name of Cortansia. She is a fair looking bitch, with the lips of a puffer fish. Much to our surprise, she is sharp, for a female. She knew exactly what we were carrying and why. Not only that, but she told us just how and where to stash our wares as not to alert the local officials of our doings.

Finch, always the skeptic, suggested that she was not to be trusted and that I should kill her, post haste. But I had to remind him of the fraulein back in Luxemburg, and just how well she was at not only giving us proper dick jobs, but also at knowing which specific areas to duck and hide in her city. It has always been a well-known truth throughout the ages that females adore seamen. Therefore, my dear brother, trusting Cortansia is almost elementary.

She not only gave all seven of us a proper evening that included multiple trains, but she also pointed us in the direction of more weapons that the city's guards have all but abandoned. Say what you will about the Greeks, they do craft proficient weaponry, if nothing else.

Once we were finished with our overnight libations and carousing, we began to set off, back for Africa, that hellhole of a nation. Upon our departure, we encountered two bastard, Negro men who happened to discover that we are headed for Ethiopia. The sorry fuckers didn't even have the gumption enough to ask, they just hopped on board as if they were coming for a pleasure cruise. Both Finch and Shaw have already declared them good as dead the moment we reach open water.

Cortansia not only gave us all sendoff whiskey, but also her two cousins by the names of Alphonse and Gregor, who themselves are cousins. Apparently they desire to hitch a ride to escape the local authorities for crimes that neither of them are willing to fess up to.

They are both a couple of ragged faggots. They have the appearance of two diseased, wispy sewer rats. For me, Gypsies have always ranked amongst the most foul of creatures, right next to those black apes. But Cortansia assured me that they know the waters better than anyone in the city, and that they are quite elegant with a rifle.

Finch has checked their bags, and he tells that they were both filled with all kinds of Ouija boards, pentagrams and other ridiculous types of medieval array. I cannot say that I am surprised, them being Gypsies and all, but I am quite disturbed, neither fools will hardly even speak with any of the crew, even the blacks are afraid of them. I never considered myself a superstitious fellow, but if we make it to Africa in one piece then I will be quite amazed.

Even their smell is vile, but once again, I must remind myself that they are Gypsies, scum among the living. At night I can hear them chanting to each other, or their "master". Yes, they both deserve a bullet in their heads, but so far they have successfully managed to navigate us through the Isles, so I guess they will be kept a while longer, for now at least.

Perhaps God, in his so called infinite wisdom, will get us to where we need to be without incident. But then again, I never did have much favor or respect for the fucker to begin with.

Captain T. Hudson

*   *   *

Printed in the United States
By Bookmasters